THE
HALLOWS

WITHDRAWN

ALSO BY VICTOR METHOS

An Invisible Client
A Gambler's Jury
The Shotgun Lawyer

Neon Lawyer Series

The Neon Lawyer
Mercy

THE HALLOWS

VICTOR METHOS

THOMAS & MERCER

Text copyright © 2019 by Victor Methos
All rights reserved.

No part of this book may be reproduced, or stored in a retrieval system, or transmitted in any form or by any means, electronic, mechanical, photocopying, recording, or otherwise, without express written permission of the publisher.

Published by Thomas & Mercer, Seattle

www.apub.com

Amazon, the Amazon logo, and Thomas & Mercer are trademarks of Amazon.com, Inc., or its affiliates.

ISBN-13: 9781542042741 (hardcover)
ISBN-10: 1542042747 (hardcover)
ISBN-13: 9781542042727 (paperback)
ISBN-10: 1542042720 (paperback)

Cover design by Christopher Lin

Printed in the United States of America

First edition

To Ms. Whiting, my high school English teacher, who let me cut my other classes and lie down in the back of her classroom as long as I read a book while doing so, and was the first person to tell me they liked my writing. How seldom we recognize the people who set the sails of our lives.

1

"Murder."

I looked into the jury's faces. Twelve men and women and two alternates, chosen at random from Miami-Dade County. My client sat at the defense table, dressed in a pinstripe suit and a Rolex watch. This was South Beach, after all, and the juries here needed to see wealth. From *The Art of Jury Trial as War* (a book I was in the process of writing), chapter 7: "In any jury trial, in any part of the country, the jury has to believe the defendant is one of their own."

I swaggered over to the table where the lead detective on the case and two prosecutors sat. Their closing had been by the book, fact after fact after fact. *The Art of Jury Trial as War*, chapter 4: "Juries can't tell an important fact from an irrelevant fact, so pick the best 'facts' you've got and run with them."

In a murder case like this one, they had to see that the victim had it coming. That the victim had done so much wrong and was such a nasty person that it was only a matter of time before *someone* killed them, and it might as well have been my client.

Of course, that didn't really apply when your client was innocent, which my guy miraculously was.

I winked at the detective.

"Murder," I said, turning back to the jury. "Just say the word. *Murder*. Sort of hangs in the air, doesn't it? Brings up these horrific images of every movie you've ever seen, all the slasher films, the assassination films, the Mafia films. But it's not like that, is it? The evidence you heard these past five days was, in the words of a wise woman from long ago, banal. Evil is banal. It's boring and tame. There's no devil with a pitchfork and fire spurring someone on. It's just men. Men and the wickedness they do." I shrugged. "Banal . . . is it, though? It takes a special kind of man to do something so heinous, strangling the victim, a young woman barely out of her teenage years, to death." I lifted my hands, simulated the strangling, and stepped closer to the jury. "To wrap your fingers around an innocent girl's throat and squeeze . . . to see life drain from her eyes, to know she's about to die, and to keep going . . . that sort of evil should never seem banal. And Marcus Green is not a man capable of that type of evil."

I looked to the judge, a cherubic man named Clemens, who appeared half-asleep.

"You were instructed by the judge that you must be impartial in your reasoning. You took an oath before this trial that you would uphold the law, that you would do what's right and what's just. And what is justice? It's doing what's fair. Don't buy into this nonsense the prosecution has fed you." I took out a coin, flipped it into the air, and caught it with one hand. Then I opened that hand, revealing that the coin wasn't there. I opened my other hand, which held the coin. "What the prosecution has done on this case is what I just showed you: a magic trick. They tried to distract you with things about Marcus's past. And it's all true. Marcus was a drug addict, and somehow, by the grace of the Lord, he pulled himself out of that life. And far be it from the government to give him a second chance, even though he's paid his dues.

"You heard from him yesterday. You saw him get up on that stand, tears in his eyes, and tell you how much he loved Mindi Bower. That he was going to marry her, that he wanted children with her and to grow old together. And someone took that away. Poof," I said, making the coin disappear again. "Just like that, the love of his life was gone. Imagine what that would feel like."

I paused and looked to Marcus, who had put his head down, just as I'd instructed him to do.

"Now imagine the police come to you and start grilling you. Where were you? What was your relationship like? Let us see the last text messages you two sent each other. Detective Pascal over there held Marcus in a room for seven hours and grilled him with her partner to the point that he broke down and wept. A man who had been through the most horrific thing a man can go through, seeing the corpse of the person he loves on his floor, and they tortured him like he was a terrorist."

I leaned forward on the banister in front of the jury. I didn't like to invade their space—jurors hated that—but I also knew that after five days of gruesome photos, a recording of a heartbreaking 911 call by a neighbor, and a medical examiner who'd gone into excruciating detail about the strangulation, they were beaten down and numb. Being right in their faces would get their attention.

"The prosecution told you Marcus has a temper and that temper flared up and he killed Mindi. Really? How do they know he has a temper? Have you seen it? Have you heard from a single witness anything that indicates he has a temper? Did you see anything on that detective's video interview that indicated he had a temper? Because all I saw was a man weeping over the loss of the woman he loved."

I took a step back. "The fact is, there is no motive, there is no physical evidence. There are no witnesses other than a neighbor who says she didn't see anything until coming into the house and discovering Mindi's body. What we *do* have is a broken kitchen window someone climbed through, missing cash and jewelry from the home, and a grieving husband who testified that he arrived during a home invasion and scared the monster off . . . but not before that monster killed Mindi." I pointed to the prosecutors. "They have nothing here but circumstantial evidence and a hope that they're right. Because that's what this is really about: hope. They hope they can get a conviction in this case because it's in all the papers, and because Mindi was an up-and-coming actress. This prosecution is grotesque, and it's enough. Marcus hasn't even had time to grieve for the loss of his love and the life he was supposed to have with her. Enough's enough. Let him go home. Please, just let him go home and grieve."

I turned to the detective and prosecutors, winked one more time—rubbing it in their faces because they knew they would lose this and had still made me do the trial—and then sat down.

The prosecutors shook their heads at the judge, indicating they were done, and the judge began instructing the jury on the deliberation process.

"I was told you were good, but I had my doubts," Marcus whispered, leaning over to me.

"Ain't over till it's over."

"I've been in sales for thirty years, and in my business it's all about reading people, and that jury is going to acquit me. You were worth every penny. Even if it was ten times what I would've paid the next guy."

"Just remember that when you get your final bill."

We rose as the jury filed out, and Marcus's girlfriend ran up from the audience and hugged him. Another young actress. They were easy to find in this town for people like Marcus, who drove Rolls-Royces and could convince girls that they knew a producer or a director looking for talent. South Beach was the new Hollywood.

I left the crowd and went to the bathroom—small but paneled with what I was sure was imported wood and accented with brass shined to a gleam. It'd be a shame for the country's wealthy to have to tolerate an average bathroom. I was splashing water on my face when the door opened and Detective Pascal walked in. She wore the leather jacket I had bought her for her birthday. She leaned against the sink next to mine and folded her arms.

"He's gonna walk," Sarah said.

"Yes, he is."

"Would it be too presumptuous of me to ask if you felt bad?"

"You know my emotions never come into it."

"Oh, I know, Tatum. That's why we broke up. You're like a block of ice. And that says a lot coming from a cop."

"I thought we broke up because you were having sex with your partner?"

A man walked in just then. Sarah said, "Find another bathroom." The man glanced between the two of us and left.

"I just thought this case, *this case*, will get to him. Nineteen-year-old girl, fresh off the bus and looking for help to make her dreams come true, and instead she finds Marcus Green, who strangles her to death in the middle of the afternoon. I thought, naively, just for a second, that you might feel bad defending him."

"Hey, if you and those clowns at the prosecutor's table had done your jobs, he wouldn't be walking. Always, always, always make sure your victim is clean as a whistle, and if they're not, you tell the jury every horrible thing about them at the beginning of the trial. After I was through with her past, it looked like you guys were trying to hide it. Once you break trust with a jury, bam, that's it. Game over. Also, not that this little detail matters to the government, but he's innocent."

"He is *not* innocent. He broke that window himself, and there is no way any jewelry and cash are missing and some mysterious man in a mask just happened to run out of the house when he came home. You're blinded on this one because you want so badly for him to be innocent."

I turned to her. "Sarah, I've done this a long time, defended thousands of clients, and I can count on one hand the number who were innocent. Trust me, I know when it happens. It's like lightning striking. Marcus didn't kill that poor girl, and if he serves the rest of his life in prison for something he didn't do, you're going to have to live with that . . . and so am I."

I wiped my face with a paper towel. "Lunch?"

"Lunch? You can eat at a time like this?"

"What? I'm hungry."

"Fine. You buy. I'm sure you can afford it, given how much you probably got from that piece of shit in there."

2

No sooner were we seated at Elevate, the top seafood place in South Beach, than Sarah and I both got the call: the jury was back with a verdict. Five-day murder trial, sixty hours of testimony, and they had returned a verdict in a little over an hour.

I insisted we at least eat an appetizer: the jury could tolerate one more hour. We had some sort of crab-and-spinach dip, and Sarah said she was sorry she'd cheated on me. That it just happened.

"No," I said. "Train accidents just happen. Letting your partner have sex with you in your own bed every weekend for months doesn't just happen."

"He decided to stay with his wife," she said, ignoring what I had just said.

"You cops are so predictable. You two will hook up again at some point, and then he'll 'choose' to stay with his wife again, and you'll be alone again. What's with you and these damaged guys? Find someone nice and settle down."

She shook her head. "It didn't even hurt you a little, did it? When you found out, I thought you would throw something at me, break something, have some sort of reaction."

"Sorry, emotions aren't something I can afford to have. *The Art of Jury Trial as War*, chapter three: 'Never, ever let your emotions cloud your judgment. If they do, you've already lost.'"

"If it wasn't so pathetic, it would almost be funny that you use your legal tactics in your relationships."

"Love is war, just like jury trials. Lawyers started as mercenaries battling to the death to settle disputes between the people that hired us. We're a guild of assassins, and assassins that feel emotions don't get very far in life. You gonna eat your roll?"

———

We got back to the courthouse about an hour after the clerk had called us. The judge was already on the bench and the prosecution was at the table. Marcus was sitting on the defense side, and I strolled up and sat next to him. The judge gave me a dirty look, but not too long of a dirty look. He wanted to retire soon, and retired judges almost always became mediators or arbitrators. And the way mediators and arbitrators got business was lawyer referrals. So they could be jerks only up to a point to lawyers like me who ran the most powerful firms in the state.

The bailiff handed the judge the verdict form, and the judge read it impassively and handed it back.

"It is my understanding the jury has reached a verdict in the matter of *State of Florida versus Marcus C. Green?*"

A slim man in a button-down shirt stood up. "We have, Your Honor."

I rose and Marcus rose with me. This was the moment of truth. The moment that I'd worked toward for the past six months. All the strategy, the research, the late nights, and the hours of grilling Marcus over and over to prepare him for the prosecution's cross-examination—it all came down to this moment. Some lawyers got so nervous at the verdict announcement they puked. I never did. Cool as a cucumber. When you'd done your work, the verdict was a given. No need to be nervous.

So why, when I glanced down, were my fingers trembling? That hadn't happened since my first trial.

"We, the jury, in the above-entitled matter, on the first count, find the defendant, Marcus Cutler Green, not guilty of the offense of homicide in the first degree. We find the defendant, Marcus Cutler Green, on the second count, not guilty of the offense of aggravated kidnapping."

Gasps, cries, whispers. The audience couldn't believe it. Marcus looked like he might faint; all the blood drained from his face. Narrowly avoiding life in prison could do that to a person. I grinned and nodded to the jury in appreciation. After a jury trial, I usually held a large barbecue for the jurors, a tactic that once had me in front of a disciplinary committee of the Florida Bar. But the case had ended, and influencing the jurors hadn't mattered anymore, so the Bar complaint had been tossed. I made a mental note to instruct my assistant to set up the barbecue.

I looked over to the prosecution, who kept their eyes forward. Only Sarah watched me, with a look of disappointment, while the judge thanked the jury and excused them.

Mindi Bower had no family here except for a sister, a young woman of about seventeen or eighteen. Blonde and petite, she looked like a child in an adult's world. Lost. She sat in the back. She got up without a word and left the courtroom, glancing at me only once. She held my gaze for a second and then disappeared out the doors.

"I don't even know how to thank you," Marcus said.

"Don't worry. We'll get creative with your billing and find a way," I said, slapping his shoulder.

His family all wanted to shake hands and spread congratulations around, and I glad-handed a bit and then sneaked out of there. Sarah was waiting by the front doors.

"Congratulations, Counselor. Hope that felt good."

"No emotions means no emotions, win or lose." I put on my sunglasses, and as I brushed past her, said, "Try not to be too sad. I'm sure there'll be more innocent people you can falsely arrest."

3

The prestigious law firm of Gordon & Graham sat in the Peterson building on Ocean Front Avenue in South Beach. The most expensive office space in this part of Florida. When Tim Gordon and I started this firm, we shared one office in a building that had been shut down by the health department twice. Within two years, we had moved into a decent office space with three associates and a few staff. Within ten years, we had moved into the Peterson with twenty-four associate attorneys and twice as many staff. Our firm was known for one thing and one thing only: winning. I had once been quoted in an interview for *Miami Lifestyle* magazine, saying, "I didn't get into this profession to lose." I hated slogans, but it had become our de facto slogan, and I swore nothing brought in more money than that little line dancing through the heads of rich and famous Miamians who'd had tin bracelets slapped on their wrists in front of the cameras. We even had it on our pens and mugs.

As I pulled up to park, I saw a small dog on the sidewalk. I stopped the car and got out. The dog was white with matted fur, all skin and bones. I had always had a soft spot for dogs in a way I didn't seem to for people. They loved you unconditionally, no strings attached. I had rarely met a person who didn't have an agenda in exchange for their love.

I bent down and he gently put his head on my foot, exhausted. I rubbed his head and picked him up.

———

Woof and Stuff, aside from the horrendous name, was the top pet day care center in Miami. The type of place celebrities dropped off their pets when they went on their fifth honeymoon or had to shoot on location in some remote spot for a few months. The owner, George, knew me from way back. I had gotten him acquitted on a pot charge, when prosecutors were still filing those.

I gently placed the dog on the counter, rubbing behind his ears, as George came out from the back.

"Another dog?" he said.

"This little guy was just sitting on the sidewalk. No tags. Looks like he hasn't eaten in a while."

George began running his hands over the dog, checking for injuries. "What is it with you and dogs anyway? You spend more here than any other customer I have."

"They're innocent in a way we're not. How long, do you think?"

"Well," he said, checking the dog's teeth, "he's beat up pretty good. Probably been on the streets a long while, so we'll need some time to get him healthy again, but he's particularly cute, so I would guess we could get him adopted in about a month, maybe."

I took out a stack of cash and put it on the counter. "Good family, Georgie."

"I know."

"I'm serious. If I find out you're giving these little guys away to some abusive pricks, you are not going to believe the legal hellfire I will rain down on this place."

"What'dya think, I got into this business because I hate dogs? Good families, I know. I even do background checks just for you. They're going to good homes. Don't worry. By the way, how come you don't got any? Someone loves these guys as much as you, I'd figure you got ten of 'em at home."

I shook my head. "I prefer to be alone."

I rubbed the dog's ear a little more, then let George take him into the back for a bath and shots while I left.

———

The firm was a mess of phone calls, faxes—because some government agencies wouldn't update the tech they used no matter how much money taxpayers dumped on them—and people shouting into phones. I tried to sneak into my office, but Tim Gordon met me in the hall.

A small man with a bald head so shiny it could burn your retinas under strong light, he ran up and hugged me.

"Dude, come on," I said.

"Sorry, I know you don't like to be touched, but that Green case was huge. *Entertainment Tonight* called and wants to interview you."

"Pass."

"Hey, come on, you can't buy publicity like this."

"I'm tired, Tim. You take it."

His mouth fell comically open. "You . . . really?"

"It's all you, buddy. Have fun."

I left before any other partners, of which I think we now had six, could stop and congratulate me. I shut the door to my office and took off my suit coat. Outside the windows, which looked down over the ocean across the street, the sunlight glimmered off the water. I hadn't even seen the ocean until I was twenty-two, and the first time I saw it, I thought it was a dream.

My phone buzzed, and my secretary said over the intercom, "It's Maggie, boss."

"Patch her through." I waited a beat and then said to the speakerphone, "Paris as fun as you remember?"

"I'm back in the States actually," Maggie said. "Why didn't you tell me you had a trial today? I had to read about it online."

I'd actually mentioned it to her three times, but who's counting?

"Sorry, must've slipped my mind."

"Well, I think you deserve a treat for that. I picked up a little number in Paris that you're going to like. Came with its own handcuffs."

I watched a couple jogging along the water. "Yeah, sure, come over tonight."

"Well, don't sound too enthusiastic."

"I'm enthusiastic. Just distracted. Guess I forgot that I can be the good guy and defend someone innocent sometimes. Last six months just kinda beat me up." I took a breath. "Looking forward to it. Really. See you then."

I hung up and sighed. Maggie was nice enough. The typical South Beach beauty with all the trappings that came with it. I was pretty sure she was cheating on me with her ex, but frankly, I didn't care enough to mention it. Besides, I'd already had that conversation with Sarah recently, and two of them in two months didn't sound fun.

My intercom buzzed. "Boss?"

"Yeah?"

"*Entertainment Tonight* again. Eddie says you owe him one, and he doesn't want to talk to Mr. Gordon."

"Ugh. Fine. Send it through."

4

We sat at Ganish, the new hot restaurant—or what I'd been told was actually a brasserie, a fancy word for *snobby restaurant*. Maggie was the expert at hot spots. Her mother had been a celebrity chef in England, and where you ate, according to her, was as important as what you ate. So Maggie dragged me to all the fancy places for peanut-butter gazpacho or roasted quail or fresh escargot that could crawl off your plate and over the table. I'd usually just move the stuff around with my fork and then hit Del Taco on the way home.

We sat with two of Maggie's friends, Dale and Cynthia something or other. Dale was telling some witty story I was reasonably certain never happened, and Maggie and Cynthia were laughing, and at one point Maggie lightly touched Dale's hand and I realized that they were probably sleeping together as well. I sighed and leaned back, looked around. The restaurant could've been ripped out of the most opulent of king's palaces. Growing up as a kid in River Falls, Utah, a town of three thousand people, I never even dreamed places like this existed. Much less that I would eat at them one day.

"Gotta use the bathroom, excuse me." I rose and circled around to the bathroom. An attendant was there. I washed my hands and noticed that his tip jar was empty.

"Nothing, huh?" I said.

He shrugged. "Some nights are more generous than others."

"You know, I used to wait tables when I first came out here, and I once worked this party of a hundred—some company on an outing. I mean, *worked*. I was dripping sweat. It took like the whole night, and I couldn't work any other tables, so these guys were basically the money I was going to make for that shift. And they stiffed me. Not because I did a bad job, because I didn't, but because they just didn't care. They thought they were so important that I was invisible to them."

He shook his head. "If that doesn't describe this city, I don't know what does."

I dried my hands. "Before they left, I got the CEO's keys from the valet and parked his car across town. Heard it took him like two days to find it."

He laughed.

I took out a couple of hundred-dollar bills and put them into his tip jar and told him to have a good night. I stood outside the door a second and decided I wasn't ready to go back to the table yet, so I circled around to the bar, but Maggie saw me and waved me over. I'd resigned myself to heading back when my phone rang. It was my after-hours office line.

"This is Tatum."

"Sir, it's Julie. We have a bit of a client emergency."

"What's up?"

"You better get down to Mr. Green's house right away."

"Green who?"

"Marcus Green. He's been arrested again."

5

Marcus Green lived on Fisher Island, which meant a ferry ride over for me. The island had the highest median income in the country. Marcus owned a line of luxury car and yacht dealerships and had bought up properties here in the eighties like it was going out of style. He managed, during my time defending him, to work in that he was worth three commas: i.e., a billion dollars. Three commas. Clever.

I parked on the street just as the sun was setting, painting the sky a deep orange. There were two police cruisers there, and Sarah's Ford Mustang was on the opposite side of the street. When I walked up to the scene, an officer stopped me, but Sarah said, "Let him through."

I ducked under some police tape and said, "What's going on?"

"I'll show you."

She led me around the horseshoe driveway up to the front door, and we ducked again before we stepped inside. In the atrium was a body. I recognized it but couldn't place it for a second.

"Mindi Bower's sister," Sarah said. "Bethany Bower. Maybe you saw her in the courtroom."

Around her throat purple and black splotches formed the shape of fingers. Her eyes were cold and distant, glossed over. Two crime-scene techs were taking samples from underneath her fingernails. She had on sparkly pink polish, the kind a teenage girl would pick. It sent a shiver down my back. I'd seen that nail polish before, on a girl from a long time ago, from a past that didn't seem real anymore. I remembered her in a hospital bed, her face bloodied and bruised.

I looked at the body in front of me and didn't see a woman; she was just a child.

I'm so sorry, kid.

"Where's Marcus?" I said.

"Your client is down at the station. I was the one that told your secretary to have you come down here. I wanted you to see this, Tatum. She's seventeen. She came down here to vent. She wasn't armed, nothing like that. A neighbor saw the whole thing. She was yelling at Green, and he punched her, knocked her to the ground. Then he dragged her inside, and the neighbor heard screaming. Looks like she's been strangled to death. Sound familiar, Counselor?"

I stared at Bethany for another second, then turned and left.

6

I texted Maggie and told her that it was an emergency and I wouldn't be coming back to the restaurant. Instead, I headed to the Miami-Dade sheriff's station. Even the police station here looked like it was owned by millionaires and billionaires. Palm trees, manicured flower beds, and a building that was a mix of old Spanish and modern eclectic. In other words, soulless style, like many of the other buildings that tried to impress people with how much money had been spent on their construction.

I parked in police parking and hurried inside. The deputy behind the check-in desk knew me and had me sign a sheet on a clipboard before I was led back to the interview room.

Marcus Green sat at a gray table. A detective was there, a decent guy named Phillips.

Phillips had his jacket off and his arms folded, and he looked frustrated. I had taught Marcus *The Art of Jury Trial as War*, chapter 5: "Under no circumstances do you talk to the police. You don't chat about the weather, you don't mention you like their shoes, you don't say anything but your name, which you're legally required to do." It looked like Marcus had followed my advice.

I stood there and stared at him. He had a smirk on his face.

"Can you get bail set, Tatum? I'd like to go home tonight if possible."

I grinned as I approached him, and then I grabbed him by the throat. I lifted him out of the chair and pressed him against the wall, squeezing his throat. He reached up and tried to remove my hand, but I was stronger and angrier than he was.

"You son of a bitch, she was seventeen. Seventeen!"

"Lemme go!" he spat.

"You killed Mindi, too, didn't you? Didn't you!"

Phillips grabbed me then, wrapping his arms around mine and pulling me off. Marcus coughed, his hand around his throat as he glared at me.

"Doesn't feel good, does it?" I said.

I pulled loose from Phillips and turned to leave. Marcus shouted, "Where you going? You're my lawyer!"

"Not anymore."

7

I made the decision about what to do next without really thinking about it. There was only one person I needed to tell. I sent the text before tossing the phone out the window into the Atlantic.

I packed casual clothes, workout clothes, and a single suit. I thought about what else to grab and couldn't come up with anything. I had a line of expensive watches, but I didn't want them anymore. A closet the size of an apartment held my shoes, of which I took only my favorite pair of sneakers and the dress shoes I was wearing. This was my entire life, and there wasn't a thing in the house that I wanted to take with me. People said that what you valued most in life was the first thing you would save in a house fire . . . I had nothing I would bother to save.

The front door opened and Sarah walked in. She saw the large suitcase I was hauling, and she leaned against the wall and folded her arms. "Just like that?"

"Just like that."

"For how long?"

I put the suitcase in front of the door. "You can have the house."

"What?" she said with a laugh.

"This house. You can have it. I'm taking the Tesla, but you can have the Ferrari. It's yours. The title's in the safe in the bedroom, and I've already signed it, and the house, over to you."

"Tatum, Tim called me in a panic and said you texted him that you quit."

"I did." I looked around the house one more time, thinking I'd feel something. Some tug of regret. I felt nothing.

"Take care," I said.

"Wait, wait," Sarah said, coming up and touching my arm. "What are you doing, Tatum? This is ridiculous. Do you want to take a vacation? I'm happy to take some time and go with you. Tim said take as much time as you need and you'll always be welcome back. I mean, when I called you down to the scene, I didn't think this was what was going to happen. I just wanted to show you . . . I don't know."

I leaned in and kissed her on the cheek. "Goodbye, Sarah."

"Wait, when will you be back?"

"I won't. Hope you find what you're looking for in life. I mean that."

I got into my Tesla, rolled down the windows, and drove away, leaving Sarah standing by the front door watching me.

8

I drove out of Miami and contemplated where to go next. Though I ran some places through in my head, my thoughts kept returning to that sparkly pink nail polish. And that led only one place: a place I hadn't been in nineteen years. The memories weren't exactly pleasant, but as I drove out of Florida, I realized I didn't have anywhere else to go. I had no close relationships, no real friends. Only then did it hit me how much I had let success seclude me from everyone.

I stopped only to gas up and sleep in whatever hotel was nearest the freeway off-ramps. As I drove into Utah a couple of days later, my guts were in knots, and I had to roll down the windows and let the air hit my face. It was dry and hot, but there was no hint of smog to it. No metallic taste of exhaust, no scent of the poison that constantly pumped into the air in Miami.

River Falls was right over the Nevada-Utah border, about an hour from Las Vegas. It was one of those small towns that had been set up for some mining operation or around a large factory, and the residents had put down roots and stayed long after the industry they'd been hired by had moved on.

A white and yellow sign said, **WELCOME TO RIVER FALLS!** Usually towns bragged about something they were known for. Even Beaver, Utah, one of the least populated cities in the nation, had a welcome sign that read, **HOME OF THE BEST WATER IN THE COUNTRY**. River Falls didn't boast anything.

To my utter shock, the town looked . . . essentially the same. A couple of new convenience stores and a coffee shop that wasn't there before, but other than that, it hadn't really changed. A freaking time capsule.

I saw a diner that had been there since I was a kid—Benson's—and suddenly realized I was starving. I made a quick turn and parked. A lot of days, I would cut class and come here. Most of the cool kids had spent time here, and I'd try to ingratiate myself with them: I had been a bookworm with no friends except a girl named Gates, and it seemed like my freshman year was spent trying to make more friends, until I'd finally given up.

I got a few stares because of the Tesla, and someone, a stranger, said hello to me.

Inside, the place hadn't changed a bit. Country music on the speakers, old wooden tables with nicks and chunks missing, waitresses in short shorts. Still no hostess. I seated myself by the window and looked out. Across the street was a series of homes, all dilapidated, with trucks and trailers outside. One of the houses had a huge yard and sheep roaming around.

"Tatum?"

I looked up to see the chubby, instantly recognizable face of Roscoe Mallory approaching from another table.

"Roscoe?"

I held out my hand and he gave me a hug. He smelled like leather.

"Easy, big fella," I said.

He wore a massive grin and sat down without being asked. While I was growing up, he lived just a few houses down from me. Aside from maybe an extra sixty pounds, he looked the same as the last time I'd seen him. The hug was interesting since I think we'd talked maybe half a dozen times our entire lives and had never considered each other friends.

"What're you doing here?"

"I don't know," I said. "Just passing through, I guess. How you been? Last time I saw you, you were trying to get onto SUU's football team."

He nodded and looked away, out the window. "That didn't work out so well. I got hurt my first year, real bad. Broken back. Had to learn to walk again."

"Oh, wow, I'm sorry."

The grin came back as he looked at me. "It worked out. I coach at RF High now. You remember Nikyee Geller?"

"Not really."

"Well, she was Nikyee Mallory for a while. We're divorced now."

"Sorry about that. I know those aren't easy."

He shrugged bashfully. "So how have you been? I know you're a big-time celebrity lawyer. I just saw you on TV with that basketball player that was caught with all them guns."

"Allegedly caught with those guns. He was acquitted."

"Yeah," he said, not really getting what I was saying. "Hey, you remember Gates?"

Gates Barnes. Probably the only girl in this town who was nice to me. Once, in elementary school, some kids had knocked the books out of my hands, and I'd stood there as all my index cards with notes went flying through the hallway. Gates had stopped and helped me pick them up while everyone else laughed. That was how we met.

"I remember," I said. "How is she?"

"She's a lawyer, too."

"Really?"

He nodded. "Yeah. She's the county attorney now."

"Wow. She always told me she wanted to get out of this town."

He shrugged. "Not everyone was as smart as you. I was really proud of you for just leaving like that and making something of yourself. I never got to tell you."

"Well, I appreciate that, Roscoe."

He nodded again and looked at his watch. "I better go. I got a class to teach." He rose from the booth and hugged me again. "You seen your dad yet?"

My guts turned to ice. "No."

"Oh. Well, say hi to him for me."

"Don't think I'll be seeing him, but it was good seeing you."

His grin went away again as he thought of something to say, and then he just patted my shoulder and left. The waitress brought coffee over, and as I poured in some cream and sugar, I thought about Gates. I'd run away from here so fast I hadn't really thought about who I'd left behind. Out of them all, she was the only one I had missed.

And the last time I'd seen her, she was lying broken in a hospital bed, and I could barely bring myself to look.

I drank the coffee and ordered a slice of chocolate cake. I'd been a kid when I'd run away from here, and what I'd felt then had come back the second I drove into town. A claustrophobic tightness like I was being crushed in some giant fist. I had a feeling that whatever demons I'd been running from as a kid were still here.

9

When I was done eating, I checked Airbnb for a place to stay, and not a single place was listed. I remembered there was an old motel down the street, and I drove past some newer-looking condominiums, white and gray. An attempt to bring some modernity to a street where people kept horses and sheep in their yards. I pulled in and spotted a sign about inquiries into leasing or buying, and I called the listed number. I told the Realtor I was interested, and she said she'd drive down in fifteen minutes. Didn't sound like there was a lot of business coming through.

A slim blonde in cowboy boots rode up ten minutes later. She saw my car and her eyes went wide, probably at the prospect that I actually had the money to buy a unit.

She led me to the third building and unlocked the door. The unit was nice, two stories, white, clean walls, new carpet. I opened the window. It looked out onto the woods behind the condos.

"There's three bedrooms, plenty of space for you and . . . the missus?"

"Not married."

She smiled. "Oh. So what brings you to our little town?"

I glanced into the kitchen and the living room. The entire place was, maybe, the size of the master bedroom in my Miami house. "You know, honestly, I have no idea." I exhaled. "I'll take it."

"This one is only for purchase, unfortunately."

"Sure. Whatever. Real estate is never a bad investment, right?"

"Oh, wow. Okay, um, well, we can head back to my office and draw up the paperwork. For the financing, do you have a preferred lender? If not—"

"I'll just put it on my credit card."

She was silent a second. "The entire purchase price?"

"Yeah."

Her mouth fell open.

I returned to the window and stared out into the woods. The trees, half-bare from the intense desert heat, were swaying in a breeze. "I, um, gotta visit somebody really quick. Just have everything drafted up, and I'll be by afterward to sign."

10

As I drove along Main Street, I saw several signs that said, **Horace Webb for County Attorney: Responsible Government**. I saw a couple of lawn signs for Gates, but there were more for Horace. It seemed like there were only two billboards in town, and Horace had them both. One of them said, **A Return to Government for Americans by Americans**. Not sure what foreign power was pulling the strings in a place where a second Walmart was the talk of the town, but all right, whatever floats your boat.

I parked in front of my father's house and sat in the driveway for a while.

The house looked smaller and more run down than I remembered. Funny that things from childhood always looked smaller when you went back as an adult. Was it just that you'd been smaller then, or was it that the world had seemed like a much bigger, more mysterious place?

You seen your dad yet? Roscoe had said. I didn't think I'd talked about my father since I moved to Miami. Maggie, Sarah, and everyone else I dated had rarely asked about my parents, and I had responded vaguely and changed the subject when they did.

I got out of the car and went to the front door. My hand hovered over it to knock, but I was having a really hard time hitting the wood. I grimaced, took a deep breath, and then knocked. I just had to convince myself I wasn't ever going to see him again, that I was here for however long and then I'd never come back. I had to see him one more time for . . . well, I didn't know what for, but I was already here.

A minute later the door opened. My father stood there. He was thinner and his hair was white. The once-prominent mustache had turned gray, and his face drooped with age. His eyes were wide, wet, and red.

"Adam," I said. "How are you?"

He didn't say anything for a second. "What the hell are you doing here?"

"Just passing through. I won't be here long, I think."

He nodded and looked me up and down. "Well, did you need something?"

"Not exactly the welcome I was expecting. Did I run over your cat or something before I left? I feel like I'd remember that."

"Always the smart-ass."

"Gee, I wonder where I got that from."

"Not from me. I show respect to this country and to people. You never had an ounce of respect for anything."

"Oh, what was I supposed to . . . no. No, it was a mistake to come here. Sorry to bother you."

I turned and left, and he shut the door. As I was pulling away I saw him peering through the window blinds.

"What a shit-show," I mumbled to myself as I wondered if I should just leave town right now. But fatigue had suddenly crept over me. Five or six hours of sleep wouldn't be a bad thing.

I went to the real estate office, signed the paperwork, and bought the condo. If I did leave soon, I'd just hang on to it for a while and sell it for a profit in a few years.

By the time I got back to the condo, it was almost eight. Someone was waiting for me at the front door. A woman in a suit.

My breath caught.

Gates.

I'd pictured her as a mother of four, married to some rough-and-tumble farmer. But the campaign signs I'd seen still reflected her maiden name.

She turned and saw me as I parked and stepped out of the car. Her red hair was straight, exactly as she'd worn it in high school. A thick leather bracelet adorned her left wrist, tattered to the point of almost falling apart.

"Still in a suit?" I said. "I think the workday is over."

"Actually I just got done."

"You always were the worker bee. You know what I figured out? I could work harder than anyone else, but if I was working at the wrong things, it didn't matter."

"I'm guessing you mean you've heard I'm county attorney. You don't approve?"

I stood close to her and could smell her perfume. Really, she didn't look that much different. A few wrinkles that weren't there before, but the youthful glow, the energy, the fierce intelligence that always had shone from her eyes, those were as bright as ever.

"Approve? I'm really proud of you. Seriously. For a woman to get to the top law enforcement spot in a town like this is incredible." I sat on the hood of my car. "Kinda surprised me, though. You were more eager to get outa here than I was."

"Yeah, well, life usually doesn't work out like you planned." She inhaled deeply and leaned against the wall of the condo. "Your Realtor recognized your name and called your dad as a reference, who told her to call me."

"Sounds about right."

"You staying awhile?"

"I don't know yet."

She moved a strand of hair away from her face. "Well, I wanted to see you to just . . . I don't know."

"What?"

"My father died shortly after you left, Tatum."

The news hit me hard. "You're kidding. Felix? He was healthy as a bull."

"Heart attack. He'd been smoking and drinking since he was nine years old. Last of the cowboys, I guess. But real cowboys don't live that long." She paused and kicked at a pebble by her shoe. "You leaving while I was still in the hospital, I got over that. But you didn't come to the funeral. You didn't call, you didn't send a card, nothing. You acted like none of us ever meant anything. My father loved you like a son."

I nodded and felt something I seemed to be feeling a lot of lately. Guilt. I didn't like it. Didn't seem to fit right, like a tight jacket that was suffocating me.

"I'm sorry. You just . . . you want to leave behind your past sometimes so bad you forget that there's people who can get hurt."

She shook her head. "Doesn't matter now. We're all different people anyway."

A woman got out of her car at the condo next door. She waved and said hello, and I waved back. "Out of curiosity, how'd you become county attorney?"

"When my father died, I was the only one that could run the ranch. Nineteen-year-old running a cattle ranch by herself. I had to get some workers and I made it happen, but I realized I wasn't my father. The ranch was always his dream, not mine. Law school seemed like a good choice. I got my degree from UNLV. Kept the ranch. Started off as a prosecutor and just kind of rose through the ranks. The last county attorney was my mentor, so it seemed like a given that I would run."

"Sounds like you got another election coming up. Saw the billboards in town."

She nodded. "I'm not sure I'm going to win this one. I think my time is up."

"Why?"

"Horace, my opponent, is well connected in this town. He came in a few years ago and bought up a lot of property and several businesses. I don't know if his plan was to become county attorney or not but seems like something he can get now."

"Just 'cause he's rich? Come on. You're a hometown girl. No way he has an advantage."

"Well, I did some unpopular things. Got a new murder case against some local boys that's proving to be a real headache and has half the town calling for their blood and half saying it's a witch hunt. I cut some plea deals on cases the public didn't want plea deals on. Of course the evidence was terrible, and I would've lost if I'd gone to trial, but they just see the headlines and don't care about the facts. So Horace has painted me as some kind of lunatic that wants criminals released into the streets. Seems to be working so far. We don't do polls out here, but from what I'm hearing, it's a fifty-fifty shot between us. But he's got the money to ramp things up before the election. Not sure I can compete."

"How much you need?"

"I'm not taking your money, Tatum."

"You're a public official seeking reelection. What do you care where the money comes from?"

She pushed off the wall. "I don't want it. I just came by to see you." She hesitated a second. "How long are you really planning on staying?"

"I don't know. Leaving tomorrow or the next day . . . maybe. Just didn't really know where else to go, I guess."

She nodded, staring down at the ground. "You seen your dad yet?"

"Yeah. Went about as well as you can imagine."

"What'd he say about his treatment?"

"What treatment?"

She paused, and I could tell she was unsure what to say.

"Gates, what treatment?"

"He didn't say anything about his health?"

"No, why?"

"I think you need to go talk to your father."

"Why? What treatment? What are you talking about?"

"Tatum . . . he has cancer."

11

Adam opened the door the next morning, still in his pajamas. He didn't say anything, just looked me up and down, and then left the door open as he went inside. I came in and shut the door behind me.

The house hadn't changed. Messier than it was when my mom was alive, but the decorations were the same, the carpet was the same, even the television was the same. An old gigantic color television with the rabbit-ears antenna. My father sat down at the breakfast table. He was eating eggs. I sat across from him and folded my arms.

"You want some eggs?"

"I'm okay."

We sat in silence a minute.

"What type?" I said.

He held my gaze a few seconds. "Lung."

"Are you in chemo?"

He shook his head. "I ain't doin' that."

"What the hell do you mean, *you ain't doin' that*? You wanna live or not?"

"You seen the side effects? Hair loss, bleeding, constipation, too much sleeping—"

"Too much sleeping? Are you kidding me right now?"

"The side effects are too much and there's no guarantee." He took a bite of eggs.

I watched him awhile. He had once been massive and strong. Not gym strong—the kind of strength that came with baling hay and building fences in 110-degree heat. The kind that came from meat and potatoes at every meal and a body hardened by twelve-hour days of constant labor. But that was a long time ago. Now he looked frail, and tired.

"Why didn't you call me?" I said.

He glanced up at me and didn't speak as he took another bite of eggs.

I exhaled and looked around the house. "House looks the same."

He shrugged. "No one comes over anymore. No need to change anything."

"Mind if I go look at my room?"

"What do I care?"

I rose and went upstairs. My room was at the end of the hall. I opened the door. Posters of Batman and *Star Wars* still hung on the walls. The clothes I'd worn in high school were still in the closet. On the top shelf was my Miami Marlins baseball cap. I put it on, grinning, and then looked in the mirror above the dresser. Seemed smaller now. I tossed it back and left the room.

My parents' room was on the right. The last place I had seen my mother. I stood in front of it a second and then went back downstairs.

"I got some things to do," my father said. "Don't stay too long."

I stood in front of him. "I, uh . . . I'll see ya."

"Yeah, see ya."

12

The Ute County Attorney's Office was in River Falls. The Realtor had also informed me that River Falls now had six thousand residents, Ute County had fifteen thousand, and they had recently added a Home Depot.

The City and County Building used to house the only courthouse and jail within fifty miles. The courthouse was still there, but they had modernized it so it looked like a medium-size office building now. You could still see some of the bolts in the ground where they'd shackled chain gangs outside.

I followed the signs for the county attorney, which pointed me to the basement. An elderly woman sat behind a reception desk loudly chewing gum. She looked up at me suspiciously and put her glasses on to get a better look.

"Can I help you?"

"I'm here to see Ms. Barnes."

"One moment."

She—painfully slowly—picked up the receiver and called someone. She spoke a few words and then realized she hadn't asked who I was. "Who are you again?"

"Tatum Graham."

She said my name into the phone and then waited a few seconds before nodding as though the person on the other line could see her.

"You can head back."

The District and County Attorneys' Offices in Florida were locked down like military bases. The insane and desperate in the cities needed to take it out on someone, and the prosecutor who had said all those horrible things about them in court was a good place for them to start. The last time I went to the Miami-Dade County Attorney's Office, I had been searched, ushered through a metal detector, and scanned with a handheld device before my identity then had to be verified. Here in Ute County, I opened the door, walked inside, and had access to the entire place.

Since no one was there to direct me, I wandered around, looking into the various offices. I came across a kid—probably early twenties—who looked at me curiously. A good-looking kid with blond hair and a pencil behind his ear who said, "Tatum Graham?"

"Yeah."

"You're . . . you're really Tatum Graham?"

"In the flesh. And you are?"

He nearly jumped out of his chair and almost tripped over it. He held out his hand. "Will. Will Aggie. One of the deputy county attorneys here."

"Well, nice to meet you, Will."

"I watched some of your trial with Marcus Green on *Court TV*. I mean, it was awful what happened and all, but the trial itself was amazing. I mean, the way you got the prior convictions for the victim in by introducing them as eleven-oh-two statements was incredible. I never would've thought that would work."

"Well, you gotta throw everything at the wall and see what sticks."

"I just read something about you quitting your law practice after that case. Is that true?"

I glanced around. "Is your boss here?"

"Gates?"

"Yeah."

"Um, sure. The big office at the end of the hall."

"Thanks."

As I strolled down the hall, I felt him looking at me. When I turned around he was leaning out of his office, staring at me.

Gates was writing something on a notepad. She stopped when she realized I was there, placed the pen down, and leaned back with a grin. "I thought you'd've left by now," she said.

I sat down across from her and rubbed my forehead. "You got any Advil?"

She opened a drawer and gave me a few pills. I took them and pointed to a water bottle on her desk. She handed it to me and I washed down the pills.

"He doesn't look good," I said.

"No, he doesn't."

"How long does he have?"

"I found out about it four months ago. When I took him some wine for his birthday. He told me the doctor said a couple years."

"You visit him on his birthday?"

"And Christmas." She hesitated. "And Father's Day."

We stared at each other a second. Luckily, Will walked in and said, "Hey, I was just—" He tripped over a box and nearly tumbled over the desk. He knocked one of Gates's little statuettes of Lady Justice off the desk. He picked it up and put it back. "Sorry."

"What is it, Will?"

He looked to me and said, "Mr. Graham, can I just say it's awesome that you're actually here."

"In body only."

He grinned and then looked at Gates. "Have you told him?"

"Told me what?"

"There's an open position."

Gates said, "He's not interested, Will. Now what did you need?"

"Are you sure?" he said. "I mean, how cool would that be? Tatum Graham in our office as a prosecutor. I mean, that'd be insane."

I chuckled. "Me, a prosecutor? Sorry, kid. But prosecutors are the tadpoles swimming with the crocodiles like me. Not my thing."

"Oh," he said, genuinely disappointed. "I just think . . . I just thought that would be great." He turned to Gates and said, "Settled the Marlow case. Just wanted to tell you."

"Thanks."

He nodded and looked to me and said, "It was good meeting you."

When he left I said, "Sweet kid."

"He is. Bit green."

"You could train him."

"I don't really have the time. All my prosecutors are new and young. People get experience here and move on to bigger and better in the cities. The two I got left, Will and Jia, are barely a year out of law school. And I already have to give them a murder case."

"You're kidding?"

She shook her head. "I don't have a choice. With the campaigning I'm doing, I just don't have the time." She paused and looked out the window a second. "You know, they could actually use someone to train them. We just lost our most senior prosecutor. If you know anyone, I'd appreciate a recommend."

I chuckled.

"What?" she said.

"It's just cute that you think you can bullshit me. Look, you would hate me working here, and I just retired from the law."

"I can understand why you'd need a change of scenery after what happened with your last case, but is retirement from the law really the answer? I mean . . . why?"

I shook my head and looked down to her desk. "Personal reasons."

"You're too young to retire."

I shrugged. "Chips fall where they fall."

She sighed and said, "Too bad. They could really use the help. This case is going to be a real bastard."

"What's the case?"

"The one I told you about. Young girl, Patty Winchester, seventeen, raped and murdered by two boys. I got no witnesses, and one of the boys is well connected in the town."

I swallowed and felt that tight suit squeezing me again. "I can't. Sorry."

She nodded. "I understand. I'm glad you saw Adam. He needed to see you one more time."

I took in a deep breath and exhaled slowly as I stared out the window. "I'll probably stick around a little longer. Another few days or whatever."

"Why?"

I shrugged. "Who knows?"

13

I drove back to my father's home, wondering what the hell I was doing here. River Falls, Adam, Gates . . . this was the past and I needed to focus on the future. But when you have nowhere else to go, it's almost as if you retreat back into wherever you knew when you were a kid. And this was the only place I'd known for the first nineteen years of my life.

The door was open and breakfast was still on the table. Music was on, a classic rock station. The Beatles started playing. My father sat in his recliner and I sat on the couch across from him, and we silently listened.

"Mom loved the Beatles," I said. "Whenever she cleaned the house on Sundays, she would put them on. I think I've heard every one of their songs like fifty times."

"They brought in the hippies and the loafers and threw good Christian morality out the window. They destroyed our culture with this crap music." He took a drink out of a glass that I could tell was filled with bourbon. "You seen Gates yet?"

"Just left her office. Why?"

"She's a sweet girl. Never misses a birthday."

"Yeah. She seems stressed right now. Thinks she's going to lose the election."

"Horace is a powerful man. And she's got Patty's murder."

"She mentioned it."

He shook his head. "I know Patty's father, Hank. Good man. Mechanic. He fixes the cars of some of the widows around town and takes cake or casseroles as payment. Don't know what the hell he's going to do. His wife left him way back, and he raised two kids on his own." He took another drink. "Poor girl. And what those two little shits did to her before she died . . ." He shook his head. "I'll never understand people." He grimaced and said, "Get me two of those pills on the kitchen counter by the sink, would ya?"

I rose and went into the kitchen. A large amber bottle of pain pills sat next to a glass. I took two and brought them to him. "You know you're not supposed to take these with alcohol, right?"

"Look who's a doctor all of a sudden." He shot the pills down with bourbon. "You've met Hank, before Patty was born. He fixed that Oldsmobile we had."

"The station wagon?" I smiled. "I spent my childhood in the back of that car, driving around with Mom. What happened to it?"

"It got old and its time came." He lifted the glass to his lips and said, "Happens to all of us."

I stared at him as he drank. "She asked me to help her on that case."

"Gates?"

"Yeah. She says her prosecutors are newbies and need help."

He took another drink, draining the glass. "You gonna do it?"

"No. I retired. I'm just passing through."

He shrugged. "Well, thanks for coming by."

He rose and went into the kitchen. I sat on the couch, listening to "Let It Be." Probably my mom's favorite song. How the hell my dad and her managed to stay married was a mystery to me.

Up on the mantel was a photograph of the three of us at a park. I didn't remember the photo and had no idea who took it, but I was smiling widely. My mother was smiling and had her hands on my shoulders, but my father had a stern face and had his hands behind his back. I stood and said, "Take care of yourself."

———

The next morning, after a restless night at the condo, I called ahead to a resort on Catalina Island that I had once been to and booked a two-week stay. Seemed long enough to relax and figure out my next move.

On the drive out of town, I debated whether to stop and say good-bye to Gates.

I couldn't decide, and I was hungry, so I stopped at the diner. I sat at the counter this time and ordered steak and eggs. It seemed like everyone was here. In small towns, people liked to eat breakfast out at the same place every day, and this was the only diner in town. It was somewhere to hear the latest gossip and news, discuss politics and the economy, and stay connected to the town. I pictured the street markets in ancient Athens and Rome serving about the same function.

While I waited, a big guy in a gray mechanic's uniform came in. The name tag said "Hank." He took a stool close to me, and I could smell the aftershave on him. He ordered some eggs and sat quietly. He didn't read the paper or look up to the television that was hanging behind the counter. He glanced at me and then looked again, this time taking a long stare.

"Tatum?"

I turned to him, making the connection: Hank, Patty's father. "Yeah."

He grinned and held out his hand and we shook. "Last time I saw you, you were trying to buy beer with a fake ID over at the Gas n' Go."

I thought a second. That's right. I had done that. "Hey, you were the one that convinced that jerk Larsen to let me go without calling the cops, weren't you?"

"Yeah."

How had I forgotten that? I'd used an ID that belonged to a fifty-year-old guy to try to buy some Budweiser. Hank had come in to get gas shortly after I'd been caught. He'd asked the owner to cut me a break.

"Wow. I completely forgot about that. You drove me home after, too."

He nodded, a grin coming to his face. "Your dad would always tell me you were a delinquent, but that you were going to accomplish great things one day."

"My dad said that? I think you're confusing me with someone else."

"No, he said it. I dropped you off, and he smacked the back of your head and told you to go upstairs. I told him to take it easy on you, that we all did stuff like that as young men, and that's when he said that."

My food came and I said, "How you holding up?" as I poured Tabasco over my eggs.

He lost the grin. I instantly knew I shouldn't have asked. I didn't have that voice in my head that other people had that told them not to say something because it might hurt someone else's feelings.

"You, uh, heard about Patty?"

"I did. My father was talking to me about it. I'm sorry."

He nodded. "She was seventeen and would've graduated a few days after . . . after it all happened. She'd applied to Dixie State and gotten in. She wanted to be a nurse." He grinned again. "She said that people were on their worst behavior when they were sick, but that the nurse could change that. That the nurse, not the doctor, was the one that made sure people felt that someone cared about them. That was her. Always worried about other people. She volunteered after school in the children's wing of the hospital. She'd bring them presents on their birthdays and Christmas, though I don't know how she managed to save up the money to do it. Do you remember her at all?"

"No, she was born a few years after I'd already left."

He nodded again as his eggs came. He stared at the plate a second and then pushed it away. He took out a ten and left it on the counter and said to the waitress, "I better run, Mary."

"You want me to box it up for you?"

"No. I don't feel much like eating right now."

He turned to me and said, "You, um, take care of yourself, Tatum. If you need anything with your car while you're here, don't hesitate to come to me."

"Thanks."

I watched him leave. His head hung low. When he reached his truck, he put his hands on the roof and stared off at nothing for a second, as if pulling together the strength he needed to get inside, and then he got in and drove away.

I turned to the steak and eggs in front of me. I didn't feel much like eating either.

14

I was back at the County Attorney's Office. Will was there, along with a young lady whom I guessed was Korean. She looked at me and said, "Can I help you?"

"Gates here?"

"She's out."

Will came out of his office and said, "Jia. This is Tatum Graham."

Her face changed and she said, "Oh. Nice to meet you." She rose and shook my hand. "I followed several of your cases very closely. We actually had the Santos case as a mock trial in our trial advocacy class in law school."

"Oh yeah? What side were you?"

"Prosecution. I got a conviction."

"Wow. That was a tough case for them. Good job."

"I'm not in the habit of losing, same as you."

I pointed to her. "You I like."

I turned back to Will and said, "You got Patty's file here?"

He glanced at Jia. "Yeah. Um, did you want to look at it?"

"No, I wanna buy it dinner and meet its parents."

He grinned but still stood there, while Jia went over to a filing cabinet and returned with a massive file.

"Paper files?" I said. "Abraham Lincoln work here, too?"

"Hey, if you can convince the county council to budget more money for us, we'd be happy to take it."

I thumbed through the file. "I'll be in the conference room."

The conference room was tiny. Six chairs around an old table made from logs with a bearskin rug under it. Photographs of canyons and cowboys in the West decorated the walls. I sat down and opened the file.

The detective's narrative was straightforward and filled with about as many errors as I expected from small-town detectives not used to homicide cases. I guessed there weren't specialists here, and these guys were used to investigating stolen bikes and fraudulent checks instead of a rape and murder. I grabbed a legal pad that was on the table, along with a pen, and took a few notes to try to boil down the essence of what had happened, since the detective, who apparently hadn't really been able to tell, had thrown everything and the kitchen sink into his massive narrative.

Essentially, Patty was found at a campground called the Hallows near the top of a secluded canyon, her body partially buried in a ditch. She was nude, and no clothes were found at the scene. The body was spotted in the early morning hours by an elderly couple taking their dogs for a stroll.

The coroner determined that she was killed by strangulation and that, based on a number of contusions and broken bones, she had been tortured before death. A SAFE kit—sexual assault forensic evidence kit—had found semen from one unsub—unknown subject—and vaginal tearing. Coroner placed the time of death about four days before the body was found and concluded that she was likely killed there on scene.

No blood spatter analysis expert was called to examine the scene. Several tire tracks were discovered, but no expert had been consulted to determine what type of car it was. They "guessed" it was a large truck. Nice, boys. Might as well say it was a car that likely had four wheels.

No scrapings done of her fingernails, in case she clawed at the assailants, no careful scanning of her body for hair fibers, no entomologist to examine the insect larvae that had no doubt taken up home inside the body and could confirm time of death. The coroner, thank goodness, at least knew what blood lividity was and had done an analysis to determine she was killed on her back and left that way.

Crime scenes were supposed to have a "safe area" for nonessential personnel, to prevent contaminating the crime scene, and the forensic techs were to keep track of who entered and exited the crime scene. Nothing like that here. No log of the people there, and no sketches of the scene, though, thankfully, there were photographs. The detectives and forensic team had phoned it in on this one.

Upon interviewing Patty's friend Cecily Gilbert, it was determined that Patty and Cecily had gone into a bar in Las Vegas called Skid Row—sounded like a lovely place—and that they'd met Anderson Ficco and Steven Brown, two kids they'd gone to high school with who had graduated last year. Cecily left early because she had a curfew. Patty had said she would get a ride home with Anderson and Steven. Her body was found four days later. The semen found inside her had degraded too much for a DNA match.

Steven had no priors, but there was a note that Anderson Ficco had a juvenile rape charge that had been dismissed. Bail had been denied, and both boys had been sitting in jail for just over three months.

The door to the conference room opened, and Gates walked in sipping a Diet Coke.

"What the hell is this, Gates?"

"Not the best investigation, I know."

"Not the best? I would get this case dismissed in a single motion. I'm not kidding. I would set an expedited hearing and have these boys back out on the street in forty-eight hours. Who'd you have working this case, Barney Fife?"

"We don't get many murders, Tatum, and we only have a handful of detectives for the entire county. They're used to credit card fraud and car theft cases. This is the first homicide they've ever worked."

"So you call in someone else from a bigger county."

"That's not how it works here. Nobody wants this case. The public is screaming for blood, and if these boys get acquitted, any prosecutor or detective working the case is going to get the brunt of that anger. I made a call up north to Vernal, Saint George, Provo . . . everyone said they'd get back to me, and lo and behold they stopped returning my calls. I'm thinking I might see if the FBI can help."

I shook my head. "With their budget cuts? Forget it. They got all their resources wrapped up years in advance."

She looked down to a photo of Patty laid out in the ditch, her milky eyes upturned to the sky. "I mean, it's not the best I've seen, but I think you're exaggerating a little. There's enough there for a conviction."

"No, there's not."

"Why not?"

"For starters, semen deteriorates extremely quickly outside the male body. In a living woman, it can last about five days. If the woman is dead and there's no warmth or blood down there, two days tops, usually one day. Your coroner says the body was out there four days after death, which means he wouldn't have been able to test for the presence of semen. It just wouldn't be there. So the day of the murder is wrong, for one. Oh, and there's the little matter that a good defense attorney is going to argue fairly convincingly that the boys didn't actually do it."

"What do you mean?"

"Look at it from the jury's point of view: Two kids that went to high school with her, that knew her, knew her family, and just suddenly, after knowing her their entire lives, decided to kill her? And not just kill her, but brutally abuse and kill her? That kinda thing doesn't happen out of nowhere. I saw Anderson's got a prior sexual assault that was dismissed, but there were no details in there. You need to get those reports right away and see if there was violence involved. Don't get me wrong, these boys did it. But I could have these kids acquitted with my eyes closed."

"You think someone else was involved?"

I shrugged. "I don't know. The Ficcos were rich even when I was here, so someone that grew up filthy rich could potentially view other people as expendable, and Anderson does have that prior rape allegation . . . but this is just blind violence. Fury and hatred. The defense will argue that this kind of fury would've expressed itself between the boys and Patty before this, but I didn't see anything in the file to indicate they didn't get along. In fact there was that statement from Patty's father that Patty liked Anderson and Steven. They probably liked her, too. Why kill her like that just for fun?"

"There's evidence Anderson was out of his mind on drugs that night. People do all sorts of insane things in that state of mind."

"Yeah, but Steven was there, too, and he wasn't high. So to buy your theory, the jury's gotta believe that they killed someone they've known almost their whole life for fun—and after being seen with her by witnesses. And then they just handed us their convictions on a silver platter." I shook my head. "It's too easy, and when it's too easy, something else is going on."

"You haven't watched the confession yet."

I nodded. "True, but I'll bet you anything it's not much of a confession. I mean, probably enough for a jury, but, I'm telling you, the defense will argue this was personal. Someone was either hurt by Patty or scared about something she knew and wanted to send a message to others that know it, too. Could also be just a random psychopath who stumbled across her, but I don't think so. The body wasn't hidden well. This is someone filled with rage masked as lust. Again, yeah, I think you got the right guys, but that has nothing to do with a court of law. A good defense attorney is going to have a field day with this case." I hesitated and felt my heart in my throat as a nervous energy shot through me, an energy from a memory that was still too fresh to analyze without intense pain. "But I've been wrong before."

She sighed. "You don't think I knew all that? It is what it is. We go forward with the case we got, not the one we want."

I closed the file. "You gotta start over. From square one. Get some real detectives down here and reinterview all the witnesses, get some people from the state crime lab, and a blood expert—but only to look at photos since the scene is deteriorated—and you got to have a medical examiner go over the body with a fine-tooth comb."

"We can't, she was buried months ago."

"Then you gotta exhume the body."

"Her father is very religious, no way he would allow it."

"Well, then get ready for these boys to walk. Your only hope is a terrible attorney that pleads them out."

She shook her head. "That's not going to happen. During the interview when one of the detectives told him he's going to prison, Anderson Ficco said, and I quote, 'Rich people don't go to prison.'"

"Sounds like a charming lad. Who's his lawyer?"

"He hired one of those celebrity lawyers from New York. Russell Pritcher."

I chuckled. "Russell Pritcher? As in the Russell Pritcher that once defended one of the Saudi princes?"

"You know him?"

"We've met. Where are you in the case?"

"We're going to have the preliminary hearing next week and then a trial after that."

"Oh, forget the trial. He'll get this dismissed at prelim. The guy's good. Not as good as me, granted, but the best your money can buy if I'm not available. Is he representing both boys?"

"Just Anderson." She glanced out the window. "If I lose this case, Horace will have it plastered in every store window, on every billboard, and running on every radio station. I'll lose my seat."

"I mean, it comes with the territory, right?"

"Do you have any idea how hard it was for me to rise to this position in a county like this? The men here still think it was a mistake to allow women the right to vote." She shook her head. "All that time, all that work . . . for nothing. To lose to a man who just happens to have a lot of money."

I stared at her a long time. "Wish I could help."

She took the file and opened it up. She removed a photo of Patty's body lying in the ditch. A necklace hung around her neck, half a heart. Something young girls share with their best friends.

I started to reach for it, then realized my hand was trembling for the second time in only a few days. I shoved my hand under the table and held it steady with my other hand, hoping Gates hadn't seen.

"I don't know who you are now, Tatum, but I know who you were. And the boy I knew would never have allowed this"—she pointed at the photo—"to happen if he could do anything about it. I'm asking for your help. But I understand if you can't. If you just want to run away." She rose. "It's what you do best, right?"

15

I sat outside on the steps of the City and County Building. Most of the men coming in and out wore suits with cowboy boots, some with hats to match. The women, down to the person, wore skirts. Except for Gates, of course. She never cared what men or society expected of her. I remembered how once—at a bar we had gotten into with fake IDs—she got into a drinking match with a burly Hells Angel. Shot for shot, she drank him under the table. On the tenth or eleventh shot, the tequila came shooting out of his mouth and he puked.

Someone came and sat next to me. I looked over to Will, who put his arms on his knees as he said hi to one of the cops going into the building.

"You leaving?" he said.

"I don't know. I think so."

"Sure could use your help. Anderson's pretty nuts. I heard he once put a cigarette out on a kid in gym class that ticked him off. If I lose and he gets off, I don't think he's done hurting people, and everyone will blame me because I don't know what I'm doing."

"Takes a big man to admit something like that. Most lawyers would never say it. It's also stupid. *The Art of Jury Trial as War*, chapter nine: 'Never admit you don't know what you're doing. Weakness attracts weakness, and strength attracts strength. You portray weakness and you entice people to attack.'"

"*The Art of Jury Trial as War?*"

"Book I'm writing. Trials are a war, Will. And wars have rules. Things that have worked over and over again. You gotta learn the rules if you wanna win. Without it you're just flailing in the wind." A woman walked past me and smiled. "What're you doing here anyway? Most kids your age can't wait to get outa this town."

He shook his head. "Not me. I love this place. My father was born here and his father and his father. It's in my blood."

"You only think that because you haven't seen the rest of the world. There's a lot out there, you know."

"I got my little corner of the world and it's enough for me." He looked at me. "Sure do wish I could get that girl a bit of justice, though."

I chuckled. "*Justice?* Forget that word if you want to be a good trial attorney. It's a concept invented for philosophers to debate. You are at war, and you're a general trying to win for your side. That's it."

"I like to think it's more than that."

"It's not."

"Yeah? Then why'd you quit after your client killed that girl?"

I stared at him a second and then turned away.

"Did Gates ever tell you how she was attacked?"

He nodded. "Up by the farm, right? Like twenty years ago?"

I looked out over the parking lot. "A guy rear-ended her on that empty road up by McCaleb's property. When she got out, he jumped her. She fought like an Amazon warrior, but he beat her until she was unconscious. Luckily another car came by, and the guy booked it before he could toss her into his car and take off. Anyway, she was in the hospital. I visited her, and you know what I remember most? Her nail polish."

"Why?"

I shook my head. "I don't know. It was . . . pink and sparkly. Something a kid would pick out. I stared at it a long time." Someone brushed past me up the steps. "And then a day later, I left, without saying goodbye. I was planning on leaving that year anyway, but I just . . .

I don't know. Froze. Something clicked in my brain. Turned off. And I left." A deep breath escaped me. "I saw that nail polish on the girl my client killed."

"Look, Mr. Graham, I don't know you, but I can't imagine that feels very good to have a guy you got acquitted go out and kill a young girl. I'm going to feel the same way if Patty's killers walk because of me. And maybe you will, too, because you had a chance to help us and you didn't."

He rose and went inside.

When he was gone, I sat on the steps awhile longer, exhaled loudly, and then rose and followed him in.

16

I came into the office, and Gates, Jia, and Will were sitting around a desk speaking. I shut the door behind me and said, "Will, task number one: get my employment paperwork drafted up ASAP and get me a badge."

He stood in shock a second.

"Should I send a stripper-gram to you?"

"Oh," he said, "sorry." He grabbed a legal pad and pen and began writing. "Um, we also get guns."

"Don't need a gun. Just get me my district attorney badge. Task number two: call Wilford Snow. He's an auto expert out of Arizona, so it's not much of a drive for him if he has to come testify. Send him the photos of the tire tracks. Tell him I need the make of the tires that made those tire tracks, and castings approximating the treads in case we need to match it to someone's car. Assuming of course he can even tell from those crappy photos. Task number three: I need the names, phone numbers, and addresses of everyone Patty Winchester saw the day she was abducted, and then I need to know the names of the owners and everyone that worked at Skid Row that day. I would normally say send out the detectives to interview them, but looks like we're going to be doing the brunt of the work ourselves. We're going to interview every employee at Skid Row and then anyone else they remember was there."

I turned to Jia. "Jia, first task: call Linda Burt in Sacramento. She's the top expert on blood spatter analysis in the country. Send her all the photos and the police reports and tell her I want the best guesses she can make without actually seeing the scene. Task two: call the Utah State Crime Lab. Tell them we have a murder down here that we want them to gather further evidence on, and we need them to look at a body ASAP."

"We don't have a body."

"Sure we do. It's just sitting in the graveyard."

Gates said, "I'm not sure exhuming a young girl is going to play very well with the mayor and sheriff."

"Hey, are you the county attorney or are they?"

She grinned. "You need her father's permission, and as I said earlier, I doubt you'll get it."

"Leave that to me." I slapped my hands together. "All right, get to it, boys and girls. We got a battle in front of us."

17

The next day, I drove out to see Hank.

Hank Winchester's mechanic shop was near the outskirts of town. One garage, and it looked like one employee, Hank himself. He was doing something under the hood of an old Toyota when he saw me. He grabbed a rag and wiped the grease off his hands and watched me as I approached.

"I took auto shop in high school," I said. "Nearly cut my hand off in a fan on a Ford truck and decided it best to let the experts do their jobs."

He grinned. "Not for everybody. Me, I love it. The smell of the oil in a hot engine, the way the engine purrs when you get it going when it wouldn't work before. Something about that, fixing something with your hands. I think these generations coming up aren't going to get to experience that."

I nodded, looking at a picture of several children in a laminated photo hanging from the car's rearview mirror.

"I have to ask you for something, Hank, and it's not pretty."

"What?"

"Probably didn't know, but I'm a criminal defense attorney and I'm jumping sides for this one case. I've decided to help Gates with the prosecution of those boys that killed Patty. We've got to rework the case from the beginning. Start from the ground up. The detectives on this case are inexperienced. They didn't do a lot of the things they would've done if they'd been working homicides awhile. The defense attorney Anderson Ficco hired is one of the best in the world. He probably charged upward of a million dollars for this case. He's the guy you hire when you got the money and you do not want to go to prison."

He nodded, continuing to wipe his hands, though the grease was already off. He leaned against the car and stared at the ground. "What do you need from me?"

I hesitated. "I need to exhume Patty's body."

He shook his head. "Isn't there another way?"

"Afraid not. I need the forensic techs and a medical examiner from the crime lab to go over the body and see if there's anything the coroner missed. Can't do it without Patty." I stepped closer to him. "Hank, these boys might very well get away with this. You need to put your personal views aside and do whatever you can to make sure they don't do this to anyone else's daughter."

He stared at me a second and then nodded. "Okay."

———

We got an exhumation order drafted, and the judge signed off on it. I knew the judge: Beatrice Allred. She had been the district court judge in this county since I was a kid, and I pegged her age now at midseventies. Judges didn't have to retire unless they wanted to, and it sounded like she was going to be a lifer. And why not? You just sit there and say yes or no to lawyers all day. Mostly no.

The exhumation couldn't wait: it had to be done as fast as possible to preserve evidence—if there was any left. Jia said the crime lab had told them it'd be six weeks before they could get someone out here, so I told her to call back and ask to speak with a supervisor. I listened while she told them that unless they sent someone out here immediately, her next call was to the news outlets to let them know the crime lab was risking two boys getting away with rape and murder because they said they were too busy, and then the call after that would be to any legislator that would answer to point them to the news story. The crime lab said they'd have an ME out there tomorrow. It made me smile.

"Will, Jia, Skid Row is in Vegas. We got a drive. Let's go."

18

Before heading out to Vegas, we drove over to the sheriff's station. The building had been constructed by the first pioneers out here and looked like a massive log cabin. Didn't appear to have been many upgrades over the last century and a half.

We went in, and I had Will flash his badge at the front desk.

"Detective Howard, please."

She directed us to offices in the back. Most detectives in major cities were crammed into a bull pen. The detectives here got their own plush offices complete with a shared secretary. In one office were two men, one young and skinny—with a desk plate that said Brett Vail—and the other middle-aged, bald, and thickly muscled, with faded burn scars on his neck—Mark Howard, I guessed. Dopey looking, guys you'd see at a frat party every night when they were in college. I stepped inside with Jia and Will and shut the door behind me. I folded my arms. The detectives didn't scream at me to get out, so clearly they knew who I was. Probably a secretary or someone at the County Attorney's Office had warned them there was a new prosecutor in the office. The two detectives glanced at each other, and Howard rolled his eyes. He had a marine corps tattoo on his forearm and was smoking; he blew out a puff of smoke toward me.

Vail said, "We're in the middle of something right now, so if—"

"Shut up," I said.

"Excuse me?"

"I said shut up. Listen, son, we're not playing nice here. Let's be straight up. You two screwed up this murder investigation worse than I've ever seen. The defense attorney Anderson Ficco hired is going to file a motion to dismiss this case and turn both of you into ground beef on the stand. And he's going to invite at least a few reporters to court so that your embarrassment can be captured for everyone in the state to enjoy."

Howard rose and got within a few inches of me. "Who the hell do you think you are?"

"Mark Howard, right, lead on the Winchester investigation? Well, I'm the guy that's trying to save your ass." I stared him right in the pupils, my gaze hard. "Those boys are going to get away with rape and murder because of you. So drop the macho act, take responsibility for your shit investigation, and let's figure out a way to get this done."

Vail laughed. "Get out of our station."

"Sure, no problem. I'll go to the sheriff's office right now and tell him how many reporters are going to be at the motion to dismiss and how his detectives are going to look like bumbling idiots, and how two murderers, whose blood the voters are screaming for, are going to walk free. Isn't there an election coming up?"

They looked at each other. They weren't laughing now.

"What do you want?" Howard said.

I leaned against the wall. "Give me what you got."

"It's all in our reports."

"Don't con me. There's always things you guys leave out of the reports. What'd you leave out?"

They glanced at each other and Howard said, "Nothing."

Jia stepped in and said, "If you guys are hiding something, now's the time to tell us. Because even if we don't know, the defense attorney will, and he's going to bring it out at the worst time for us."

They glanced at each other again and Howard sighed. He looked at me and said, "There's a couple of things."

"I'm all ears."

"Patty was . . . I mean, everyone loved Patty because everyone knows and loves Hank." He looked to Vail and then said, "There were some things we didn't include in the reports and asked the coroner not to include. Just for Hank's sake."

"Well? Like what?"

"Patty had cigarette burns all over her body. Like all over."

"Cigarette burns," I said, glancing at Will.

Jia said, "Are you kidding me? You left that out of your reports and told the coroner to leave it out? You didn't think that'd come out in court? What about the photos?"

"We kept the photos showing the burns out of the file. We thought . . . I mean, we just didn't want Hank to know. It was bad enough what he had to learn. See her all busted up and bloody like that. We thought the case would be pled out early on."

Vail now said, "There's more. She, um . . . they cut her up pretty bad. Cuts all over the body." He swallowed and looked away. "Like someone wanted to hurt her for a while or something. We couldn't hide the bruising or broken bones, obviously, but we did what we could for Hank."

Jia looked like she was going to throw something at him, so I spoke before she could.

"Boys," I said, "listen to me because kindergarten is over: You're the prime cops in a murder investigation. Anything you do or say affects this investigation. I've known Judge Allred since you guys were in rookie diapers. She's tough and fair and hates crap work. What you two just told me is crap work."

"Hank is a fellow marine," Howard said. "A good, God-fearing man. I just wanted to spare him some pain."

I stared at him a second. "Detective Howard, you are going to file a supplemental narrative to your report and put in there what you just told me. You're going to say you misplaced the reports and the photos and filed them as soon as you found them."

They glanced at each other. "That's lying."

"Yeah? Well, you can go get hugs from your mommies after you do it. Now do it. What else you got?"

They were silent a second. Howard said, "We found a toy near the crime scene."

Vail added, "Like a little monkey action figure. It was near a picnic table where the body was found. We took some photos, but we just figured some kid lost it, so we didn't mention it."

"What else?"

"That's it."

"You're sure? There's nothing else I'm going to get surprised with in court?"

Howard shook his head. "No. Not that I can think of."

I looked between the two of them. "Time to take the diapers off and get in big-boy pants, guys."

We left, and out in the hall Will said, "That was amazing."

"What was?"

"The way you handled them. I've never seen them so rattled. Howard especially. He's tough as nails."

"Listen to me—you've got the law degree. The cops are there to gather evidence. If they can't do their job, it's your job to tell them how to do it, or find some other cops that can." I put on my sunglasses. "Now let's go. Police stations give me the creeps."

19

We drove down to Vegas while I played Creedence Clearwater. Jia sat in the passenger seat consumed by her phone; I figured she was texting or on social media, but when I glanced over, she was reading a book on the forensics of murder investigation. I looked back to Will, and he was staring out the window.

"So what's your story?" I said to Jia.

"No story."

"Everyone's got a story. Why'd you take a job at the County Attorney down here? You go up to Provo or Salt Lake you could make a lot more money."

She shrugged. "Better to be a big fish in a small pond. I've been out of law school fourteen months. How many lawyers fourteen months out do you know that handle murder cases?"

"Almost none. Except me."

"Really?"

I nodded. "My third case was a murder. A homeless guy that was taking shelter under a Hummer. When the owner came by to get in, the guy grabbed him and pulled him down to the ground. Robbed him and stabbed him in the chest. I was five months out of law school."

Will said, "You must've been terrified."

I shook my head. "No, not even a little. It was exactly what I wanted. A chance to prove myself. *The Art of Jury Trial as War*, chapter two: 'No risk, no reward.'"

Jia said, "Nice. You're writing a book? How many chapters like that does it have?"

"See, Will? That was the right question to ask."

"Did you do the case for free since he was homeless?" Will asked.

"No. You always charge a client what you want them to think you're worth, not what you're actually worth. The guy turned out to be the mentally ill son of some big-shot accountant. We had no experience and no money, but I quoted him double what the big firms were charging. He paid right up. People judge the quality of a lawyer on how much they charge, at least at first. Then you get a reputation and people will know your track record. So you better have a damn good one."

———

We drove into Las Vegas, and Google Maps led us off the strip into what was known as the Old Strip. The section of Las Vegas that the gangsters, bikers, and pimps used to run before the corporations moved in and wanted to make Vegas more family friendly. I parked at the curb, and in front of us was a brick building with a giant sign that said **SKID ROW** over the door. We got out of the car to find the front door locked. I pounded on it.

"Don't think anybody's home," Will said.

"They restock and clean up during the day. Someone's here."

I pounded again and someone answered, gigantic black guy in a tight T-shirt. Probably a bouncer.

Without my having to ask, Jia flashed her badge. I was liking this girl more and more.

"We'd like to speak to the owner, please," I said.

"Why?" he said, glancing between us.

"It's about a murder that probably started off here. Owner, please. Or whoever actually runs the place."

He hesitated and said, "That'd be Farah."

We stood there a second. "Well? Lead the way, Incredible Hulk."

He stared at me, then turned around and led us inside.

The place was about as divey as I expected. The windows were blacked out, what few there were, the floors were scraped and dirty, and the section with the tables near the back looked like it hadn't been cleaned since the sixties.

The bar was huge with a mirror behind it and rows of booze stacked neatly. A sign said, GETTING YOU DRUNK SINCE 1992.

I distinctly smelled the stench of at least two or three different people's vomit wafting around.

The Hulk led us around the bar to a door painted black. "Wait here," he said. He knocked and then went in and shut the door.

"We don't have jurisdiction here," Will said.

"They don't know that. Nice job flashing the badge and putting it away before he got a good look, Jia."

She grinned. I figured neither of them got much feedback on their jobs. Gates wasn't one to compliment much.

The door opened, and the giant motioned with his head for us to go in. The office was lit with a red light that shone on the stacks of papers all around. Behind a large desk sat an attractive woman in jeans and a white long-sleeve shirt. She was writing in a ledger and put her pen down before leaning back in her chair.

"Haven't seen you guys before. You're not Vice."

"No, we're not."

"So who are you?"

"We're prosecutors investigating the murder of one of your customers."

She nodded. "The young girl. I read about it. That was in Utah, though. You guys are out of your little section of the playground."

She had a keen intelligence in her eyes. If there was one thing I was good at, it was reading people, and this lady was not going to give us anything if she could help it. Threatening subpoenas wouldn't accomplish anything. Time for a different tack.

"You're probably dealing out of here, my guess is both meth and cocaine, although meth is much more lucrative and easier to get your hands on. I don't care. And even if I saw a giant bathtub full of meth right here in front of me, I still wouldn't care. Drugs should be legal, in my both humble and expert opinion, and I don't care how much of the stuff you deal. What I care about is that girl's murder. If you can help me and you don't, then I care about the meth and I call the DA out here and see about a little raid. You're thinking right now, 'Hey, that's fine. We'll get everything outa here by then.' But sorry, genius, your place will be monitored until we get a warrant, and that's when we'll do our search. Maybe take in a few of the regulars and see what they remember. Never know, we might get lucky and find someone that knows a lot about other things going on here and wants to cut a deal."

I put my hands on the desk and leaned in.

"You have nothing to gain by stonewalling me and a lot to lose. You're clearly intelligent, and I'm sure you see there's no incentive for you to lie to me."

She smiled. "I think I like you."

"I tend to grow on people." I sat down in one of the chairs. "What do you know about her?"

She inhaled and put her feet up on the desk. She was wearing Converse sneakers without socks, and I could see her smooth, tanned ankles. "One of the boys they say killed her, I don't know his name, we've had to throw him out of here a couple of times."

I snapped my fingers and said, "Photos, kids."

Will fumbled with his phone, but Jia had photos of Anderson and Steven right up on her screen. I showed them to the woman and said, "Which one?"

"The skinny, good-looking one."

"His name's Anderson Ficco. What'd you have to throw him out of here for?"

"You name it. He chopped a line of coke out on the bar once and just started snorting it up in front of two hundred people, he broke shot glasses on the floors, got so drunk once he pissed on a pool table . . . I mean, I only remember because I had to take a photo of him around to the staff to make sure they knew who he was."

"Knew who he was? You mean after all that you didn't ban him from the bar?"

She shook her head. "Kid could easily spend two or three grand in a night. As aggravating as he was, he would buy drinks for everyone in the bar for hours. He was well liked."

"Two or three grand? No offense, but this isn't exactly the Ritz-Carlton. Why would he come here if he had that kind of dough?" She didn't say anything. "Oh, he was a customer for the *higher-end* merchandise I mentioned earlier. What was his poison of choice?"

Again she didn't say anything.

"Off the record, I pinky swear."

She grinned. "I would normally tell someone in this situation to get out and call my lawyer, but I have a feeling you and I might become friends."

"Great. We'll exchange Christmas cards. What drugs was he into?"

"Everything. You name it, he would take it. He was particularly fond of cocaine."

Jia asked, "Was he ever violent?"

She nodded. "He dated one of our bartenders for a while. She came in one day with a broken nose and blackened eyes. Wouldn't talk about it, but I knew she wasn't dating anyone else at the time."

"We're going to need her name and address. What else?"

She inhaled and said, "Are you married?"

"Kinda personal for a first date, isn't it?"

"Is that what this is?" She chuckled. "Our first date? Oddest one I've been on."

"I've had worse. Now what else?"

"That's it. Believe it or not, he's not our only customer."

I nodded and rose. "Will, leave her a card in case anything else pops up."

She picked the card off the desk and held it in her hands as she smiled at me. "Is that the only reason you'd like me to call?"

"Unless you've got a line on who I should bet on in the World Series, yes. Now I'll need your info and the bartender's."

20

We sat at a fashionable restaurant at the Bellagio. I ordered the most expensive wine they had and steaks for everyone. Will said, "No wine, thanks."

"That's idiotic. Have a glass. It lubricates conversation."

"He doesn't drink," Jia said. She took a sip of the wine and said, "That's the best wine I've ever had."

"Maybe, maybe not. The question is, if I had told you that wine was eight dollars a bottle at the grocery store, would you still think that?"

"Probably not."

"Perception is everything. Forget reality. Reality has no place in life or in a courtroom."

"Is that in one of your chapters?" Will said.

"No, just a fact. But when you get into that courtroom, remember that the perception of how the jury sees the defendant and the victim is all that matters. That *is* one of my chapters: juries vote with their emotions. Forget legal reasoning; perception is what molds emotion, and emotion tells the jury how to vote."

Will took a bite of his steak and said, "How'd you guess the owner of Skid Row was dealing out of the bar?"

"She's surrounded by fifty casinos and probably a hundred bars better than hers, but that sign behind the bar said they've been in business for twenty-five years. Now how's a little crap bar surrounded by better bars survive for twenty-five years?"

Jia said, "If the bar is just a front for something else."

"Bingo."

Will shook his head. "That's crazy. So are we going to call the LVPD?"

"Hell no, we're not. Farah'll clam up and not tell us anything ever again. And since we don't have jurisdiction, the defense might be able to get anything she said to us suppressed, and then fruit of the poisonous tree would apply to anything we found. Russell Pritcher is the smartest attorney, with the exception of *moi*, that you'll ever meet."

Will took some fancy ketchup that was on the table and poured it over his steak like it was ambrosia. He tore into it, and Jia and I stared at him. He wiped his lips with a napkin and said, "What? I like ketchup."

Jia said, "Are you five years old?"

"Don't knock something till you try it."

I had bought a replacement phone and got a call from Gates.

"Hey."

"Hey. You know when you're going to have my team back? We got a motion hearing at four."

"What type of case?"

"Drug distribution."

I checked my watch. "I'll have 'em back by then."

"Thanks. Will said you guys are in Vegas."

"Gotta start somewhere. Did Tweedledee and Tweedledum file that supplemental narrative I told them to?"

"No, but I'm sure they'll get it in by the end of the day. Kind of weird they would misplace it on the biggest case they've ever had, isn't it?"

"The universe is a mysterious place. And the more mysterious it is for you on this case, the better for your deniability and reelection, if you know what I mean." I watched as Will took a bite of ketchup with a little bit of steak on it, and it made me gag. "We gotta run and hit one more interview. See you in a few."

I hung up and said, "Get the steaks to go. I gotta have you kiddos home by bedtime."

21

The bartender lived in an area of Las Vegas that looked about as normal as anywhere. Kids' toys outside, minivans in the driveways, and clean sidewalks. Diana Trees lived in an apartment complex tucked away behind a grocery store.

Her apartment was on the second floor, and I knocked and pressed my ear against the door. I heard her inside, and then I said loudly, "Diana, this is Tatum Graham. I'm a prosecutor working with the police on a case. Please open up."

A few seconds later the chain slid off, and the door opened a crack. Jia flashed the badge, and I said, "Diana?"

"Yes."

"Mind if we chat a minute?"

"About what?"

"Anderson Ficco."

She hesitated and then opened the door a little more. "Is it about that girl?"

"Patty Winchester? Yes."

She opened the door all the way and let us inside. She was young and wore a tank top with shorts, her blonde hair streaked with red. A tattoo of someone who looked like a sister or cousin adorned her right shoulder, dates underneath indicating the woman had died at twenty-two.

The apartment was immaculately clean with few decorations. We sat on a sofa and she sat across from us on a love seat. She rubbed her hands together, and I noticed a slow tap of her foot on the carpet.

"Why did you choose *Trees*?"

"What do you mean?"

"I mean, it's not a real surname. Maybe it is, but not for you. Why did you choose that?"

She shrugged. "When I was a kid there was a tree outside my room. I could see it from my window. When my father would drink and . . . get in one of his moods, I would just go there and watch the tree."

"Is that why you changed it? So your father can't find you?"

She nodded and stared at the floor.

"I'm sorry," I said, and then cleared my throat, regretting having asked. "Um, I'd like to ask you some questions about Anderson if that's okay."

Her foot began to tap faster and she crossed her arms. Not good. Before I could say another word, Jia said, "Why don't you guys wait outside?"

I looked at her and then to Will. I nodded and rose. "It was nice meeting you, Diana."

Will and I went outside and down the stairs to the car. I sat on the hood and Will looked toward the apartment.

"What was that about?"

"She was terrified. She wasn't going to give us anything. Jia sensed that, too. It's better she do it." I glanced at a mom and her daughter going into one of the apartments, then back to Will. "Can I ask you something? You looked familiar, but I didn't place it until you made that goofy face inside the apartment just now. Your last name's Aggie. You Darrell Aggie's son?"

He nodded but didn't smile or grin at the recognition. "I am."

"Darrell was one of the richest guys in town when I was growing up."

"Yeah, that's my dad. Mr. Moneybags."

"He had ties to Harvard. Is that where you went to school?"

"Nope. I went to the University of New Mexico."

"Why?"

"Because I had to pay for it myself."

"He wouldn't cough up the dough, huh?"

He shook his head. "No, he would've. I just didn't want his money. I wanted to do it myself."

"Well, that's both admirable and dumb. You could have a degree from Harvard right now."

He grinned then. "Some people don't care about stuff like that, Mr. Graham. Whenever I do anything, I just think, 'How am I going to sleep tonight if I do this?' I don't think I'd be sleeping well if I let my dad do everything for me."

I nodded. "He moved to Arizona, I'd heard."

"Yup. Haven't seen him since, actually. When I turned down entering the family business, he didn't really call anymore."

"I'm sorry. We get the fathers we get, not the ones we want."

"That's life, I guess. Can I ask you something now?" he said.

"Only fair."

"Why'd you really leave Miami? You're the top criminal attorney in the country, defending rock stars and models. Why would you abandon all that over just one client? I'm sure you've had other clients do horrible things after you got them off. What was different about this one?"

I inhaled deeply and said, "You ask this many questions of everybody you meet?"

He smiled. "Just the people I admire."

"Well, don't get too comfy with that. People don't admire me for long."

After a while, the door opened upstairs and Jia came out. She walked up to us and said, "Good news and bad news."

"Good news first."

"She said they dated for about a month. That he would drink and get high and become violent but then buy her things the next day and cry and apologize."

"Sounds like a typical scumbag domestic abuser. What else?"

"Get this: One time he thought she had cheated on him with the manager at the bar. After slapping her around, he began choking her and said he would dump her body in the forest where no one could find it."

"The proper term is *strangle*, not *choke*, don't ever say *choke* in front of a jury. They'll think about chicken bones. And nice work."

Will said, "When'd she break up with him?"

"About four months ago, and she hasn't talked to him since. Couldn't give me anything relevant about the day of the abduction. She wasn't working that night."

"What's the bad news?" Will asked.

"That wasn't the first time Patty was at Skid Row. In fact, Diana says she was there a lot. They would talk sometimes while she sat at the bar. The last couple times she mentioned someone stalking her."

"Stalking her how?" I said.

"Showing up at her school, driving by her house, following her around when they didn't think she would notice. She told Diana it was a guy she had hooked up with, and she was getting freaked out. Asked if Diana thought it'd be a good idea for her to carry around a gun."

"Anderson?"

Jia shook her head. "Diana said Patty talked about it in front of Anderson once. Not him."

"Great," Will said. "So she had a creepy stalker that isn't one of the guys sitting in jail right now for her murder. Jury will love that."

I shrugged. "I don't like being convinced of guilt and then having another suspect pop up either. Gives me indigestion. But we'll work it and see what shakes out. Take some notes and let's get back. I wanna see you guys in action."

22

We got back to River Falls, and Jia and Will grabbed their files and headed to the courtroom. I sat behind the prosecution table as they got ready.

The defense was a private attorney, an older man with glasses and a gray beard. The defendant was a middle-aged man wearing cowboy boots who smirked as he checked out Jia's legs.

"Lemme see the police report," I said.

I scanned it. Standard drug case. Utah Highway Patrol trooper pulled over a truck for speeding, and the defendant, Chad Irwin, and his passenger, Todd Hales, were acting nervous and the trooper thought he smelled pot. He took them out of the car after calling for backup and found a burned joint in the ashtray. As the police were inventorying the car and preparing to just write them a citation and send them on their way, the trooper that had pulled them over checked the trunk and found a brick of meth. The defense attorney had filed a motion to suppress the meth, saying they didn't have probable cause to open a locked trunk, even though they'd gotten permission from the defendant. That Chad had been coerced to open it against his will because he was already in handcuffs and sitting on the ground and didn't feel like he had a choice.

Not a bad motion, but not great either. The better tactic would've been to waive every court hearing and set it for a bench trial—trial with a judge instead of a jury—to resolve the case as quickly as possible.

Courts could usually set bench trials within a week because they didn't have to call in any potential jurors. Then, you'd have Chad testify that the drugs were Todd's, and Todd testify that the drugs were Chad's, and that neither knew the other had it. Bam. Reasonable doubt handed to you on a silver platter. And if the judge refused to let them go because of such legal trickery, the appeals court would certainly slap the judge down and either reverse the verdict or grant a new trial, at which time a jury would very likely acquit, or the judge might just grant a motion to dismiss. There were few things as embarrassing to a judge as being told by the court of appeals they were wrong and needed to try again.

The first witness Will called to the stand was the trooper. He testified about why he pulled the men over, the search, and why he checked the trunk. They'd found a knife on Chad that had to be removed. Routine stuff. The defense attorney grilled him on cross about why he searched the trunk, but not too hard. A good tactic since he was putting Chad on the stand: just establish that the trooper may not have had enough reason to search the trunk and then put Chad up there to say he was intimidated and frightened and didn't have a choice in opening the trunk or not.

After the trooper was done, Will said, "State rests, Your Honor."

The defense attorney stood and said, "Defense calls Mr. Chad Irwin to the stand."

Chad got up and walked over to the witness stand, winking at Jia. I saw her jaw muscles flex and imagined her pounding him to death with the thick *Utah Rules of Criminal Procedure* book in front of her.

"State your name for the record," the defense attorney said.

"Chad Irwin."

"And, Chad, you remember the events we've been discussing?"

"I do."

"Now don't worry about the stop—I mean, you were speeding, right?"

"Right."

"Let's just focus on when the trooper forced you to open the trunk. What do you remember about that?"

"I was sitting on the ground behind my car, and my hands were cuffed behind my back. The cuffs were so tight I had bruises on my wrists for like a week after. And so they find a little bit of pot, and Todd says it was his and that he'd smoked it like a day ago and that I hadn't had any. So the cop said he would give him a ticket and let us go. He tested my eyes and made me walk in a straight line and things like that, but said I was fine and that they were gonna let us go."

"Then what happened?"

"When I was sitting down, he came over and said that he wanted to search the trunk."

"What did you say?"

"I first said no. Then he leaned down like really close to me. Like really close. Right in my face. And he said he's searching that trunk one way or another, and that I could make it easy or I could make it hard. I seriously thought he might tase me or break my arm or something. He's a big dude, too."

"Were you nervous?"

"Hell yeah, I was nervous. When a cop gets in your face and tells you he's gonna hurt you, you do what he says. So I said the keys were in my pocket, and he took them and opened the trunk."

"Would you have given him the keys if he hadn't threatened you?"

"No way. That's why I told him no that first time."

"Thank you, nothing further."

The judge looked at Will and said, "Any cross, Mr. Aggie?"

"Yes, Judge." Will rose and stood at the lectern. He was reading off a sheet where he'd written his questions. *The Art of Jury Trial as War*, chapter 27: "Never read from anything. You should be looking at the witness and glancing at the judge or jury when there's something important being said that you want them to take note of." Also, dirty little trick that works most of the time, when you want someone to say yes to something, you nod. When you want them to say no, you shake your head. I've gotten affirmative answers from people on questions they should've said "I don't know" to just because of a little head nod. The unconscious mind: what a trip.

"So you said you were nervous?" Will said.

"Yes."

"But I mean, you've been pulled over by cops before."

He thought a second. "No. Not really."

"You've never been pulled over by a cop?"

"I don't think so. I mean, I think I had a speeding ticket in high school. I don't remember."

"But you didn't tell Trooper Harvey you were nervous that night."

"Yeah I did."

"You did? Then why isn't it in his reports?"

"I don't know. But I told him. I told him several times actually. He must've not written it in there."

The Art of Jury Trial as War, chapter 6: "You never, never, ever ask an open-ended question of a witness unless you know the answer." Every question is a yes or a no, and you tell your story through those yes and no answers. Basically, you wanted the witness to barely be a participant in what you were doing. I once had a DEA agent after a cross tell me that he didn't even see why he showed up.

I leaned forward to Jia and said, "He's losing."

She nodded. "We anticipated losing."

"What? Why would you do that?"

"It's a bad search."

"So?"

"So there's no Perry Mason moments. Unless we can get him to confess the drugs were his, there's not much we can do."

I rose. "Your Honor, sorry to interrupt, Tatum Graham. Hi. I'm the new guy over at the County Attorney's Office. I'm their supervisor and will be taking over the questioning for a moment if I may."

He shrugged. "It's your dime, Mr. Graham."

I walked over to Will and said, "Watch."

Turning to Chad, I could see the little grin on his face as he stared at me. He knew he was winning and this case was getting tossed. I grinned back at him, took a second, and then said, "You carry a knife, right?"

"Um, yeah."

"Hunting knife or combat knife?"

He glanced at his lawyer. "Hunting knife."

"In your boot or a strap on your hip?"

"In a strap."

"You carry a gun, too?" I said, taking a guess. More than half the people in this county were hunters and carried.

"Sometimes."

"You carry this knife and gun for protection, right?"

He thought a second. "Yeah. I guess."

"And the trooper, the night of the arrest, searched you for weapons like all good troopers do, right?"

"Yeah."

"And he didn't find the gun."

"No, I didn't have it on me."

"It's a felony to possess a firearm with illegal drugs. You're aware of that, right?"

"Um. No."

"No you are, or you aren't aware of that?" I took a step closer to him. His grin was gone.

"Um, no I didn't know that."

I lifted the police report off the prosecution table and stepped closer to him. "Show me in this inventory of the car where your gun is listed."

He glanced down and said, "It's not there."

"You left it at home."

"Yeah."

"And if the trooper had found the gun in the car, they would've charged you with a felony possession of a firearm, right?"

"I don't know."

"They could even charge it as a federal offense."

He shrugged and his eyes had grown wide. He kept glancing at his lawyer, but I wasn't saying anything objectionable, so there wasn't anything he could do.

"Where did you learn that possessing a gun around drugs was a felony offense? On a website or from a buddy?"

If you wanted more than a yes or a no, you always presented the witness with an option and let them pick. It was like choosing the two best outfits for your kid to wear and letting them decide so they thought they had the victory. He had already stated he didn't know it was a felony, but you just had to rephrase questions a little bit and people didn't realize what they were being asked.

"Um, I don't know . . . I don't know."

"You don't know or don't remember? Go ahead and jog your memory. We'll wait."

Silence in the courtroom while we sat there. I folded my arms and stared into his pupils. "Well?"

"Um, I guess I heard it from someone."

Bingo.

"And your buddy that told you having guns near drugs was a felony told you that you should leave the gun at home when transporting drugs anywhere."

He looked to his lawyer and I stepped between them. The lawyer stood up and said, "Objection. Relevance."

I looked to the judge and said, "Do I even need to respond to that, Judge?"

"Overruled," he said without looking at either of us.

I turned back to Chad. "So your buddy with experience in these things said transporting drugs with a gun is worse than drug dealing and you should leave the gun at home."

He shrugged. "I guess."

"You left the gun at home."

"Yeah."

"Because it's a felony to have a gun near drugs."

"If you say so."

"If I say so or it is?"

He first shook his head a little and then nodded and then didn't know which answer was appropriate, so he just sat there.

"You were nervous because of the trooper that night."

He nodded. "I was, like I already said."

He seemed to relax a little, thinking he had dodged the bullet. I liked to change lines of questioning suddenly. It forced the witness to answer without the time to think or plan what to say.

"You and the trooper are about the same size, right?"

"He's bigger."

"And you're scared of bigger people, right?"

"No, but he made me nervous. He had a gun."

"You had a gun you left at home, right?"

"Right."

"Because you knew that transporting drugs with a gun is a felony."

He didn't say anything.

"You a pussy, Chad?"

The defense lawyer stood up. "Your Honor!"

"Sorry, Judge, withdrawn," I said without looking at the judge. "'You a coward' is what I meant to ask."

"Hell no, I ain't a coward."

"You just said you were scared of the trooper because he's a little bigger than you. You get beat up a lot?"

"No."

"You get pushed around by the big boys in high school? They shove you in lockers?"

"No."

"No dates, I bet, huh? Hard for cowards to get dates."

"I ain't a coward."

The defense attorney stood up and said, "Objection."

I said, "You afraid of me? I'm a little bigger than you."

"No, I ain't afraid."

"But you crapped your pants with the trooper."

"I didn't shit my pants. He ain't nothin'," he said, his face turning red. "He's lucky he wore that badge or we coulda gone toe to toe. I ain't scared'a his goofy ass."

I glanced at the defense attorney, who sighed and sat down. I winked at Chad and said, "No further questions, Your Honor. Unless Mr. Irwin would like to go toe to toe with the trooper right now like he was prepared to do that night."

23

We went back to the office downstairs from the court, and Will said, "What just happened in there? How did we win?"

I sat down on the edge of a desk. "We won because technology changes, society changes, everything changes but one thing: people. We never change. We're still hunter-gatherers out there on the plains. And one thing you can count on in people is ego and insecurity. Chad Irwin is the type of guy that would rather get convicted of a drug charge than admit in open court that he's a coward. You just gotta read people and find that one thing. That little point in them that they try so desperately to hide from everybody. You find that point, and you'll get your Perry Mason moment on the stand. Witnesses will forget they're in a courtroom and shout at you like you're in the street."

Jia sat down. "That was pretty remarkable. Have to admit."

"Why do I get the feeling you don't compliment often?" I checked my watch. "Better run. Clock-out time."

"Not for me," she said. "I got motions to write."

"Me too," Will said.

"Well, shit rolls downhill for a reason. Have a good night."

———

When I left, it was getting dark. I headed to a furniture store. The place was all bears, cowboys, Indians, and sunsets. I bought a painting of wild horses and then pointed out several couches, chairs, a table, a bed, and a few other things. The owner said they could deliver them in a few days, and I told her I'd throw in an extra five K if they delivered it tonight. I thought her eyeballs might fall out of her head. I gave her the key to my place, and when I was leaving, my cell phone rang. It was Gates.

"Hey," I said.

"So I heard an interesting story about court today."

"Oh yeah? Did it involve a devilishly handsome Miami attorney displaying his genius in front of the world?"

"Maybe. Or maybe someone that just got lucky."

"No such thing as luck, Gates."

"Maybe."

I hesitated. "What are you, um, doing for dinner tonight?"

"Nothing. You hungry?"

"I am."

"Come over. I'll make something."

"You sure? We can just eat out."

"No, come over."

"Okay. See you in a bit."

I hung up and couldn't wipe the silly grin off my face.

———

Gates's ranch was on the outskirts of town and had been in her family for four generations. It looked about the same as I remembered it, maybe a bit more run down, but still up and running.

I parked in front of the house and strolled up to the door. Gates opened it without me having to knock. She wore jeans and a slim button-down shirt and was wiping her hands with a dish towel.

"Come in. Dinner's almost done."

The house smelled like old wood. It was decorated exactly the same. Nothing had changed. I sat down on the couch and watched her stirring food in a pot over the stove.

"So you're famous," she said. "My opponent, Horace, was interviewed for the local paper saying I've brought you on as a ringer to get a conviction against two innocent young boys."

"Innocent? Really? I thought the town is calling for their blood?"

"I said half the town is, and if we lose this case they'll eviscerate me. And now if we win, I'll be accused of railroading innocent boys and leaving the real killer on the loose. Horace just found a way to put me between a rock and a hard place. Anderson's father is one of the wealthiest men here, and I'm sure Horace is getting some nice little donations from him, because I certainly am not."

"Aren't you curious how much Horace is getting from him?"

"I could find out. Wouldn't be too hard. Maybe I'll poke around a little. Hope you like chili."

"Sure. You know I haven't had a home-cooked meal in . . . man, I can't even guess. Almost twenty years, probably. Since I left."

"No girlfriends cooked for you in Miami?"

"Not really how it works over there. At least not in the circles I ran in."

"Well, never too late to start over."

"Is that what you think I'm doing? Starting over?"

She looked to me. "Isn't it?"

"Maybe I'm just passing through. One last goodbye to the old haunts."

She grinned. "You never were very good at having insight into yourself. You could read other people better than anyone I've ever met, but it could never be focused inward."

"Man, you sound like some yogic guru."

She chuckled. "No, just an observation."

"Can I ask you something? Why'd you never get married?"

She hesitated. "Just never met the right person, I guess. And when my dad got sick, there wasn't much time for dating. I had to take care of him. I got close once, though. Food's ready."

I went over to the dinner table, a table I remembered her father carving from a tree he'd cut down himself because it had gotten crown rot and was withering away. "Who was it?"

"You wouldn't know him. He was only here a couple of years. A doctor from up north."

"Wow, Gates Barnes, I had no idea you were into doctors."

The table was already set, and she brought over the pot and spooned chili into the two bowls. As she sprinkled in a few garnishes and cheese, she said, "I couldn't have cared less what he did. He was nice, treated me well. He proposed to me."

"What'd you say?"

She sat down across from me. "I said no."

"How come?"

She stared at me a second. "Just wasn't the right person."

We watched each other a moment, and then I looked down at the chili. "Smells good."

"My dad's recipe. Would you like to say the blessing?"

"No."

She grinned and folded her arms. I watched her close her eyes and say a blessing for the food, thanking God for it and for the other blessings in her life.

I took a bite. The chili was hot and melted in my mouth like warm cake. It was sweet and spicy at the same time.

"Wow, that's good."

"Glad you like it."

"Your father made this?"

She nodded as she ate. "He learned it from my grandfather. My grand-dad left the ranch for a while when he was a teenager—this must've been in the thirties—against his father's wishes and worked cattle drives in New

Mexico. Out there all they had was whatever they could carry that wasn't perishable." She grinned. "He told me all of them were constipated on the drive, so he learned to make a chili that would take care of the problem."

"Oh. Delicious and will clean me out. Consider me sold."

"You know I like to be practical."

A silence passed between us then, and I said, "Gates, when I left, while you were in the hospital—"

"No, don't."

"I want to explain."

"There's no reason. You were nineteen, a kid. It doesn't matter now, and I don't want to ruin a perfectly good dinner with talk of things neither of us can change." She took a bite of the chili. "Will told me about Patty's stalker. How do you suppose Howard and Vail missed that?"

"I can tell you exactly how: they don't care. It's open and shut to them, and they want it done and to go back to their stolen-candy-bar cases. Murders are hard work. Doesn't mean Anderson and Steven didn't do it, but I'm not getting up in that court and convicting two innocent men or taking the chance that two guilty men walk. We gotta find this guy and rule him out."

She grinned. "I'm sure you will. Somehow I don't think you fail much."

I watched her. The way her eyes reflected the light, her milk-white skin burned just a little from working the ranch, the way her hair danced on her shoulders. Up behind her near the front door I saw a large blown-up photo of her and her father hugging out in the fields, her father's sun-beaten face like leather and his meaty arm around her thin shoulders. "You miss your dad a lot, don't you?"

"Every day." A sigh escaped her lips, though I didn't think she meant it to. "Don't take it for granted that they're always going to be around, Tatum. They won't, and by the time they're gone, it's too late to do anything about it."

We ate and talked for a good two hours. She caught me up on how she became county attorney. She hadn't been kidding earlier when she'd alluded to many of the good ole boys out here not trusting a woman in such a powerful position. At a town meeting, one man had asked if people would be randomly arrested when she was on her monthly. Gates had said, "Only registered Democrats, sir," and had gotten a laugh from the crowd.

We finished up, and at the door I stood there a second before saying, "Thanks. I needed this."

"Come by anytime for a home-cooked meal."

"Nah, I don't wanna put you out."

"You're not. It was . . . nice. To have someone else here. The house is usually so quiet."

I nodded and said, "Better go," and headed to my car.

"You still going to be here tomorrow?"

I turned around and said, "Never really know what the gods will bring, do you? But probably."

———

I contemplated driving to my condo but went the opposite way, to Adam's house. When I got to the door, it was unlocked. I went inside and said, "Adam?"

No answer. The house was quiet. I waited a beat and said, "Adam, you home?"

I heard something from upstairs. A quiet moan. I took the stairs up to my parents' bedroom. My father was in his pajamas on the floor.

I ran to him. "What happened?"

"Help me up, damn it."

Wrapping my arm around his back and waist, I hoisted him up as he groaned. I got him onto the bed, and he lay back and took a deep breath.

"Hand me those pills."

The amber bottle was on the nightstand, and I passed it to him. He took two and a sip of water out of a glass next to the bed.

"What happened?"

"Nothin', just fell."

"And you couldn't get up on your own?"

"Just caught me by surprise is all."

"Falling catches everyone by surprise, but we can get up. Do you need help?"

"Help? Like what?"

"Like a nurse."

He waved his hand dismissively. "I don't need a damn nurse. Just some rest. What're you doin' here anyway?"

I pulled over a chair and sat down. "Just . . . I don't know, was in the neighborhood."

"I thought you'd be long gone by now."

There was a ball of yarn on the nightstand. My mother's. I took it and twirled it in my hands. "So did I."

He looked down to the yarn. "Your mother was making me a scarf when she . . ."

I nodded. "We didn't talk at the funeral."

"Nothin' to talk about. It happens to all of us." He inhaled deeply and closed his eyes a second. "Turn out the light, will ya? I need to get some sleep."

I put the yarn down and rose. He was almost out just from the exertion of falling and getting back in bed. A blanket was at the foot of the bed, and I laid it on top of him. I stared down at him awhile. I had never realized how alike we actually looked.

He slept on the far left side of the bed, as if to give someone else room.

I crept downstairs and watched TV on the couch.

24

It was half past ten that night when I turned off the television and checked on Adam. I went outside and stared up at the moon a second before deciding it was time to take a little drive.

The stretch of I-15 to Vegas was pretty empty, but ominous because of all the canyons you had to weave through to get there. Canyons interspersed with long stretches of nothing but sand and cactus. At night, you couldn't really see anything but road and jagged shadows protruding out of the ground where the mountains should've been.

I arrived at Skid Row before midnight. The bar was hopping. A line had formed outside that went nearly to the intersection. Bars did that even if they weren't at capacity. It made people driving by think the place was exclusive and built up hype. Still, there were far more people waiting than a little dive like this warranted, and I wondered exactly how much product Farah was moving. With this much exposure, she had to have a deal worked out with the local Narcs unit. Otherwise they would've busted her a long time ago.

I parked in front and got out. The Incredible Hulk was working the door again. I smiled at him and said, "Miss me?"

His lips pursed into a slight frown before he stepped aside to let me in.

"Not even the cover charge? I knew you liked me."

The space looked a lot different at peak hours than during the day. The line outside wasn't a ploy: the bar was literally packed to capacity. A band blared some indecipherable metal song as I made my way through the crowd, which stank powerfully of marijuana and sweat, and over to the office. The door was open a crack, and I knocked and poked my head in.

Farah was there, dressed in a tight black dress with heels. She was sitting at the computer, and when she saw me, she leaned back and crossed her legs.

"People will talk about us if you keep showing up like this."

"Couldn't possibly be worse than what they're saying about me now." I shut the door behind me, raised my brows, and tilted my head toward the chair.

"By all means, please."

As I sat, she took out an unlabeled bottle of booze and two tumblers from her drawer before pouring and sliding one to me. We tapped glasses and she said, "To happiness."

The drink tasted like gasoline mixed with cinnamon.

"That is just about the worst thing I've ever had."

Farah shrugged. "My own recipe I've been working on. I'm trying to get into the booze business and go legit."

"That's the way to do it. If it's not on the up-and-up, it won't last."

She poured a little more for herself and then leaned back in her chair with the glass between her hands. "So what brings you back? I can't imagine it's just to see little old me, although that would make my night."

"Unfortunately, no." I took out my phone and pulled up a photo of Patty, a school picture. I laid the phone down on the desk between us. "That's the victim."

She nodded. "I know."

I didn't want to throw Diana under the bus for telling us Patty was a regular, so I said, "So here's the thing, Farah, my dear, what are the odds that an underage girl is at this bar for the first time ever and just happens to get abducted and murdered that night?"

She grinned. "You're wondering how often she came."

As sharp as I'd thought. I had a feeling that she would've excelled in any business, and I wondered how it was she fell into the drug game.

"I'm guessing she was here a lot."

Farah nodded. "She was a siren."

"A what?"

"Well, that's just what I call them. A girl that sits at the bar and gets men to buy her drinks all night. The drinks are how bars make money, not the cover charge. I paid her fifty bucks an hour, and she easily made ten times that for me. I mean, men would fall over themselves for the privilege of buying her a drink." She took a sip of her moonshine. "She hadn't even grown into her beauty yet. Imagine what she would've looked like at twenty-three or twenty-four."

"You hired an underage girl to work at your bar? That's a dumb move, and you don't strike me as someone that makes dumb moves. I'm guessing you've got the Narc and Vice guys wrapped around your little finger."

"This is Vegas. We pay lip service to not breaking the law, but we all know why we're here. The police aren't looking too hard at any place that provides this much . . . entertainment to the tourists."

"Did Patty ever complain to you about anybody maybe getting too handsy with her, or maybe calling her or following her around? Not leaving her alone?"

Farah grinned. "You mean every man that's ever met her? Beauty is the trait that lasts the shortest amount of time and brings the least satisfaction, and it's all men can think about." She placed the glass on the desk. "I thought you had your killers already?"

"Probably. I'm just making sure all our bases are covered."

She chuckled. "You don't think they did it."

"I didn't say that. But I need to find this guy. Her stalker would be someone older, I'm guessing, that maybe was rebuffed when they wanted to go further than Patty was comfortable. Maybe someone with a history of instability. Patty ever talk about anyone like that?"

"Honey, everyone in her life was like that. She was a sweet girl born with the curse of looks, and every piece of human garbage she met tried to take advantage of her. You really need to go talk to her friends and the people that knew her."

"What do you mean?"

"I mean you need to look at everyone in that little hick town of yours. A man came in here one night looking for her, drunk out of his mind. He grabbed her arm and tried to pull her out of here. My bouncers tossed him out on his ass, but he kept shouting that he was a mayor and would have their jobs. Patty said he had told her that day he was going to leave his wife for her and wanted to marry her and all this nonsense. She was seventeen and he was almost sixty. How he thought that would turn out well I have no idea."

"The mayor? You're kidding?"

She finished the booze left in her glass and then what was left in mine and put both glasses back into the drawer with the bottle. "Like I said, you need to look at everyone."

I glanced around the office. "You know, you made it sound like only men abused her. You abused her, too. I highly, highly doubt you stopped with men paying for her booze. You're not the type of person to see someone like Patty and not use her up as thoroughly as you can. Did you set her up on dates as well? Was she an escort for you?"

She smiled and said, "Take a look at your own house before you start judging other people's."

25

On the drive back from Vegas, I called Gates and she picked up.

"Hello?"

"You're not gonna believe this. I hope you're lying down in bed."

"Tatum? It's like one in the morning."

"I know, I'm a night owl. I just got out of a little conversation with the owner of Skid Row, and guess what she told me? Our little Patty was a siren for her, someone that sits at the bar and gets men to buy her drinks, and I got the really strong impression, though Farah didn't come out and say it, that Patty was escorting for her on the side. So I went back to that bartender's apartment, Diana. Scared her half to death waking her up in the middle of the night, but she broke down and confirmed everything. Said she didn't tell us because she didn't want to get in trouble."

"Wait, hold on, escorting? What do you mean *escorting*?"

"Just what I said. Escorting."

"Patty was a prostitute?"

"I personally prefer *escort*, but if you want to put it that way, yeah. And that's not all—Farah said the mayor, or *a* mayor, came in drunk one night after telling Patty he was leaving his wife for her. She didn't say it was River Falls' mayor, but I think we should have a chat with him. I asked Diana how much Patty was charging, and get this: two grand a date. That's high end for New York, forget River Falls. There's like maybe ten people in River Falls that can afford that. And Diana said Patty was uncomfortable going on dates with people she didn't know, so her dates were almost always the same handful of older men from River Falls. The richest ones, I'm guessing."

"Yeah, the ones that run this town and the county."

"Don't wuss out on me now, Gates. You got me to stay and you wanted this worked right. We're working it right."

"I'm telling you, Tatum, I interviewed Anderson myself once. He killed her."

"Probably. Look, everything points to him, and I think we can get a conviction, but we gotta be sure. This one is too important not to be sure."

She sighed. "We can't let this get out. I know Hank, and he did everything he could to raise Patty well. If he found out she was escorting, it would kill him."

"We got a bigger problem than that. When Russell Pritcher finds out she was an escort, he will make her look like Jack the Ripper. He'll paint her to that jury as the worst person in the world and Anderson as a savior that was trying to help her and got blamed for a murder he didn't commit. We need to figure out who was stalking her."

"Well," she said, exhaling loudly, "for now, we can't hit those men up. I know them all. They have attorneys on retainer. If we go to them, they'll clam up. Get me some more evidence, and I'll see what I can do."

"I will. And, um, be careful around those guys, huh? Never know."

She chuckled. "I can handle myself, old man. Just get me that conviction."

"Haven't lost yet," I said, no longer sure that was a point of pride.

———

My suit was wrinkled beyond repair, and I had brought only one with me. Didn't think I'd be needing one at all. In the morning, I googled the nearest clothing shop and found it was in the next town over, about a half hour away. I bought the most expensive suits and shirts they had and drove back to River Falls.

When I got into the office, Jia and Will were already there.

"All right, boys and girls, time for business. Jia, where we at on the ME?"

"He finished the autopsy this morning. Said he'd be down at the coroner's."

"Will, how are we on witnesses?"

"Tried to interview the elderly couple that found the body, but they weren't answering. Was going to go over there today."

"Any new motions from the great Russell Pritcher?"

Jia said, "Got a call from his office asking if we needed to get any discovery to them before the preliminary hearing. Said I would check with you first."

"I checked this funky state's rules, and we're under no obligation to give them anything before the prelim."

Will said, "That doesn't sound right."

"Check rule seven. It's right. Remember, this state is descended from cowboys and pioneers. Justice moved slow in the Wild West. So that means we need to get done as much as we can before the preliminary hearing next week so we know where we are and what we got. If there's any way for this case to get dismissed, Russell Pritcher is going to find it." I checked my watch. "Where's Gates?"

"Meeting with the mayor."

"The mayor, huh? Well, I've got some news on our dear old mayor. I'll tell you on the way. Let's go pay the ME a visit and see what he found on our girl."

———

The coroner's building looked like something you would see in an old Western movie. The interior was filled with paintings of cowboys and buffalo. A prayer carved into a wood block hung over the door. I didn't see a single science journal or book on any of the bookshelves.

I walked over to the desk as Will went to find the coroner. Staring at his degrees, I saw only an undergraduate degree in biology. I checked the rules for coroners in Utah on my phone and confirmed what I'd already guessed: in Utah, you didn't have to be a doctor to be a coroner. Another gift from the frontier towns of the 1800s. There weren't enough doctors, so anybody who could fill in was allowed to run and be elected.

An older man with glasses, dressed in a vest and a white shirt, came in and said, "Damn rude to be interrupting a man's breakfast to talk about the dead."

"That's what the taxpayers are paying you for, right? You're the corpse whisperer." I turned to his degree and pointed. "Tell me you spilled prune juice on your medical degree, and it's just drying off somewhere."

He took out a soda from a small fridge behind his desk and said, "I ain't no doctor."

I rubbed my head. Russell Pritcher was going to eat this guy for a snack. Our only hope was the medical examiner.

"Where's the ME?"

"Your fancy doctor is downstairs. Feel free to find your own way."

Lawrence Bryce, from the Utah Office of the Medical Examiner, was a tall guy with sandy-blond hair and glasses. I'd met him once before, on a case that involved a banker accused of killing his business partner. Lawrence had flown out to Miami to testify in the case, and, well, I hadn't exactly been kind to him on the stand.

Lawrence stood beside a metal gurney containing a tarp over what was clearly a body. The room seemed sterile and smelled of antiseptic.

"Larry, how are ya?"

He looked at me and shook his head. "I was told you were the prosecutor on this. I was hoping it was just someone with the same name."

"Hey, we both had jobs to do and I did mine."

"You called me the Curly of medical examiners in a courtroom full of people."

"Hey, Curly's everyone's favorite Stooge. It was a compliment." I folded my arms and looked down at the body. "Let's set that aside and try to put away the boys that did this, shall we?"

He had been filling out a form on a clipboard, which he set down on the counter. He pulled back the tarp.

Patty's body had severely decomposed. Will groaned and looked away. Jia didn't flinch. The Y-shaped incision was fresh, sewn over for the second time. I looked at her nails. They were still painted a fading pink.

"Tell me you got something."

"Some. Why they let people without medical degrees become coroners in these rural counties I'll never understand."

"Yeah, it's a real mystery. What'dya got?"

"Well, there's not going to be much forensic evidence after an autopsy and burial, so you can forget about that. But there were a few interesting things. For one, she's got cigarette burns over her body. That wasn't in the initial reports."

"Yeah, goof up by the boys in blue."

"They're fairly egregious injuries. I counted twenty-one cigarette burns over her body from head to toe. There was one on her right cornea."

Will said, "Bastards."

Lawrence glanced at him and then looked down to the body. "We had a couple fractured bones that weren't in the coroner's report. Her navicular bone on her right foot was fractured. Something heavy was probably dropped on it."

"Or maybe someone stomped on it wearing a boot."

"That would also explain it, yes. The lacerations across her body were also not mentioned."

"It's fixed now. But what I'm really concerned with is the time of death."

"Hard to tell at this point, but I did send some photos to my entomologist on the larvae that the detectives took at the scene. He thinks they were too young for her to be exposed to the elements for four days. Lividity suggests she was killed at the scene, so more than likely she was dead less than a day before the witnesses found her."

"He'll testify to that?"

"I suppose, for what it's worth after just looking at a few photos."

"So if that's accurate, it means she was probably tortured somewhere else." I turned to Jia. "We need to find that somewhere else. Tweedledee and Tweedledum's search of Anderson's and Steven's homes said they didn't find anything. But if those boys killed her, I'll bet you if we go through the basements, and I mean really go through them, we'll find something. Get the forensic team from a bigger county down here, and tell them it's high priority. We can't trust our dear old mayor right now, so if they drag their feet, tell Gates to get our state rep to call their state rep or district attorney or sheriff or whatever. Just get them down here."

"On it," she said, taking out her phone and leaving the room.

"What about the rape?" I said, turning back to Lawrence.

"That I can't help you with. The body is simply too degraded."

I nodded, looking down at Patty's ghostly white face, one eye closed and the other halfway open and rotted away. "What else?"

"That's it. There's just not enough for me to work with here."

"Did you review the tox report? Anything I should be worried about in there?"

"No, luckily the coroner sent that to the state lab, so everything's good there. Alcohol in her system but no narcotics."

I nodded. "I appreciate you coming down, Larry."

"I came down for her," he said, pulling the tarp back over the body. "Not for you."

26

With Jia running down a forensic team to search the boys' homes, and a request from me to interview Patty's best friend Cecily to see if she knew anything about Patty's stalker, Will and I headed to the scene. Many lawyers didn't visit the scene of a crime, but I always did, no matter what type of case. If it was shoplifting, I went to the store and wandered around; if it was a DUI, I went to where they were pulled over; if it was murder, I went to the scene and took my own photos and tried to imagine what my client and the victim felt.

"Up here," Will said.

We were in a wooded area with a few clearings here and there. It was up a canyon so there weren't that many people, and I'd only seen a few cars on the drive up. When we got out of the car, I could smell the pine trees and hear a stream nearby. Peaceful and quiet. A couple of picnic tables were near the stream.

We walked a trail through some trees. A small clearing about the size of a basketball court with tall grass was just beyond. A breeze blew, and the grass swayed with it. I tapped one of the pine cones at my feet with my shoe. The Hallows hadn't changed even a little since I'd seen it last almost thirty years ago.

"I forgot how secluded this place is," I said. "It hasn't been developed at all."

"No one really wants to move here, so there's no need to build anything. We used to think the place was haunted when we were kids."

"I remember someone killed themselves here when I was in elementary school. All the kids would go up after school to see if there was a ghost."

"I don't remember any suicides, but there was another murder here a while back," Will said. "Some teens up here drinking, and one just, outa nowhere, smashed a bottle and stuck the business end into this other kid's throat. Couldn't even explain why he did it after. Said he just felt like he had to. I don't blame people for not wanting to develop here." He stopped, pointed. "Patty's body was found over there."

We walked to a small ditch in the middle of the clearing. It wasn't wider than a couch, and it was about as long as one. I knelt down and looked from one end to the other. Then I looked from one end of the clearing to the other. It was a perfect spot for this kind of thing: far enough from the road and civilization that no one could hear screams. For this type of killing, with this type of brutality, I had no doubt that the killer or killers would've enjoyed hearing the screams before she died.

I looked out over the Hallows. The last time I had been here, I was eleven and with a group of friends. We left soon after coming here because we heard rocks falling down the hills, like someone, or something, was climbing down toward us.

On the north end of the clearing was a picnic table. The only indicator that this place was anywhere near civilization.

"The detectives said they found a toy near the picnic table, right?" I said.

"Yeah, a little monkey. Like an action figure."

I rose and stared at the picnic table. It was maybe thirty feet away. Heading over there, I listened for cars but couldn't hear them this far in. Nothing but the tall grass rippling in the breeze and the occasional bird.

Sitting down at the table, I placed my hands on the worn wood. The table tilted slightly to the right; the ground had moved underneath it. To the left, a trail led back into the woods.

"Where does that go?"

"A parking lot."

We followed the path through the trees, and sure enough, there were a few parking spaces. A dirt road behind them led out through the forest and back into town.

I took out my phone and pulled up the file for the case. I'd had the secretary scan and email me all the reports. I looked at the photo of the doll: a white monkey with swords in its hands.

"There's no dirt on this toy."

"So?"

"So it means it wasn't out here very long. In fact it looks brand new." I looked up and around at the parking spaces and the trail leading out of the forest. "Why would a kid leave a brand-new toy? They usually hang on to these like gold."

He shrugged. "Kids lose stuff all the time."

"At a picnic table with nothing else around? I mean, he would've realized at some point the toy was missing, and his parents would've driven back here, right?"

"Maybe."

I nodded. "Yeah. Maybe."

I looked back to the ditch, and I remembered the photo Gates had shown me, Patty lying there with a child's heart necklace around her neck. I wondered if her father had seen that photo.

I took a deep breath and then said, "What stores around here sell toys?"

27

Only two places in town sold toys: the Walmart and a small hobby shop. We drove to Walmart and walked up and down the toy aisles but didn't see anything like the monkey. We asked a clerk if they carried anything similar, and she said she didn't think so.

Next we hit the hobby shop. Walking in, Will said, "They could've ordered it online."

"They could've. Make a note to check which stores carry it and might have shipped it here."

Will made the note as I glanced around the store. I saw a bar with a soda fountain behind it and several stools in front of it. Posters of old science fiction movies were up on the walls. It was the type of place that probably had been on every street corner seventy years ago but seemed a relic of ancient history now.

The guy behind the counter had curly hair and glasses and a blue shirt with stains on the front. I approached him and showed him a picture of the monkey.

"You got this here?"

"Yeah," he said, coming around the counter. He went back to the action figures aisle and pulled one down. I compared the photo and the toy: identical.

"Someone bought one of these here within the last few months. I need to know who it was."

Will came up and said, "He's with us, Mel. He's good people. So far anyway."

I grinned. "Nice."

Mel rolled his eyes and said unhappily, "Let me go through the receipts, I guess."

———

Luckily, Mel kept electronic receipts and was able to pull up the information before long.

"One person. Roscoe Mallory."

"The football coach? You're kidding me?"

"That's what it says."

My old pal Roscoe. I glanced at Will and then turned to Mel and said, "Thank you."

We left the store and I put on my sunglasses. "I'll go chat with him. I want you to help Jia with interviewing Cecily and getting a forensic team here ASAP. Something might be in one of those boys' homes, and I want to know what it is."

———

I imagined being back at your old high school was a nostalgic, pleasant experience for most people. For me it dredged up memories better left forgotten. Small-time jocks pushing me around, girls laughing at me, teachers that would throw erasers and hit us with rulers. I stood out on the field. The buildings looked run down, and the pavement in the parking lot was chipping with massive cracks running its entire length, but the football field was well manicured and taken care of. Not a blade of grass out of place.

As I entered, I stared at the lockers on either side of the hallway and at the trophy case off to the right near the gym. Classes were in session.

I could hear the hum of teachers speaking in several rooms. I went to the front office and asked for Roscoe.

"He should be teaching social studies right now. Upstairs, second door on the right."

"Thanks."

In his classroom, surrounded by students, Roscoe looked even bigger than he had at the diner, with arm muscles that bulged underneath a white T-shirt with red trim and a ponderous belly that stretched the shirt to its limits. I stood at the doorway and smiled and said, "Just need a minute, Coach."

He told the class to hang on and came out into the hallway.

We shook hands, and he asked how I liked being back in River Falls so far and I said, "Fine."

He put his hands on his hips and glanced over his shoulder at the class. "What's going on, Tatum?"

"I'm helping out Gates, prosecuting Patty Winchester's case. I'm guessing you heard about it."

"Small town, everybody knows everything."

"What do you know about Patty? She went here, right?"

He nodded. "Yeah. I knew Patty pretty well. She was in my class a couple years back. Sweetest girl. The room would just light up when she came in. She helped one of the kids that was struggling. Tutored him every night so he could pass the class. Didn't tell anyone, just did it. That's the kind of kid she was, never wanted any credit for anything. She did it because it was the right thing to do. And her father—" He shook his head. "I can't even imagine what Hank is going through. He's got a big heart, and I'm afraid he'll never recover. If it wasn't for the fact that he's still got his boy to look after, I mean, who knows what he would've done by now."

"Do you have kids, Roscoe?"

"Yeah," he said, folding his arms. "Why?"

"How old are they?"

"Got a boy that's ten. Lyle. Why?"

"When was the last time you were over by the Hallows campgrounds?"

"Hallows? Where Patty was found?"

I nodded.

"Oh, jeez, I dunno . . . last year maybe."

Damn it.

"Last year? You're certain of that?"

"Yeah, we went camping up there during the summer."

"Did you buy Lyle a toy monkey a few weeks ago from the hobby shop? White with plastic swords in its hands?"

He shook his head. "No."

"You're sure? Because the owner has a credit card receipt with your name."

"My ex and I have a joint account still. Might have been her."

"Roscoe, which of you has custody of your boy?"

"She does."

"I'm going to need her address and phone number."

28

Nikyee Geller lived in an upscale condo across the Nevada border. Mesquite wasn't a large town, but it looked new enough and had several casinos along with a new marijuana dispensary. I drove through residential neighborhoods filled with stucco homes with red Spanish-style roofs. I parked in front of one with a red Mercedes in the driveway. The porch had several toys on it, something younger kids would play with. Nikyee was expecting me, but she didn't answer after several knocks. I rang the doorbell a few times, and she answered in workout clothes.

She was my age but looked a helluva lot better. I guessed several hours a day of working out, tanning, and fruits and veggies would do that—all things that belonged in hell as far as I was concerned.

"Hey, Tatum Graham. We spoke on the phone."

"Yeah," she said, pulling her hair back with a rubber band. "Wow, you haven't changed since high school."

"Not true, but I appreciate it."

"So what can I do for you?"

"I spoke with Roscoe, and he said you liked to go camping up at the Hallows. That right?"

"Yeah, we go up a few times a year."

I looked inside the home. Over the mantel was a large photo of Nikyee, a child, and a buff dude with slicked-back, greasy hair and a tight shirt. The new hubby, I guessed. I could see her entire relationship with Roscoe in a flash: she married young to get out of the house, only to realize that he bored her, and Greasy there was more exciting. And given the fingerprint-shaped bruising I saw on her arms, I guessed exciting wasn't the only thing he was.

"Those are some bad bruises. You okay?"

She crossed her arms. "Fine. What is this about exactly? I'm in the middle of a workout."

"When was the last time you guys went camping up there?"

She shrugged. "I don't know. Few months ago."

Might be around the time Patty was killed. "You're sure?"

"Yeah. My husband likes to take our dirt bikes up to the dunes. Why?"

I pulled out my phone. "This toy look familiar?"

"Oh yeah, you found it." She smiled. "My son was a mess."

My stomach dropped. "This is your son's?"

"Yeah, Lyle. I bought that for him because monkeys are his favorite animal. He cried for like two days that he'd lost it."

"What time does he get out of school?"

The smile fell, and she leaned against the doorframe. "I don't think you can talk to my boy until you tell me exactly what this is about."

"I'm guessing you've heard about what happened to Patty Winchester. I'm with the County Attorney's Office prosecuting the case. I'm just following up on a few things. This toy was found up there in the Hallows. Near the body."

Her eyes went wide. "You think Lyle saw something?"

"I don't know."

"There's no way. He tells me everything. He certainly would've told me."

"Never hurts to ask, right? I don't want time alone with him. We can do it together, and it won't take longer than a minute."

"Well, he's in extended day today. He has a short day tomorrow, so you can come by then and see him if you want."

I nodded. "Tomorrow then." I turned and said, "And, uh, if it gets worse than bruising, you call me at the Ute County Attorney's Office. Ask for Tatum. I'll take care of it."

She rubbed her arms over the bruises and then shut the door.

29

Back at the offices, I got an update that a forensic team was coming down but wouldn't get here until the next morning. Jia and Will had also interviewed Cecily. She denied everything at first, and then admitted that Patty had, indeed, been escorting for Farah. Apparently her dad's mechanic shop had been failing and money had been getting tighter, and she'd thought it was a way she could help out the family. She'd never given her dad money—it would have raised too many questions. Instead, she'd paid bills behind his back or stocked the fridge with groceries when he wasn't around. Hank had no idea what his daughter was doing.

Unfortunately, Patty had refused to tell Cecily much about that part of her life, so she had no idea if Patty'd had a stalker or not. Patty, it seemed, had been living two lives and had wanted them kept as separate as possible.

I leaned back in a chair in the conference room, which apparently was my office for now, and put my feet up on the table. I stared at a painting on the wall of a cowboy sitting on a horse, its head dipped in a stream. The cowboy was looking off at the horizon. The painting had struck me as tacky the first time I saw it, but staring at it, I felt there was something haunting there. A man alone in a desert with nothing but his animal.

A knock on the door snapped me out of it. The secretary stood there and said, "Phone call for you."

I rose and followed her to the lobby. The secretary was working on a crossword puzzle, and she put her glasses on and went right back to it.

"This is Tatum."

"Mr. Graham," a male voice said. I'd recognize that raspy little weasel's voice out of a hundred voices.

"Russell. How nice of you to call. Are you congratulating me for putting your client away? Little early for that, isn't it?"

"Oh no, I wouldn't quite bank on that yet. Just wanted to touch base and make sure there wasn't any discovery I should be receiving."

"As I'm sure you're aware, I have no obligation to give you anything until the preliminary hearing. Be grateful you got what you got."

"The prelim's in a few days. You'll have to hand it all over then. And the fact that you haven't feels to me like something nice and exculpatory is in there."

"Yeah, well, feelings can be deceiving. What the hell are you doing out here anyway? I thought you stuck to the coasts."

"I could say the same about you. Imagine my surprise when I learned you were not just an attorney on this case, but the prosecutor." He chuckled. "I never thought I'd see the day. Frankly, I think you're a bit of a traitor to the criminal defense profession. Let me give you a bit of advice, and I won't even bill you for it: people do insane things. Your client killed that girl. So what? You didn't kill her. You did your job. The fact that you don't see that shows your weakness. And guess what, Tatum? I'm going to exploit that weakness, and when my client is acquitted, you'll leave prosecution, too. Where you going to run then?"

"I don't know. There's always your mother's house. She seems to always welcome me."

He laughed. "I'm glad we talked. This will be even easier than I thought. Goodbye, Tatum. See you next week."

I hung up and took a deep breath. The secretary had a little stress ball, a green goblin with bulging eyes. I grabbed it and angrily squeezed it a dozen times before plopping it back on the desk and returning to the conference room.

———

I couldn't just hang out all afternoon and do nothing, but as I was stepping out of the building, I ran into Jia, who said, "Leaving already?"

"Nothing to do here. Want a drink or an early dinner?"

"Sure."

I drove us to Benson's, and we sat in a booth near the window. I ordered a whiskey and water and Jia ordered a hamburger and beer.

"Why are you here?" I said.

"I'm hungry."

"You know what I mean. You're smart, far smarter than anyone in that office knows. I can see it clear as day. You could be at the feds prosecuting terrorists and serial killers. Why waste time on drug offenses and DUIs in a small hick town?"

"You say that like it's not important."

"Is it?"

"It is. And I'm not stuck. One day I'm going to be county attorney. Or maybe I'll go somewhere else. I've always wanted to work at a big firm, too, and see what that was like. I like it here for now, though. I just need to figure out what I'm doing as a lawyer."

I smirked. "Let me tell you something, Jia. No one knows what they're doing. Not the judges, not the prosecutors, not the defense attorneys, or the cops. We're all just winging it."

"I looked you up, and your Wikipedia page said you've never lost a trial. That doesn't sound like winging it to me."

"I'm an exception, but that's not something you learn. You're born with it. I have it, and Russell Pritcher has it, too. He's never lost a case either, you know. That isn't something they teach you in law school."

"So you're saying I don't have it?"

I shrugged. "I'm saying you're not going to find out if you got it or not by prosecuting horse thieves. You need to test yourself."

"Well," she said, taking a bite of burger, "lucky for me, we have a rape and murder case thrown in our laps, right?"

I watched her eat a minute and then finished my drink.

"What do you know about Patty's love life?"

She shrugged, taking a napkin and wiping at her lips. "Just what you told us. I didn't know her. When we got this case, I asked a friend of mine that does hair that knew her, and she said Patty dated a lot. All older guys. She didn't like guys her age."

"She give any names?"

Jia shook her head. "No, but honestly, if she was charging two grand a night like you said, and she only went on dates with guys from River Falls, there's not that many people here that can swing that. Top of my list would be Nathan Ficco, Horace Webb, and the mayor. How the hell do you even get rich as a mayor? He makes like twenty-five grand a year."

"Being mayor of anywhere has perks. Like buying worthless property and then getting it zoned commercial and selling it for ten times what you bought it for." Outside the window, a woman was walking her large black dog without a leash. I watched the dog a moment and then said, "Do me a favor; when you get back to the office, get me an appointment with our dear mayor. And don't tell Gates for now."

30

The mayor's office wasn't in the City and County Building like the other city administration offices, but in an old Victorian-style home that had been converted to office space. The home was redbrick with white pillars out front and an American flag by each pillar.

Inside, law books took up massive floor-to-ceiling shelves and the furniture looked imported. A receptionist led me back to the mayor's office; he was at his desk, on the phone. He held up his finger, indicating he'd be just a minute. I stood by the window, watching his reflection in it.

He was a large man that overflowed from his chair, and sweat glistened on the thick mustache that decorated his upper lip like a small rug. He wore an immaculate suit with a pocket square and had a ring on three of the four fingers of each hand.

When he hung up, he came over and thrust out his hand. "Roy Dawson, so nice to finally meet you."

"Tatum Graham. Likewise."

"Have a seat."

I sat down across from him. The chair groaned as he sat and put his hands across his prodigious belly, a grin on his lips.

"So what can I do ya for?"

"Honestly, Mayor, I just wanted to come meet you. I figured there'd be cases we would want your input on, and I just wanted to get the meeting in first."

"Well, I appreciate that. I've known your father for forty years. Good man, hard worker."

"Yeah, thanks."

I looked at the photos on the wall behind him. "Wife and kids?"

"Yes, yeah, four kids. You?"

"No. I can barely take care of myself."

"I know the feeling," he said with a chuckle.

A moment passed in awkward silence.

"So how long have you been married?"

"Going on twenty-four years."

"Long time. Congrats. Most marriages that I've seen, at least in Miami where I lived before coming out here, were in shambles by then. It was typically the husbands cheating and the wives finding out and either sticking around because it was more comfortable than leaving or just not caring enough to leave."

Another silence. The grin on his face was gone.

"Well, this isn't Miami," he finally said. "People out here respect their wedding vows."

"I know. I love that about this place." I brushed a piece of lint off my pants. "I guess you've been keeping up on the Patty Winchester case."

"Who hasn't? We haven't had a murder here in over ten years. That one was at the Hallows, too. We should just close down that damn place. But yes, I'm familiar with Patty's case from Gates."

"Yeah, it's really a shame, too. She seemed like a really pleasant girl. Beautiful, too. In fact I'd say one of the most beautiful girls I've ever seen."

He looked away from me, to his computer screen. "I couldn't tell you. I don't judge women on their looks, being a married man. 'Nother difference between here and Miami, I guess."

"Guess so."

"Look, Mr. Graham, it was nice meeting you, but I've really got a packed—"

"Did you know her?"

"Excuse me?"

"Patty Winchester. Did you know her?"

"What is this? Why are you asking me these questions?"

Time to rattle the cage with a lie and see what shook out.

"We, um . . . look, you're the mayor, so I wanted to bring this to you. No one else knows about this. This is just you and me as far as I'm concerned. But there's a video of you at a bar in Las Vegas. Skid Row. I was up there talking to the owner, and she mentioned that someone had come in there and assaulted Patty, shouting about how they were the mayor. They keep all their recordings in case there's ever any investigation for anything, and they showed it to me, Mayor."

The color left his cheeks, and he instantly slumped down into his seat. His fingers started to tremble.

Got you.

"I, um . . . could use a drink. You want a drink, Mr. Graham?"

"She was seventeen, Mayor. What were you thinking?"

"It, um . . ." His eyes rolled up to the ceiling. "I was in love with her. It just . . . I mean, it just happened. You can't plan for something like that, it just takes over and happens. I mean, you saw her. You're right, she's one of the most beautiful women I've ever seen."

"Girl, actually. She wasn't a woman yet."

He swallowed. "When she broke it off, I just kinda lost it. I went out there to tell her that I loved her, that I wanted to be with her."

"That you wanted to leave your wife?"

He sat stunned a moment and then nodded slowly. "I'm not proud of it. But it happens. Someone like me . . . that someone like her would even pay attention to me . . . I mean, no man could say no." He chuckled mirthlessly. "You want to know something funny? I swear it made my marriage better. After being with Patty, I could go home and just be home. Be with my wife and kids."

"Did you hire her as an escort?"

He nodded, staring down at his desk. "It started that way. It was, um, known that Patty was . . . you know, and that she had someone helping her with all that. I was given the information of who to contact. Some woman. But I promise you it wasn't like that between me and Patty. She loved me, too. I think she was scared to commit because of what her father would think about her being with a man my age. She had all these dreams, all these plans, and I think she thought an older man would slow her down."

"She was with you for the money, Roy. That's it. She didn't love you. She was working to support her father and brother the only way she thought she could. It was a job."

He sat silently awhile, and I could see the sweat droplets that had formed on his forehead dribble down to his collar and leave little circular stains.

"Were you following her around? Showing up at places you thought she might be?"

"I don't know. Some. The Vegas thing, I suppose."

"Where were you on May fourteenth?" I asked.

"What?"

"The night Patty was killed. Where were you?"

"That's ludicrous. I would never hurt Patty in a million years. I loved her and she loved me," he said loudly, and then immediately recoiled when he realized his door was open.

"Where. Were. You?"

His eyes turned to slits, and the confidence he had lost when I shook him had returned. He stood up and said, "This is my town. You're just a visitor here. Get the hell outa my office. And if that video ever makes the light of day, I swear to you I will sue you into the Stone Age. I'll make the DA file so many charges against you for criminal defamation you'll spend the next year in a cell eating porridge and beef jerky. And I have connections to the Utah Bar, too. I'll make sure you never practice law again."

I rose and buttoned the top button of my suit coat. "It's always nice meeting those who so selflessly serve their communities. Have a good one, Mayor."

I glanced back once as I was leaving. He stood with his hands on his desk, his cheeks flushed red, his lips straight and narrow with anger. When he saw me looking at him, he barked, "Marcy! Shut my door and hold all my calls."

31

I took a drive back to the Hallows after meeting with the mayor. I wanted to be out there by myself. The breeze hadn't left, but the sun was so bright overhead I had to squint even with sunglasses. The Hallows had a cold, calm feel to it, like how a city got quiet after a snowstorm. It seemed like there was a bubble up here that shielded it from the rest of the world.

I went over to the ditch and sat on the edge, staring down into it. I wondered what the last thing Patty saw was. Did she look up and see the stars behind the faces of her killers? Was it painful, or was she in such shock that she was numb? It made me uncomfortable to think about her last moments, so I rose and left.

My father's house wasn't far, and though I didn't entirely want to, I stopped there. The door was open. I went inside and didn't hear anything. The silence in the house made it seem like a crypt; dust swirled in the sunbeams coming through the windows.

I saw my father sitting at the kitchen table, his back turned to me. He was coughing and wiping the blood from his lips on a handkerchief.

In his other hand he was holding a picture of my mother. He wiped his tears away with the back of his hand. I backed out of the front door and quietly closed it.

I sat on the porch a long time and watched the sunset. When darkness had fallen, I heard the door behind me open and my father said, "How long you been sittin' out there?"

"A while. I like it, it's quiet."

"Well, come inside."

"It's nice out here."

He disappeared for a bit and came out with two bottles of beer and handed me one. He sat behind me on the bench. He sighed and drank a big gulp.

"I liked this beer," I said. "I would sneak some and replace it with water when I could. Did you ever notice?"

"Of course I did. You don't drink your entire life and not know when your beer tastes like water."

"How come you never said anything?"

He hesitated. "Kids gotta grow up on their own. Not my place to say things like that." He drank some more. "You got any?"

"Kids? No."

"Any plans to have any?"

I shook my head and took a sip. I set the bottle down next to me. "Not really. I'm good where I am."

"If that were true, you wouldn't be here."

We sat silently a few minutes.

"How long?" I finally said.

"How long what?"

"You know what."

He didn't answer. I glanced back at him, and he was staring down at his beer bottle, picking at the label. "They said a year without treatment." He coughed again and pulled out a fresh handkerchief. No blood came out now. Just a dry, hacking cough that looked painful.

"So get the damn treatment."

He inhaled and looked up to the sky. "You're not old enough to feel this yet, but you just get tired of life. You just say enough's enough, and you're done. It's not sad or disappointing or anythin' like that. You're just tired."

He finished his beer and went inside. I watched as he struggled with the stairs up to his bedroom. After a few minutes I went up there to check on him and he was already asleep, fully clothed. I took off his shoes and put a blanket on him, careful not to disturb the picture of my mother resting on the pillow on the other side of the bed.

32

I didn't feel like going to my condo so I went to Gates's ranch. She was at the stables with her horses, brushing a beautiful brown mare under a portable light. She tossed a brush to me.

The other horse was black and eating some hay. I set my hand on his head, gently running my fingers down before starting to brush his body.

"Haven't done this for a minute," I said.

"You used to love it."

"What ten-year-old doesn't love playing with horses?"

"Hey, wanna go for a ride?"

"Now?"

"Yeah, now."

"I haven't ridden a horse in twenty years."

"It's fine, riding a bicycle."

"It's dark."

"Quit being a sissy."

After letting the horses drink some water, we saddled them. Slowly, I climbed on top of the male horse and followed Gates. It felt like I was on top of jelly that could go either way and toss me off.

"Grip with your knees."

"I am gripping with my knees."

"You're scared. He can sense it, and it makes him tense. Close your eyes."

"Um, no thanks."

She stopped and turned her horse around as she watched me. "Close your eyes, Tatum."

I exhaled and closed my eyes.

"Feel his heartbeat?"

"No."

"Then you're thinking too much. Calm your mind and feel his heart."

I took a deep breath and didn't feel anything for a bit, and then I felt the slow pulsing of a heartbeat. Once I felt it, I couldn't believe I didn't feel it before. It was like a drum against my legs.

"Is it fast or slow?"

"Fast."

"He's tense. Take a deep breath and rub his back and tell him it's okay."

I did as she said, and I could feel the heartbeat slow after a moment.

"Horses are perceptive. They feel what you feel."

"Yeah, well, he must feel confused as shit."

We began trotting along a dirt path that led behind the ranch to a grassy clearing that seemed to go on for miles.

"What're you confused about?"

"Russell told me today he thinks I'm a traitor. That somehow my switching to prosecution is saying that our profession as defense lawyers was so awful that I needed to jump ship to live with myself."

"Do you feel that way?"

"No. We're not a dictatorship. Everyone gets a lawyer."

"Then why let it bug you?"

I was quiet a moment. "I don't know."

We followed the dirt trail and began climbing a hill. I looked back to the ranch house and could just see the bright portable light by the stables. The house was dark, but the moonlight lit up the valley enough that I could clearly make out the flowers in the grass and the red rocks of the nearby mountains.

"Did the mayor call you?" I asked.

"No. Why?"

"I met with him today. I lied and told him I had a video of him assaulting Patty at Skid Row."

"And?"

"And he cracked and admitted he'd hired her as an escort. When I asked where he was the night she was killed, he threw me out and said he'd arrest and sue me if the video ever came out. I'm going to, with your blessing, have Will dig a little bit into his life. I need to know where he was the night she was killed. He also said he got the information about how to set up a date with Patty from someone else. I need to know who that someone else was, though I got a pretty good guess who."

She shook her head. "That poor girl. Yeah, do what you have to do, I guess. But nothing public, not yet. Oh, I asked around about Horace. No one would say much, but it's pretty clear he's getting huge donations from both the mayor and Nathan Ficco. Looks like the powerful in this town don't want me in the top spot anymore."

"They don't want whatever they're hiding to come to light."

We rode a little in silence.

"I used to come up here for hours," she said. "Just sit on a ledge and let the world disappear. You have a place like that in Florida?"

"The pier near my house, I guess. I mean, it was always crowded, but there was something about being near the ocean that . . . I don't know. It does something to you."

"Do you know I've never seen the ocean?"

"What're you talking about? You've never been to the beach?"

"I've never been more than a couple hundred miles from River Falls. Went to law school at UNLV and would just drive down every morning. I had a plan to study abroad, but Dad got sick." She glanced at me. "How's Adam?"

"Not good. He's coughing up a lot of blood, but he refuses to get treatment. And he's got a little arsenal of pain medication. I think his plan is to take the pain meds until it's time to check out."

"He's not that old. He's got time left if he started treatment."

"Said he's tired of life. Don't think that's going to happen."

"Well, you need to talk him into it."

I chuckled. "Since when does anyone talk Adam into anything? He does what he does, and the world be damned."

She smiled. "Gee, who does that sound like?"

We dismounted and sat on a small rock ledge that overlooked the entire ranch. There was no breeze, no cars, no crickets or katydids, nothing.

"Tonight he asked me if I wanted kids," I said.

"What'd you say?"

"I said no. Too late anyway. I'm an old man now."

"Pushing forty is hardly an old man. Besides, you started everything else over. Maybe not having kids is something you need to rethink, too."

I looked out over the green plains. In the moonlight, they were the same aquamarine as ocean water.

"I don't belong here," I said. "It feels like I'm in a play. I should've just kept driving through."

"I don't think you believe that for a second. I think you're scared of something, and you're not used to being scared."

We stared at each other a second, and she said, "We better get back. I have an early meet and greet with the old fogies in town."

I rose and watched as she nimbly hopped onto her horse like it was the most natural thing in the world.

"Last one back has to unsaddle them."

I scrambled to get on my horse as she took off down the hill, a woman in her most natural environment. It put a smile on my face to think what the women I dated back in Miami would think of someone like Gates.

Then I raced after her.

33

The next morning I got a text from Jia that the forensic team was down at Anderson Ficco's house. I rushed there as quickly as I could, and as I got out of the car, Jia handed me something. It was a gold shield in a black wallet.

"Welcome to the County Attorney's Office," she said.

"Nice. Now I need my Mayberry uniform, and I'm officially in." I grabbed my jacket out of the back seat and put it on. "What've we got so far?"

"Nothing yet."

We walked up to the home. It was a mansion, which probably wasn't easy to pull off in River Falls. The city council, I guessed, didn't like monster homes being put up in a town where people prided themselves on being salt-of-the-earth types.

We took the steps up and went inside. White carpets, crystal chandeliers, spiraling staircases on both sides of the room leading up. Dining room with marble table to the right, and library to the left. This wasn't a River Falls home: this was something someone from a big city flew down whole. It felt out of place here, like some colossal red tree in a green, level forest.

"Are you the asshole that authorized this?" a man said, walking up to me.

"You must be the father," I said.

Nathan Ficco folded his arms, his eyes narrowing to slits as he stared at me. I could almost feel the anger bubbling off him like heat. His gray hair was combed to the side, and I could see the outline of a vein popping in his forehead. I thought it might burst and we'd have to give this guy CPR right here.

"I've called my lawyer. If there's so much as a broken plate—"

"Mr. Ficco, the judge signed the warrant. Take it up with her. Now if you'll excuse me, I'm going to sift through your underwear drawer."

I brushed past him and into the dining room, Jia right behind me. "They won't find anything here."

"What makes you say that?" she asked.

"Look at this place. It's like something Marie Antoinette would own. Look at the crystals in that cabinet; there's not even dust on them. Anderson had to have known Joseph Stalin over there would somehow find out if he did anything like that here."

"If he kidnapped a girl that everyone knew he was with, he doesn't strike me as the type of person to plan ahead."

I folded my arms and went over to a photograph of the family. To the right, apart from the rest of the family, stood Anderson Ficco. I recognized him from the photo in the police file. He had a bad teen-age mustache and a grimace. One eye was uneven with the other and drooped down. A tattoo on his lower arm poked out from his T-shirt, though I couldn't make it out.

"What's the tattoo?"

"Oh, it's charming. It's a stripper on a pole with a snake going between her legs and up into her . . . well, places it shouldn't go."

"A snake?" I said, looking at her.

She nodded. "I told you, he's just a little charmer."

I turned back to the photo and stared at him. The rest of the family, his parents and three siblings, were all smiling and dressed in their Sunday best. Anderson wore torn jeans and a Cannibal Corpse T-shirt.

I shook my head. "No. He's not bringing Patty back here. Not with his parents. He's got somewhere."

"Like where?"

"Kid like this has access to a lot of money. He's got an apartment or a house somewhere."

"We ran his name and did a background check. He's got his car and a credit card, that's it."

"Subpoena the credit card company. Get me all his statements going back two years, and I need them today."

"You got it."

Will turned a corner just then, wearing a bulletproof vest that said RFPD on it. I chuckled. "Planning on going down in a hail of bullets, Wyatt Earp?"

"Hey, when in Rome. We don't get to raid a home often down here. All the cops were excited."

"It's not a raid. It's a search, and next time, wear a suit. It'll make you look more respectable and less intimidating."

"Tatum Graham."

I turned around. Russell Pritcher stood there in a black pinstripe suit. He had long silver hair pulled back in a trademark (or at least he thought so) ponytail, and a face that looked like a skull with skin pulled tightly over it. His hands always had these protruding blue veins that I couldn't stand. He put out his hand, and I shook, feeling as if I were holding slimy bird bones.

"Wasn't expecting you out of your coffin this early, Russell."

"Well, I thought I'd come see the sights before the prelim." He looked me up and down. "You shopping at Super Target for suits now? I know government doesn't pay quite as well, but I'm happy to recommend some affordable tailors for a man of your modest means, if you like."

"I don't know. Your mom picked it out, and I think she did a pretty good job."

He lost the smirk on his face and stared at me a second. His eyes were steel gray, a color I didn't see often, and added to the impression that he was a zombie in a $4,000 suit. He took a step forward and looked me in the eyes. "That joke has run its course. Much as you have." He grinned, adjusted my tie, and said, "Now, please, if you haven't found anything, I'd like you to leave my client's house."

"Not quite done yet. Pull up a chair, might be a while."

He turned and went to talk to Nathan Ficco. Will said, "What was that about?"

"Old grudges."

"About what?"

"I hit on his mother at a restaurant just to annoy him."

"You're kidding?"

"Just words, nothing else." Will watched me. "What? It drove him nuts that she thought I was charming. Also, I stole a client from him that he really wanted. Hale White."

"The director?"

"That's the one. Huge case. We had our pick of clients after I won that one. Russell did everything he could to get Hale to sign on the dotted line, but Hale said he got a creepy feeling from him. Russell of course blames me."

"Hale's right. The guy gives me the creeps."

"Well, get used to him, because you're going to be in court with him a lot if any of his past cases are any indication."

He watched Pritcher a second. "Looking forward to it. Hey, anyway, we're done here, boss, and haven't found a thing. There's no reason not to leave."

"Tell Forensics to go through everything again."

34

Jia got me the credit card statements within an hour. Don't know how she did it because credit card companies loved dragging their feet, but she got it done. We sat down in the conference room and began reviewing them. Will sat at the end of the table, and every once in a while I would catch him glancing at Jia, who seemed oblivious.

"You know, I knew Anderson's older brother pretty well," Will said.

"From high school?" Jia said without looking up from the copies of the credit card statements.

He nodded. "Nice guy. Totally laid back, nothing like his brother. Don't know what happened there."

"If Anderson tortured and killed her along with his buddy, he's a psychopath. It's a pretty common phenomenon for psychopaths," I said. "We don't know the causes, and you'll find people with great childhoods and no abuse who turn into monsters. The *why* isn't our concern. Our concern is the *what* and *how*. Assuming he killed her and it wasn't our mystery man stalking Patty, he took her somewhere after the bar, but it wasn't his house."

"They could've gone to Steven's house," Will said.

I shook my head, flipping the page I was on. "He lives with his parents and five siblings. No, Anderson's got some place. If the ME is right, then they kept her for at least two days somewhere. Forensics will still check Steven's place out, but they wouldn't have wanted to risk someone stumbling across her. It has to be somewhere private."

"Got something," Jia said.

"What is it?"

She slid the page she was on over to me. "Ten-thousand-dollar charge to a REU Realty."

"Is that in town?"

"One town over, in Loxum."

———

I remembered Loxum as a little dirt town with one gas station, but when we pulled in, it had a strip mall, several grocery stores, and tons of ongoing construction for new office and residential buildings. Apparently they had been doing something right while River Falls stayed the way it was.

REU Realty was on the first floor of a white office complex. A thin blonde woman in a gray suit met us at the door, and I said, "Tatum Graham."

"Suzanne, hi, nice to meet you."

"You as well. Not to seem too blunt, but we're in a little bit of a time crunch."

"Of course, I have what you requested, but unfortunately, we need court documentation that we were forced to hand it over. I have to keep my clients' purchases private."

I stared at her a second. "You're kidding."

"Afraid not."

"Now, correct me if I'm wrong, but when someone buys a piece of property, they have to record it at the county recorder, right? That's public information."

"Yes, well, it's company policy."

Ah. I had a feeling it was only company policy for the rich, who may or may not have registered the property under their own name.

"It's not under his name, is it? Look, I don't give a crap. I'm going to search that property, and if I have to have you arrested for obstruction of justice to do it, I will."

"Excuse me?" She bristled. "You don't come in here and talk to me that way. I think it best you speak to our company attorney from now on."

She shut the door on us.

"Obstruction?" Will said, staring at the closed door.

I shrugged. "Rolled the dice and lost. It happens." I put my hands on my hips and glanced around the parking lot. "Well, I'm open to ideas."

Jia said, "We could try to meet with Anderson and pretend we know about it already. See if he might give up some information."

"No way Russell lets us talk to him, and there're rules you bend and rules you break, and speaking to someone that's represented isn't either of those. Good way to get the case tossed and you disbarred. What else?"

Will said, "We could ask around to some of the girls he's dated. Dollars to doughnuts he's brought them to his condo or whatever before if he has one."

I pointed at him. "That is a great idea. And don't ever say *dollars to doughnuts* again. All right, Jia, I want you at Steven's house. They should be wrapping up by now. He's got his own lawyer, but I bet you Russell will be there, too. Let them know we're not giving them any easy outs. Will, you know these people. Talk to anybody Anderson's dated." I checked my watch. "I got an appointment to keep."

35

I went to the home of Nikyee Geller, who I'd learned had adopted her new husband's name of Ellison, and waited in my car the half hour until our appointment. I watched the neighbors coming and going; several of them were retired elderly. One guy kept glaring at me.

I got a text from Will:

Sorry, boss, Mayor was at a charity dinner in Mesquite the night Patty was abducted, and at a family reunion the night before her body was found. There's photos of him at both with his wife and kids. Wife says they went home after both and he was with her both nights the entire night

Damn. It would've been so much more satisfying to get a conviction against a corrupt jackhole mayor than two kids barely out of high school.

A black SUV pulled into the garage and Nikyee stepped out. A young kid with floppy brown hair jumped from the passenger seat with some drawings in his hand. I got out of the car and grabbed a brown paper sack from the back seat. Nikyee saw me and grimaced. I guess she'd thought I wouldn't actually show up.

"Hi, Nikyee." I smiled at Lyle and said, "Lyle, how are you, pal? My name is Tatum and I'm a friend of your dad's."

"Hi."

I turned to Nikyee. "Should we talk inside?"

"Sure."

We went inside through the garage, and she did a few things in the kitchen while Lyle and I sat in the living room. Nikyee came in a second later and sat down next to him. She was wearing workout clothes and had sweat stains on her chest. She folded her arms and said, "Lyle, Tatum has a few questions to ask. Just be honest with him, okay?"

"Okay."

I opened the bag and pulled out his monkey.

"My monkey!" he said. He grabbed it without hesitation, and I saw his mother smile.

"Left it at the campsite," I said. "Do you remember when you went camping up there, Lyle?"

He nodded.

"Did you have fun?"

"Yeah, we made s'mores."

"Oh yeah? I love s'mores. I put extra chocolate on mine."

"I like the marshmallows."

"Marshmallows are good, too." I glanced at his mother. "Lyle, something very bad happened up there when you were camping. Somebody got hurt. A very nice girl. And I'm trying to figure out who was responsible. Do you know what *responsible* means?"

He lost his smile and nodded without looking at me. "Yes."

"What does it mean?"

"It means someone did something."

"That's right. It means someone did something." I hesitated. "Did you see anyone up there? Someone that could've hurt someone else?"

He didn't answer. His mother looked worried now and said, "Lyle, did you see something?"

He blinked and nodded.

"What did you see, pal?"

"I . . ."

"Hey, it's okay. I'm a friend. I'm here to help. So you take all the time you need. Just think about it and put it into your own words what you saw."

He looked to his mom and then said, "I heard someone getting hurt."

I glanced at Nikyee again. "How do you know they were getting hurt?"

"They were screaming."

"Was it a girl?"

He nodded.

"What was she screaming?"

"Just screaming. And she said, 'Please stop.' She was crying and screaming."

Nikyee looked like she might faint. "Why didn't you tell me, sweetheart?"

He shrugged.

I leaned forward and said, "Did you see who was screaming?"

He shook his head. "Not really."

"Did you see anyone else up there?"

He played with his monkey a minute and then nodded.

"Pal, if you saw these people again, do you think you would know it's them?"

He nodded.

I looked to his mother. "Can we talk in the kitchen?"

We went in there, and I looked back to make sure Lyle couldn't hear us.

"We need him to do a lineup."

"No way," she said, folding her arms. "I'm not making him a part of this."

"Did you know Patty?"

She stared at me a second. "I don't see what that has—"

"They tortured her for days before taking her up to the Hallows to kill her. You think that's the type of thing you do once and then stop? They got a taste for it now. How're you going to feel when you see the next girl on the news? How's Lyle going to feel when he sees their faces splashed everywhere and hears what they did?"

She sighed and leaned against the wall, her gaze drifting to the ceiling.

"What would he have to do?"

36

As I was leaving Nikyee's house, I called Jia. She didn't answer, so I left a voice mail. "Get a lineup set for Anderson and Steven. We got a witness."

I was about to get into my car and join them at Steven's house when I got a call from Gates.

"Hey," I said.

"Tatum, you need to get down to the hospital."

"Why? What's wrong?"

"It's Adam."

———

I rushed down to Saint Mark's and left my car in ER parking. I went inside and asked for Adam Graham's room. He was down the hall to the right, and when I went in, he was lying in bed with a hospital gown on and Gates was sitting in the chair next to him. She was wearing a blue suit and glasses and quietly talking with him.

"I told her not to call you," he said.

"What happened?"

"Nothin'. Just a dizzy spell."

Gates rose. "I need a Diet Coke. Come with me, Tatum."

I followed her out as Adam turned his attention to the IV sticking out of his arm. We walked down the hallway.

"You remember that time you had a concussion and I brought you here?" Gates said.

"Yeah, I got into a fight with some football player, and his girlfriend popped me in the back of the head with a baseball bat."

"You remember what the fight was over?"

I shook my head. "No. I assume my natural charm just got to him."

"He grabbed my ass."

"Oh, right. I do remember that."

"When you were unconscious on the ground, I maced him and his girlfriend."

I chuckled. "I remember thinking you'd thank me, and all you said was you could take care of yourself, and then you drove me to the hospital. I was trying to impress you with my manliness. Boy, that backfired, huh?"

She smiled as we got to the vending machines. "I was grateful, I was, but the guy was twice your size. You gotta fight battles you know you can win."

"If I did that, I'd still be stuck in this town." She glanced away, toward someone coming through the emergency room entrance. "Sorry, I didn't mean it to come out that way."

She grabbed her drink and turned to me as she opened it. She took a sip. "He's not well, Tatum."

"What happened?"

"He fractured a rib from coughing so hard, and it caused him to pass out. He called me when he woke up. I found a towel covered in blood. I spoke to the doctor, and they said he needs to begin treatment immediately. If he waits much longer, it'll be too late."

"What do you want me to do? He doesn't want it."

"You're his son."

"We barely know each other and he hates my guts."

She shook her head. "I swear, you're the smartest dumb person I know. Look in the top drawer in his desk at home."

"Why?"

"Just do it." She eyed her watch. "I gotta run. I'll be back to check on him tonight."

I watched her walk away and then turned back to Adam's room. He was already asleep. I spoke to the nurse, who told me they'd given him some pain medication and that the doctor was at dinner but would be back soon to discuss his case with me. I took a breath and sat down in the chair Gates had been sitting in and stared out the windows at some trees.

By the time the doctor got in, I was nearly asleep. He was a younger guy, and he smiled widely as he shook my hand. Adam was still asleep, so we spoke there. He told me that the cancer was advanced and he was worried that without starting treatment right away, it would progress to the point that they couldn't really do much to extend his life.

"The outcomes with treatment are good. With treatment and catching it as early as we did, I'd put it at a sixty percent chance for remission. Without treatment, I'd put his odds at five percent that he survives a year once it develops into its later stages."

"But I mean, I know he's coughing a lot, but he doesn't look *that* unhealthy to me."

He shook his head. "This type of cancer is very aggressive. The coughing is already nearly uncontrollable. In mere months, breathing without aid will be almost impossible. He needs to start the treatment protocol as soon as possible." He grinned. "When I told him that, he said that I was just trying to buy another Ferrari."

"Yeah, that sounds like him." I glanced toward Adam. "I'll talk to him."

He nodded. "Well, he seems to be better now. You can take him home when he wakes. Make sure to keep him hydrated. I'll prescribe a stronger cough medication with codeine, but he's already on so much pain medication that we can't get too strong because it might affect his breathing. Just make sure to keep an eye on him and contact me if it's not working." He looked over to him. "The elderly, in my experience, are frightened of this type of treatment. They know they don't have long left, and they don't want to spend it in a hospital bed. It's a very human emotion, so it's up to the family to help them overcome it."

"Not sure he sees me as family, but I'll try."

———

When I got Adam home, I helped him up the stairs to his bed. He was still groggy from the morphine, and he sat on the edge of the bed while I took off his shoes and belt. He lay back on the pillows and groaned. I put a throw blanket over him and he said, "She would leave notes for me."

"Who?"

"Your mother. She'd leave them in the house. Hide them places she knew I would eventually find. Under the cushions of the couch or in the pantry. I would find them all the time." His brow furrowed and he said, "I found one a few months ago in one of my dress shoes I never wear. It just said, 'I'm proud of you.'" A tear rolled down his cheek.

I wiped it away with a clean handkerchief I found on the night-stand. "Get some rest."

I left the room and watched him from the hallway. He was out almost instantly. I went downstairs and was about to flop on the couch when I remembered what Gates had said.

My father had a small office next to the kitchen. I sat down at the desk.

I opened the top drawer. Inside were newspaper clippings from all the major papers I had been in: a piece in the *LA Times* about a rap star I defended. A piece in the *San Francisco Chronicle* about a corrupt cop I had gotten acquitted. A mention in the *New York Times* about a politician I was defending on a gun charge. There were at least twenty pieces in there. Pretty much all the national newspaper attention I had gotten was accounted for.

I put the pieces back and shut the drawer, looked around the office, and then left the house.

37

I got a call from Jia while I was at Benson's eating a turkey sandwich.

"Yeah."

"Nada on Steven's house. Nothing there. What's this about a lineup?"

"The monkey. Belonged to a kid that heard Patty screaming. He said he saw who was hurting her. Did you get the lineup set?"

"Yeah, tomorrow morning at eight."

"Man, I am just loving you more and more every day. I'll call the witness's mother and see you there."

I hung up and dialed Will.

"Nothing yet, boss," he said by way of greeting. "Trying to track down an old girlfriend of Anderson's to see if he took her anywhere other than his father's house. I'm waiting outside her work. Shift doesn't start until eight."

"Keep me posted. I want Anderson's place, Will."

"I'll stay on it."

"I also want a list of everybody that could've been one of Patty's clients: older men with big disposable incomes. The mayor's been ruled out, but everyone else. We need to go through them one by one and establish if they went on dates with Patty and where they were on the night she was abducted and the night she was murdered. Then get photos of each of them and show them to Diana. Maybe she saw some of them in the bar when she was working."

"Will do. What about Farah? I can live with turning a blind eye to drugs, but she's basically pimping out minors, boss."

"I know the prosecutor at the Attorney General's Office that oversees the sex trafficking division. Once we're done with Farah, I'll put in a call. But until then, we may need her, Will, so play nice."

"Hey, I'm nice to everyone. Better run, think the ex just rolled up."

Next I called Nikyee and told her when to be at the station, and all she said was "Okay."

I hung up and stared out the window. I had an urge to go see someone, and I didn't know why I wanted to see him right now.

———

Hank Winchester was working on an old truck when I showed up to his house, which was a large trailer in a trailer park not far from the mechanic shop. Nearby, a boy of nine or ten sat on an upside-down crate and played on a phone. He looked like Patty.

"I love these older trucks," I said, walking up. "Reminds me of something from better times, maybe. More innocent times."

"Don't know about that. These models were first used by people in the Depression coming out west to find work. They got a history of moving desperate people from place to place. You seen the new color videos they got of the Depression?"

"I haven't."

"You can see it in black and white and think it's from way back, but when you see them starving faces in color, it hits home. Think that could happen again? Where the country falls apart and people gotta fight for everything?"

"Don't see why not. Cell phones and self-driving cars don't change human nature."

He nodded and looked to his boy. "Corbin, say hi to Mr. Graham."

He didn't say anything and didn't look up. Hank stared down at his boy awhile.

"Come inside. I wanna show you something."

I followed him in. He didn't seem surprised that I was there and didn't ask why I'd come. In the kitchen, he reached in a drawer and pulled out a photo. It was of Patty, him, and Corbin at an amusement park. Patty wore a wide smile and had her arm around her father's neck.

"That's the last photo I took of her. She was teasing me because I still like using real cameras instead of phones." He smiled as he stared at the picture. "Her mother left us when she was eleven. Said she wasn't happy and just left one morning. Went into the kids' room and kissed each of them, came to me and kissed me, and then just left with one bag."

His face went stern, and he put the photo down on the desk. He ran his hand along the stubble on his face. "Helluva thing to think your life is going one way and in just a few minutes it's all gone. That's all it was, just a few minutes."

I stared at him a second while he took a deep breath. "Was she out for the funeral?"

He shook his head. "I don't know where she is. For the first few years, the kids would get cards on their birthdays, but then that stopped. I don't know if she's alive or dead, or has another family. People say change is a good thing, but it sure ain't for the people you leave behind."

"If she was the type of woman to run out on her kids, maybe it's for the best."

He glared at me. "Yeah, maybe."

"Look, um, I just came by to tell you we're doing everything we can. We may have a witness."

"A witness? What the hell are you talking about?"

"There may have been a family up there at the time, and their child may have seen something."

Anger flashed across his face. "Why didn't the cops tell me?"

"They didn't know."

He was silent a second, fury building in his face. "You telling me they missed someone that saw my little girl get killed?"

"In their defense, Hank, they're not experts in this. This type of thing just doesn't happen out here, and these investigations are very complex."

He calmed and nodded. "Well, you're here now, and I know you're gonna do everything you can for Patty."

I swallowed and had to look away. The pain he was going to experience when it finally went public that she was escorting would be excruciating. He would blame himself for not knowing, and by extension, for her death. I wanted to just tell him now and get it over with but knew I couldn't.

"Yeah . . . I promise I'll do everything I can," I said. "Um, look, Hank, did Patty ever mention anybody maybe following her around?"

"What do you mean?"

"Like someone that maybe was following her around that she didn't want following her? Or did you ever notice someone around the house? Maybe just waiting outside in their car?"

I wanted to add, *Someone like our dear mayor*, but held my tongue.

"No. Why?"

"Just following up on everything. I gotta be thorough. Look, I gotta run. Duty calls. Call me if you need anything."

I turned to leave and he said, "Tatum? Thanks for coming here. I mean, to the town, but also here today. It's nice to talk about it sometimes. Everybody else in town walks on eggshells around me."

I nodded and left.

38

A lineup could be done in one of two ways: a photographic lineup or an in-person lineup. *The Art of Jury Trial as War*, chapter 20: "Always, always, always—if you have the choice as a defense attorney—go with a photographic lineup." Human memory is enormously fallible, and false identifications happened all the time. A photographic lineup was the best way to confuse the witness since people rarely look the same as in a photo. A lot of times, lazy cops didn't even take new photos. They just used old booking photos or even crappy DMV photos from years ago.

So as a prosecutor, I wanted a live lineup, and I worked fast enough that Pritcher couldn't file a motion to object. It would be fruitless to do so, since he'd for sure lose, but stalling tactics to wear down the prosecution worked more times than not. But he'd never been up against someone like me before.

I got to the station in the morning, and Jia was waiting for me outside. Her arms were folded as she paced, completely lost in thought. She struck me as someone who lived mostly inside her own head, for which the outside world was almost a distraction.

"Is the party ready to start?" I said as she followed me inside.

"Everyone's here. Russell's threatening to file a motion objecting to a live lineup."

"Of course he is."

"Can he even do that? Seems frivolous."

"There's a Supreme Court case that says he can object on the grounds that it's overly suggestive, which violates the accused's due process. So let me do the talking. One misstep and Russell will get the entire lineup tossed."

We went inside the station, and near the back I saw Russell sitting with two other people in expensive suits. A tall woman with brunette hair and flashy earrings, and a younger man with a gold Rolex that gleamed in the sunlight coming through the windows. I caught a few of the officers glancing at them when they thought no one was looking.

"Tatum," Pritcher said. "Looking sharp as ever. Did you raid your father's closet?"

"Funnier every time. Let's do this."

"I haven't made up my mind whether to file an objection yet."

"You're going to file one after the lineup saying I was overly suggestive, so let's not bullshit each other. Shall we begin? I'm sure you've got flies to pick the wings off of or puppies to kick."

We headed back to the lineup. The viewing room was darkened, and Lyle and Nikyee were there, as was Detective Vail, who was standing with his arms folded in the center of the room. Lyle was hugging his mom's leg.

"Where's Howard?" I asked Vail.

"Car theft uptown. We still have other cases, ya know."

I turned to Lyle and said, "Hi, Lyle."

"Hi."

"You ready to do this, pal?"

He glanced at his mother and then nodded.

I looked to Vail and he left the room to bring in the men.

When the first group walked into the room on the other side of the two-way mirror, I stood next to Lyle, blocking him from Pritcher's view in case ole Russ got the idea that maybe he could intimidate the little guy.

Seven men came in. All white, all with dark hair and builds like linebackers. On the far right was Steven Brown. The kid was taller than the rest and had a thicker body, probably from football or wrestling. He was unshaven and, I could see it from a mile away, scared. He was fidgeting and kept glancing around.

Vail looked to Lyle and said, "Do you recognize anybody standing here?"

He clutched his mother's hand and buried his face in her leg. I looked to Nikyee, who I could tell understood that I couldn't be the one to help him.

"It's all right," she said softly. "Tell him if you recognize anyone here."

Slowly, he turned his head and shook it.

"Are you sure?" his mother said.

"It was dark. There were two of them. I don't know."

Crap.

I looked to Vail, who led the men out and brought in the next group.

In the middle was Anderson Ficco. Seeing him in person was something . . . different. I felt anger, and I didn't want to. Anger was temporary insanity, and it was the worst of all the emotions for a trial attorney to feel, since it blocked all reason and clearheadedness.

Unlike Steven, Anderson had a smirk on his face. No fear at all. Steven was the weak link, and I made a mental note of that.

Lyle glared at Anderson. It was clear, I'm sure, to everyone in that room that he was terrified of him, and I wondered just how much Lyle had seen that night.

"Do you recognize anyone, son?" Vail said.

He buried his face in his mother's leg again, and this time, he nodded.

"Which number is he holding?"

He slowly turned and looked at Anderson and then dug his face back into his mother's thigh. "Three."

Pritcher stepped forward and said, "Lyle, are you sure you recognize number three? It seems like you hesitated a little bit."

He gripped his mom's leg tighter. "Yes. Three."

I nodded and turned back to Detective Vail, who left the room again to take the men in the lineup away.

"Thank you," I said to Nikyee as everyone filed out. Only Pritcher, his two associates, and Jia and I were left.

"Agg homicide," I said, "and I'll take the death penalty off the table."

He chuckled. "You're kidding, right? They'd never let him out. That's as good as a death sentence."

"Russell, we're not in downtown Miami or Compton. This is rural Utah. The cops here are treated like saints, and everything they say is scripture. That jury's gonna want to fry him the second I rest my case."

"Manslaughter, five to fifteen."

"Get outa here. I'm not giving him manslaughter. He tortured and murdered a seventeen-year-old girl."

"Now don't tell me you've already forgotten the use of the word *allegedly*, Tatum. You gotta prove that before you start throwing it around. And you're right. We're in rural, pro-police, pro-prosecution Utah, which means the jury's already going to be against us before my client even sits down in that chair. But it also means these detectives botched this homicide investigation, your coroner doesn't have a medical degree, and I'm just willing to bet there were tidbits the detectives left out of the report or overlooked. And when I find them, I'm going to tear you and this case apart."

One of his associates opened the door and held it for him. "See you in court."

He left, and I clicked my tongue against my teeth.

"He's right you know," Jia said. "We got a botched case. If I were to bet—"

"If you were to bet, always bet on me."

I texted Will. Anything?

Yes. Texting you an address now. Get down here, and get that forensic team here.

39

The forensic unit had been put up in the only motel in town by the taxpayers of Ute County. They reached the scene in about half an hour: an apartment complex in the nearby town of Glassdale, about twenty miles south of River Falls, over the Nevada border. A detective from the local sheriff's office had come out, but he was sipping coffee with some of the other cops and didn't seem to care about what was happening.

As Jia and I stepped out of my car, Will came up to us and said, "Bebe Stewart, her real name, dated Anderson for four months. He'd bring her here most nights because he said his dad would beat the sheesh out of him if he brought, in his words, *white trash* to the house."

"Would beat the what out of him?"

He glanced at Jia and said, "I, um, don't use profanity. Just a personal choice."

I shook my head. "Utah, man. Okay, where's Bebe?"

"At her house. Told her we would be stopping by."

I looked toward the complex. Didn't appear especially upscale. They were three-story townhomes for sale, and on a purchase sign up front, I saw what I needed to see: one of the bullet points said they had large basements.

We entered the unit. The townhome was sparsely decorated, really just a couch with a TV and an Xbox next to it. The stairs leading down to the basement were off to the right. I got some paper booties from one of the forensic techs and slipped them over my shoes and made Jia and Will do the same.

Vail and Howard showed up, too, and stood at the door. Vail said, "Be nice if you called us first since this is our case and all."

"Hey, back when I was a defense attorney, we were enemies, and I would do anything to win. But now I'm on your side, and I'm still going to do whatever I can to win. So cut the whining and be glad I called you at all after you hid evidence."

Howard stepped right up to my face and said, "You know, I might get sick of your bullshit one day and decide to do somethin' about it."

"Well, until that time, Detective, please put some paper booties on your feet before you kick another crime scene in the balls."

I went into the living room and watched a tech spray something on the couch and then go over it with a heat lamp. I opened the sliding glass door and stepped onto a small patio. The air was hot and dusty, and a fence blocked the view of the neighbors. A bag of charcoal lay on the ground against a wall, but I didn't see a barbecue.

Back inside, the techs were working feverishly to finish up a scan of the house, and I watched them for a while to make sure the speed wasn't interfering with the quality, and it didn't seem to be. One tech, a woman in a blue jumpsuit with CRIME LAB emblazoned in bold lettering on her back, was vacuuming a section of carpet with a small handheld vacuum.

"Why you guys in such a hurry?" I asked.

"We're not really," she said without looking up. "None of us expected to have to stay the night, so it's throwing a little bit of a wrench into some of our other cases, but we'll deal. That's why they pay us the big bucks, right?"

Jia was speaking with Howard, and the detective glanced at me before leaving.

"Where's he going?" I said.

"Talk to the neighbors. See if anyone heard or saw anything."

"You mean he's actually doing his job? I'm impressed."

"He's not so bad. You guys might actually get along if you talked to him."

"Doubtful, but thanks for the vote of confidence."

"Detective," one of the techs shouted from the basement, "we got something."

Since Vail had left by then, too, Jia and I headed down. Prosecutors had to be enormously careful at crime scenes, since, at the very least, they were witnesses to the scene itself. If the defense wanted to disqualify a prosecutor from a case, all they had to do was say that a conflict was created because the prosecutor is both the prosecuting attorney and a witness. It was easily avoided, though, if it could be shown that another witness could provide the same testimony without the prosecutor's involvement. There were enough people here that it wouldn't be a problem if I was careful.

"What we got?"

The tech, a burly guy in a coat, flipped on his black light. The basement didn't have any windows and was naturally dark. The blue-tinged light lit up a space of about four feet, revealing dark splotches that ran in a horizontal line along the floor.

"What am I looking at?" I said.

"Blood. It pooled here before someone cleaned it up. Looks like probably with bleach. It's a common mistake: bleach doesn't actually destroy the blood. But they probably used something more powerful, too. It's really degraded."

"You got enough for a DNA match?"

"Doubtful. Bleach contaminates the blood. Only one of the three types of blood tests could work with stains this old anyway, what's called PCR."

"Polymerase chain reaction, yeah, I know it. It got one of my former clients falsely accused of a crime he didn't commit."

"Well, no method's perfect, but that's a pretty good one. Anyway, I'll keep looking. There might be some arterial spray or something that got elsewhere that they didn't use bleach on. But keep in mind, these stains are months old. My guess is nothing usable's left."

"Well, good work nonetheless."

"Thanks. And who are you again?"

"I'm the babysitter for this investigation, apparently. Just keep me posted on what you find."

We left the basement, and I went outside and called Gates to give her an update, but she didn't answer. I looked back to the town house as Will came out. He slipped his booties off and said, "I was going to head over to Bebe's."

"I'll come with. These guys might be a while."

———

The three of us drove to a house in River Falls that I recognized. A girl I'd had a crush on growing up had lived there. The house was run down, to the point that it looked like it could fall over, and a car that was missing its two rear tires was up on cement blocks, which I didn't know was actually a thing that happened outside of movies.

"You guys stay here," I said.

Will nodded and Jia was already lost on her phone. I got out of the car and headed for the house. Just in case Pritcher decided to try to get me off the case by saying I coerced or intimidated a witness, I opened the recording app on my phone and hit the record button before slipping it back into my pocket.

I knocked and a beautiful—stunningly beautiful, really—brunette wearing a Lynyrd Skynyrd shirt answered. She must've been twenty-two or twenty-three, and she said, "Yeah?"

"Bebe?"

"Yeah."

"I'm Tatum Graham. I'm a deputy county attorney." I took out the badge for the first time and flashed it, felt like I was on some terrible seventies cop show, and quickly put it away. "I'm prosecuting the Patty Winchester case."

"Oh."

Huh. That's it? Conversation was not going to flow easily with this girl. "Can I come in?"

"I guess."

The house looked like a hoarder's dream. Piles of everything from toys to letters filled boxes stacked on top of each other against the walls. The orange carpet was shaggy and thick, with stains spread out through the room. The walls were the fake wood wallpaper, and duct tape held together one of the lamps.

"You live alone?"

"Nah, my mama lives here, too, but she's at work." She sat down on the couch and curled one leg underneath her. "Anderson didn't do it, you know."

I went to sit down across from her, but the sofa had dried food on it, at least what I thought was dried food, so I stood and folded my arms instead. "Oh yeah? Why do you think that?"

"Because he ain't nothin'. I dumped him and he was cryin' and stuff, wouldn't let it go. Kept showin' up at my work and almost got me fired. He's a chickenshit, couldn't kill nobody."

"You dumped him? See, because I got the impression that he was a bit of a player."

"Yeah, he gets girls 'cause'a his money and all, but he ain't no player. He's weak as a turd. Like a little kid."

"Really? Because that's not what I heard."

She shrugged. "Believe what you want. I'm just tellin' you. He ain't nothin'. Steven, though, that fool's an idiot."

"How so?"

"Just gettin' all stupid wherever we go, you know? Pickin' fights with Hells Angels and all sorts'a people. He's got that temper."

"So you think Steven was the one that killed Patty?"

"I mean, I don't know, but that makes more sense. You seen Anderson? He like ninety pounds soaking wet. We got into it once, and I smacked him around like a bitch."

I nodded and looked around the house. "What was Anderson and Steven's relationship like?"

"I don't know. Didn't hang out with Steven too much. Seemed like a bully to me, so after a couple months I told Anderson I didn't want to be around him no more."

"What'd he say about that?"

"Said it was fine. I think Steven picked on him so he didn't mind."

"Picked on him how?"

"He would just be smackin' him around sometimes. He tried to have sex with me right in front of Anderson, to show him, you know, whatever. Damn fool was lucky I didn't claw his eyes out."

"Did he stop?"

"Yeah, I got him good. Made his eye bleed, and he jumped off and was hollering and wakin' up the dead. If my mama woulda woken up, he woulda been in a world'a hurt."

"Did Steven or Anderson ever mention anything about Patty to you?"

She shook her head. "No. I was surprised as hell when it was on the news. I could see Steven, but Anderson? No way. If he was there, the coward was probably hidin' in the car or somethin'." She began looking at her nails. "Anyway, that's all I know. I can't really help you none."

"What about Patty? You know her?"

"Little."

"Any guys she was dating you knew about? Older guys, maybe?"

She shrugged. "I don't know. I think she said somethin' once 'bout some guy that was married and obsessed with her. Wouldn't leave her alone."

"Did she say who?"

She shook her head. "I don't think so. I don't remember, though. She was kinda quiet. Didn't talk much. Can't blame her, though, for goin' after older guys."

"Why's that?"

"Guys our age are damn fools 'round here. Don't do nothin'. Get married and expect their wives to pay the bills. A nice sugar daddy would be somethin'."

I nodded, staring at her. "Well, thanks for your time."

"No worries."

I left the town house. Steven, at the lineup, had looked like he was about to piss his pants. So she was either lying, or he was an even more convincing psychopath than I thought. No way that oaf would be that slick, so she was probably lying, which then begged the question, Why? If she'd broken up with Anderson months ago, she didn't really have a reason to lie to law enforcement for him. Which meant someone either had paid her or scared her into saying that. Could've been Anderson, but he'd been in lockup with his calls and letters monitored for three months. The person with the most incentive to see Anderson acquitted other than Anderson was his father, Nathan.

I texted Will.

Get me a file on Nathan Ficco. Everything you can find out about him.

40

After convincing Steven's attorney to agree to let us meet with him tomorrow morning, I headed home. The forensic team hadn't found any uncontaminated blood, but they would still try to test for a DNA match. I could still introduce the blood at trial, but Pritcher would say it came from a deep cut, or the previous owner of the town house, or it was too contaminated to be trustworthy, or a million other things. If we weren't able to identify it as Patty's, we didn't have a way to place Patty at that townhome.

I stopped at Adam's house. When I went inside, music was playing, and he was sitting in his recliner. He didn't turn around. I came up and sat on the couch again, and we listened quietly to some jazz before he turned the volume down and said, "I don't want to go back to that hospital."

"It's not really up to you at this point."

"The hell it ain't," he said, turning around, fury in his eyes. "I don't see you for twenty years, and you come in here and think you can dictate what I do or don't do?"

I leaned forward. "You're dying, Adam."

"I know I am. And I won't spend the small sliver of time I got left in a hospital bed puking and shitting my guts out."

"It's your only shot to live longer."

"Maybe I don't want to live longer."

"Hey, any life is better than no life."

He was quiet awhile. "You'd be surprised how different you feel at the end of your life than at the beginning." He zoned out for a second and then said, "I'm hungry. Make me a sandwich, would ya?"

I wanted to say something, anything, that would convince him to start his treatment, but I could tell there was no talking him into it. I rose to make his sandwich.

"Hey, you've known Nathan Ficco for a long time, haven't you?" I said from the kitchen.

"Thirty years. I worked for him for a while, too."

"Oh yeah? Where?"

"He started a landscaping company. When me and your mom were first married, I picked up a job there for some extra cash."

"What was he like?"

"He's a son of a bitch, that's what he's like. Violent as a pit bull in heat."

"Violent?" I said, slathering some mayonnaise on bread. "Violent how?"

"One time this young fella might'a stole some cash out this change box we carried with us to make change for the customers. Not much, just a few bucks. Poor kid had a wife and daughter at home and couldn't make ends meet. Anyway, Nathan found out about it and had him taken into the middle of the road and held down, put his knee on one of the kid's arms to pin it in place, took a hammer, and broke each of his fingers."

"Yikes."

"Yeah. Did it in front of all of us, too, just to show us who we were dealing with. Nathan Ficco is no one to mess around with."

"Huh."

"How's Gates?"

"Good. Stressed with the election, I guess."

161

His question made me wonder what Gates was doing. I finished putting some chips on a plate to go with the sandwich, and before I could text her, she texted me and said, Sorry I missed your call today. What did you need?

Nothing. Just was going to give you an update. You wanna meet for dinner?

Sure. Come over.

No, let's go out. I feel like being out right now.

K. Tell me where and when.

After making Adam food and helping him to bed, I freshened up in the bathroom and straightened up the house a little. Before leaving for dinner, I had a feeling I should check on him one more time. When I went upstairs I heard him in the bathroom. The door was open and I could see him over the toilet. He was vomiting, but it wasn't vomit coming up; it was blood.

I put my arms around him and said, "We need to go."

"I'm not going to the hospital."

"You're coming to the hospital."

He pushed me off. "I ain't goin'."

"Damn it, Adam, if I have to bash you over the damn head and drag you there, I will."

———

I was sitting outside the hospital room when Gates arrived. She carried two bags from Chick-fil-A, and she handed me one and sat down next to me.

"How is he?"

"He's asleep. In addition to the cancer, apparently he has a vicious ulcer, hypertension, and diabetes I didn't know about."

"You say that like it's his fault he didn't tell you. You were gone a long time."

"Oh, not you too."

"Not me too what? You left him, remember? And you're mad at him for not telling you every one of his ailments? Do you know Adam? You think he's the kind of guy to call his son and complain about his health?"

"So what, I should've been here, is that it?"

"I'm not judging you, Tatum."

"It sure as hell sounds like you are."

We sat silently a moment, and I sighed and looked in the bag. It was a kid's meal with a little toy. It made me chuckle.

She smiled. "I thought you would like the toy."

I lifted it out of the bag. A tiny doll. "I do."

She reached over and slipped her hand into mine, and we sat there waiting for the doctor.

41

I woke up to the vibration of my cell phone. It was Will, and he'd sent me a text saying, Where are you?

"Oh, crap," I said.

Gates was in the seat next to me. We were still in the waiting room of the hospital somehow, even though I thought I remembered going home to sleep. She woke up and rubbed her face, pulling her hair back over her shoulder.

"I gotta run," I said.

She stretched. "Where you going?"

"Interviewing Steven Brown at the jail." I kissed her cheek. "I appreciate you staying here with me."

"I'll keep an eye on him until you get back."

"You don't have to. I'm sure you've got fund-raising or something to do."

"This is more important."

———

The jail staff let me in without searching me, and I was led back to an attorney-client room. Steven's attorney was a young woman, tall and black with a nice gray suit. We shook and I sat down across from them. Will stood in the corner.

Steven was huge. Much larger than he seemed in the lineup. Even sitting down I could see the bulge of muscles in his shoulders. His hands were like meaty claws, and I saw dried blood around the edges where he had picked off the skin.

"Steven, I'm Tatum Graham. I'm the prosecutor on this case. Do you know what that means?"

"Yes."

"Good." I glanced at his attorney. "I read the statement you gave the police, but I thought maybe I should hear in your own words what happened that night."

The attorney said, "One second, Steven." She looked to me and said, "We want a deal."

"Deal for what?"

"You're obviously here because you want to cut a deal in exchange for testimony against Anderson. Which is the right move. My client was, hypothetically for the sake of this discussion, there, but just there, and had nothing to do with the murder."

My heart thumped against my rib cage, and I felt that familiar tingling of adrenaline. Gates had been right; we had the two jerkoffs who'd killed Patty in lockup.

"I disagree, but go ahead, Steven, I'm all ears. If you tell me something good, I'll think about a deal."

He put his hands together and said, "We were all just having fun at the bar. It was the same as it always was. We'd partied with Patty and Cecily before."

"So what happened?"

He looked to his attorney, who nodded. "Anderson was on some crazy binge, brother. I don't know what it was. Mescaline and coke, or something. He took anything he wanted. I mean, I've seen him wake up and roll over and take a few hits of meth. He just don't care. So he was on it, man. I mean outa his head. So I'm just tryin' to get with these girls, and he just messin' it all up. Just acting like a jackass, grabbin' 'em and sayin' stupid shit. So Cecily left, but Patty said she'd stay. We were gettin' along, but I had Anderson with me, so I said we should go drop him off and go back to my place. She said yes."

"Let me guess, big guy, she was asking for it, right? It was consensual and she wanted to be raped and tortured?"

"No, no, it wasn't like that. We was drivin' back, and Anderson was in the back seat just out of his head. I mean, sayin' all sorts'a things 'bout the government watchin' him and how people knew about nine-eleven before it happened and all that. He wasn't makin' any sense." He swallowed and glanced at his lawyer again. "And then he told me to pull over."

"Where?"

"Just on the side of the road. I thought he needed to piss or somethin', so I did. Then he pulls out a hammer from the back seat."

"A hammer? What kind of hammer?"

"Just, like, a hammer. I had my tools back there. He hits her in the head with it and knocks her out. And there's blood comin' out of Patty's head." He looked down to the table and swallowed again. "I thought she was dead."

"What happened then?"

"He said we needed to drive to his place. He has his own place. And I said we needed to take her to the hospital, and he pulled out a Smith & Wesson. He stuck it right in my face and said, 'You gonna drive to my place, or do I need to do it?' He said it just like that, too. So I drove there."

"The place in Glassdale?"

He nodded.

"What happened when you got there?"

He looked down to the table and wasn't speaking.

"Steven, this is where the boys become men. Tell me what happened. If it's good, and you're truthful, I will cut you a deal to testify against Anderson. You might be able to get out of this place with a good chunk of your youth left. If you're convicted, you're never going to get out of here."

"He . . . he kept her there."

"For how long?"

"Like I said, I wasn't there. I promise. I helped him take her up to his place, and then I left. I don't know what he did after that."

"What he did after that was rape and torture her for two days, and you let it happen."

The lawyer said, "Save the drama for the jury, please."

Steven said, "I didn't want it to happen. But you don't know Anderson. He's crazy. I seen him put a cigarette out on some dude's face. Like just did it."

"Yeah, I heard about that one."

He swallowed. "He . . . he almost killed someone once. Stabbed him right in the throat."

"That's not on his record. Where was this?"

"When we was huntin' up in Montana. We took off right after, never got busted for it. He told me if I ever told anyone he'd kill me. Patty was just like that, sayin' he'll kill me if I say anythin'. And I believe him."

"So she's there for two days, and you, allegedly, don't know what's going on and don't call the police. How'd you end up dumping the body?"

He exhaled loudly and glanced at his lawyer. "He called me and said I needed to come over. That he was ready to take Patty to the hospital. I drove down and Patty was . . . was . . ."

"What?"

"She was downstairs in the basement naked. There was blood everywhere. She was barely breathin'." Tears came to his eyes and he started sobbing. His attorney put her hand on his shoulder. "I just . . . I just wanted to have some fun. I liked Patty. I liked her. I would never hurt her. He made me go up there with him, to the Hallows. He said he would hurt me if I didn't. I thought he was just gonna leave Patty up there, and when he sobered up he'd let her go. But when we got there he tossed her in this ditch and then jumped on top of her and was chokin' her. I was tryin' to get him to stop, but he said he would shoot me dead right there. I backed off and he killed her. He killed her for no reason."

He was crying now, and I waited while he composed himself. He finally took a deep breath before his attorney said, "What can you offer?"

"Assuming I can verify some of this . . . homicide without the aggravation tag. Fifteen to life with parole."

"Attempted homicide, one to fifteen."

"No way. He'll be out in three years."

"He didn't do it, and what he did do was while he was under threat of being shot. I'll add it as a lesser included charge in his trial and have him take the stand to tell the jury what he just told you. There's a good chance they convict him of a lesser included or even a full acquittal, and you know it. One to fifteen is a good deal."

I let out a long breath of my own and looked toward Will, standing in the corner. "What do you think?"

Will shrugged. "I know Anderson's a psycho."

I looked back to Steven, who was wiping at his tears with the back of his arm. "Let me think about it," I said.

The attorney nodded and rose. She called the guard over, and before Steven was taken out of the room, he said, "If you see Hank, can you tell him . . . I guess just tell him I'm really sorry."

The attorney left her card on the table. "Call me when you want to talk."

When we were alone, Will said, "That doesn't sound like the worst deal."

"Assuming he's telling the truth."

"Seemed like it to me."

"Don't trust your first instincts. Despite what people say, they're usually wrong. Sociopaths can lie through their teeth about everything, and you'd have no idea." I thought for a second. "Go over to Cecily's and ask if what Steven said is true, if he and Patty really were into each other and Anderson was the violent third wheel. And get someone from Forensics to test Steven's car for Patty's blood. See if you can find the hammer, too."

"You got it."

I left the jail wishing like hell I could interview Anderson. I looked back to the monolith of steel and cement and thought, *He's in there, right now.* That he was breathing and living while Patty was rotting in a grave seemed unfair, and it had never struck me as unfair before, just a part of life.

I had to watch myself. *The Art of Jury Trial as War*, chapter 1: "Under no circumstances, ever, ever, ever, feel emotions toward anyone in a case. It will only lead to disaster."

42

Jia was at her desk with her head down over some paperwork, and I headed past her to the conference room. The Winchester files were laid out on the table, and as I sat staring at them, I realized I hadn't had a lawyer pro hac me into the Utah Bar: a procedure where a lawyer could practice in another state he wasn't licensed under the "supervision" of an attorney licensed there.

"Jia," I called. "I need you to pro hac me in for this case."

"Already done."

"Without asking? Look at you. You know I would've killed for an associate like you in Miami."

She set her pen down and looked at me. "The Yale guys you hired weren't to your liking?"

"They were fine if you have to draft a legal thesis on the origins of replevin. Not so great if you need someone to make an armed robber look sympathetic to a jury, or need to tail a cop for two days to see if he's having an affair you can use against him. Successful trial lawyers just have some innate dispositions other people don't. You can't be taught it, and no amount of book knowledge is going to get it for you. I think you might have it."

Will came in just then and said, "Hey."

"Tell me you got something good."

He sat on Jia's desk facing into the conference room, and I rose and leaned against the doorframe.

"I got something good. Talked to Cecily. She said Patty and Steven were definitely flirting that night. That Patty had a little thing for him since high school. And she said Anderson was acting really strange."

"Strange how?"

"She said he was high and then got progressively more and more drunk through the night. That he was saying all kinds of nonsense, and sometimes it didn't even sound like words."

"Okay, so that's a plus one for Steven's story checking out so far. Now, ladies 'n' germs, we need to see if Anderson actually has a gun. I want another warrant executed for his parents' house and his truck, this time specifying we're searching for a gun. And get it on the drive over 'cause we need to leave right now."

———

Our arrival at Anderson's parents' house gave Ficco Senior a little scare. He swore at me to get off his porch, and I retreated to the driveway. The warrant was on the way, so we couldn't just barge in, and unfortunately Pritcher pulled up before the warrant did.

"You have no right to be here," he said, coming up to me.

"Warrant's on the way."

"You've already searched. I'm filing an objection and asking for anything found in here to be suppressed."

"We weren't searching for a gun before, and we didn't have a warrant for the mother-in-law apartment in back."

"A gun? Why would you think there's a gun here?"

"His buddy Steven is quite the talker. Had some interesting things to say."

Pritcher's face hardened for a moment. "It won't work."

"We'll see. He seemed pretty believable to me."

Pritcher went inside and shut the door.

"That guy just can't help giving me the creeps," Will said.

"He should. He's dangerous. Killed a guy once."

"No way."

I folded my arms and paced in front of the massive home. "When he was twenty-five, someone said something in a bar that he didn't like, apparently. Russell kicked the man to death. Magically, in a bar full of people, no one wanted to come forward. Apparently, our young Mr. Pritcher had mob connections. His father was a lawyer for one of the families and represented their interests in Atlanta. Don't kid yourself, the guy does not care one ounce about the law. I wouldn't be surprised if he's in there right now looking for the gun himself. Where the hell's the warrant?"

Will called the detectives, and a full half hour later, Howard showed up with the warrant.

"Stop for doughnuts?" I said as I took it from him.

He grinned. "See, now, it's comments like that that make it so I just don't want to hurry."

———

Howard and two uniforms searched the house, and the mother-in-law apartment, which we didn't have authority to search last time since Nathan's younger sister lived there. I stood in the study with Pritcher as he sat in a large Victorian chair near the window, sipping coffee. Behind him were three massive bookshelves and a ladder to reach the top shelf. The books looked brand new, unused. We were alone.

"Where are your two thugs?" I said.

"Tomomi and Jordan? Hardly thugs. They're quite incredible actually. Jordan was a marine captain, and Tomomi was the archery champion of Japan before law school."

"Sounds impressive."

"Oh, they are. They're also willing to slit their mothers' throats if I tell them to. That's something you never seemed to understand: you can get a lot more out of people with fear than you can with respect. You were spineless with your associates and had high turnover as a result."

"We had average turnover and mostly because associates eventually go off to open their own firms and make more money."

He shook his head as he sipped his coffee. "Not mine. They know I'll destroy them if they leave me when I don't want them to."

"How gracious of you. Did you threaten their firstborns, too?"

He laughed. "No, but I certainly would."

I folded my arms and walked to the window, which looked out over the pines near the house. "Can I ask you something, and I give you my word it stays between us?"

"That's cute that you think your word means anything to me, but sure."

"Michelle Keri."

He grinned. "What about her?"

"You know what. She's the top divorce attorney in the nation. If she opened her own firm, she could pull down five times what you pay her, but she still sticks it out with you."

"And your point?"

"Now, I heard that she did want to open her own firm. That she came and told you and you were kind and supportive."

"I certainly was."

"But then I also heard that while she was driving around in Boston one day after a couple drinks at a bar, she ran over somebody. Allegedly killed the guy. So she called you in a panic about what to do. And lo and behold, Russell Pritcher fixes the day. You dumped the car and the body, and she owed you big time. Decided to stay with you and keep her mouth shut about any shenanigans your firm might ever do. And, again allegedly, the guy she quote 'killed' was seen by someone in the know going about his business in a Miami coffee shop."

He smiled. "You are quite well informed, aren't you?"

"You're not the only one with connections."

He nodded. "Yes, it's true."

"Wow. An honest answer. I didn't know we were that close, Russell."

"No one would believe you anyway. And I'm presuming it would be impossible to get out of you who told you all this, though I can guess. Only three people know, and I'm one of them. Seems my tight ship isn't tight enough." He set his coffee down on a side table. "Now let me ask you something that's had me curious."

"Shoot."

"Billy Rowford."

My mouth felt dry, like I'd licked sandpaper.

"Oh," he said, chuckling, "that name make you uncomfortable?"

"No. What did you want to ask?"

"See, now I heard, allegedly, that Billy murdered his lover when he found out he was cheating. Young man that was his personal trainer, was it? Anyway, again allegedly, I heard that he ran straight to your office, the murder weapon in a bag, a nice large kitchen knife." He folded his hands in his lap, a wide grin on his face. "Now as a good lawyer, you convinced him to turn himself in but not say anything. And miraculously, the police couldn't find the murder weapon. With no confession, no murder weapon, and the victim killed in his own apartment, the case was dismissed at preliminary hearing."

"What's your point?" I said sternly.

"My point being that someone saw him bring the knife into your office, but he didn't come back out with it."

I flexed my jaw and then released it, but the tension was still there. The scene he was describing had happened on a Saturday, and the only other person in the office with me was my partner, Tim. "That little prick."

He cackled. "You and I are not so different, Tatum. We do what we need to do to win. I can read the disdain on your face when you look at me, but it's the disdain of looking into a mirror. People don't change and they don't start over. You might be on the other side for now, but you're just like me, and we can't change who we are."

Jia poked her head in and said, "Umm, bad time?"

I turned away from Pritcher. I was nervous I might vomit if I had to stare at him any longer. "No. What is it?"

"I got it."

We went out to the living room, and Detective Howard walked in with an evidence bag containing a black-and-gray Smith & Wesson handgun.

"Where'd you find it?"

"Mother-in-law apartment out back."

I looked at Pritcher and said, "Rookie mistake to keep that thing around."

"Every person in this county has guns. That adds nothing to your case, if it's even his to begin with, considering it was found in his aunt's room. But feel free to use it in trial. I think you're going to find, Tatum, that your case is not as strong as you think it is."

43

Gates came into the office that next afternoon, after we spent a couple of hours with Adam at the hospital. He seemed better and was joking with some of the staff and even ate a little.

I'd been reviewing the *Utah Rules of Criminal Procedure* when Gates came in. I had looked through Utah's evidentiary rules, and nearly all of them were identical to Florida's, but the *Rules of Criminal Procedure* had pronounced differences. It seemed almost like these rules were made for a Wild West town rather than modern cities.

Gates sat across from me in the conference room.

"You look tired," she said.

"Haven't been sleeping much."

"Really? You? I would figure you sleep like a baby."

"Why would you figure that?"

She shrugged. "Doesn't seem like there's much that bothers you enough to interfere with sleep."

I leaned back in my seat and rubbed my eyes. "I wish. What're you doing here? It's clock-out time."

"Actually, I need a favor. I have a fund-raiser tonight and . . . I thought maybe you would want to come with me."

"Wow. Gates needs a prop, huh?"

"Look, you wanna come or not?"

I chuckled. "I'm kidding. Of course I'll come."

She stood up. "Good, go put on something nice. I'll swing by and pick you up."

———

I went back to the clothing store and bought a new blazer and, Lord help me, cowboy boots. I asked for the nicest and most expensive shoes they had, and the cowboy boots were it. When I was back home and sitting on the bed, slipping the boots on, I wondered how people walked around in them all day. They hurt like a mother.

Gates texted that she was here, and when I got in her truck, she grinned and said, "Are you wearing boots?"

"What? I gotta blend in with the local color here."

She pulled away. "You wouldn't wear those as a kid for some reason."

"I never rooted for the cowboys in movies. I always wanted the Indians to win, so the cowboy stuff never appealed to me."

She glanced at me. "You look nice. Really."

I put one boot up on her dash and tried to wiggle it around to make it more comfortable. "I can sympathize with you women having to wear high heels. We men demand too much."

"I haven't worn high heels since high school prom." She hesitated. "You never came to prom."

"Nope, I did not. I was working. Saving up money for the move I knew was coming."

"You know, I . . . um . . . I waited for you to ask me. Up until the last day, I waited."

"Really? Why? Every guy in school would've thought they'd won the lottery if you'd gone with them."

She shook her head. "You're such an idiot."

We talked about my father and then her father, and how she had managed to work as a prosecutor and keep up the ranch at the same time. When we got to the conference center, cars lined the street, and the parking lot was full. She parked in a nearby lot behind an appliance store, and we crossed the street.

Inside, the place was decorated like a country music concert. They didn't wear tuxedos or have champagne or maintain all the pretenses people in South Beach would've for something like this. I got the impression no one had memorized quotes by George Bernard Shaw to pass off as their own or was telling fake or embellished stories of things that happened on ski trips to the Alps. Everybody here was focused on having fun, laughing genuinely while sipping beer out of bottles.

"What?" she asked. "Don't tell me this is too lowbrow for the great Tatum Graham?"

"Not at all. The opposite."

We mingled for a bit, and at one point Gates had to leave me to glad-hand. I stood at the bar and sipped a Miller while I watched her. She moved adeptly through the crowd, knowing exactly who she needed to speak with and who she could avoid since time was limited. The men were clearly infatuated with her, and ever so subtly she would touch them on the shoulder or the elbow. And as she left them and walked away, they would stare at her.

"She's something, isn't she?" the bartender said.

"She certainly is."

"I asked her out once."

I turned to him: young guy with blond hair. "Oh yeah?"

"Yeah. She said no. She said she didn't really date. One of the guys here, Mr. Long, he went out with her a few times. He said that Gates doesn't like men, if you know what I mean."

"Ah. Claiming someone is a lesbian. The last refuge of the failed suitor."

"Um, what?"

"Nothing." I threw a twenty on the bar. "Thanks for the drink."

I worked my way back to her, and she took my arm and said, "Tatum, this is Horace. He's running against me."

Horace was a slim guy with bad breath and a thick gold chain around his wrist. He had a diamond ring on his pinky and a gaudy Rolex on his other wrist, and I thought maybe him and the mayor went shopping together.

"Oh, right! Saw the billboard. It was great. I thought you were hocking used cars at first but was more impressed it was an election."

He grinned and then lost the grin as he realized I was insulting him.

"So you're the hotshot we've been hearing so much about, huh? Well," he said, smile returning, "I'm not sure how the mayor feels about a pinch hitter coming in from the outside on the biggest case this town has ever had. I'll tell ya what, though, this case has been mishandled from the beginning. It was a mistake to put a woman in the county attorney position, and the handling of this case shows it. If you'll excuse me."

He hobbled away, but not before checking out Gates's backside as he went around her.

"That guy has douchebag dripping off him like he took a douchebag shower," I said.

She chuckled and wrapped her arm through the crook of my elbow. "Come on. I have a few more people for you to insult."

———

First I met the county recorder, a cute little old man who combed his hair to one side to cover a massive bald spot that had clearly been sprayed with some type of black paint. Two Utah state representatives were there: one looked like he was twelve years old and the other like he was a hundred. He began telling me what it was like to live through the civil rights movement, which "started all the problems this country now has." At that point I basically zoned out, and by the end of the night I couldn't really remember who I had spoken with.

The mayor was there, saw me, and flipped me off.

We climbed back into Gates's truck when it was time to leave and sat there a bit. She turned on some music, a country station, and then said, "Sorry. You've probably outgrown this, too."

"It's fine. Reminds me of the drive to Florida. I turned on some Merle Haggard, rolled down all the windows, and just let the wind whip my face."

"Must've been scary going somewhere you didn't know anybody, with no idea how to make money."

"Oh, it was terrifying. But I knew I had to get out. I had to go as far away from Adam as I could. After my mother died, our relationship got worse and worse, and I was just counting down the days."

She thought for a second. "So you didn't miss us at all?"

I looked over to her and she was looking at me. Perfect in every way.

"I missed some more than others."

My cell phone buzzed.

"This is Tatum."

"Mr. Graham? This is Dr. Langley at Saint Mark's."

"Yes, hi."

"We need you to come down to the hospital right away. It's about your father."

44

We sat in the lobby a long time. The doctor came over and sat down on a chair, same young guy as before.

"I'm sure you know this type of cancer your father has is called small-cell cancer. It's inoperable. I know he's been resistant to treatment, and I fully understand that. The elderly population has a difficult time with the side effects caused by this treatment, but he simply needs to decide whether he wishes to live or not."

I don't know why it dawned on me then: maybe it was seeing the blood my father now constantly coughed up, or the fact that I understood there was no changing his mind about treatment, but now I knew what I had to do.

"Start the treatment."

"I can't begin any treatment without his consent."

"I'll be filing a motion tomorrow morning to have him declared incompetent. Start the treatment then."

He nodded. "I know that's a difficult decision, but it truly is for the best if he's going to survive this."

We asked a few more questions, and the doctor left us to attend to some other patients. Gates took my hand as I leaned my head back against the wall.

"He's going to be fine. He's as tough as a bull."

I shook my head. "He doesn't want to live. That's why he's been denying the treatment. He's been trying to tell me that the past few days, and I haven't listened. He hasn't been the same man since my mother died."

She was silent a moment and then said, "Your mother's death really shook him. More than you know. He would come over and drink with my dad, and I'd hear them talk."

"What about me, Gates? You think it was easy for a ten-year-old kid to lose his mother and be left with an alcoholic father? And instead of getting better, he became even more of a prick."

"You can't judge someone until you've been in their position."

"I can judge," I scoffed. I blew out a long breath and leaned forward, staring at the floor.

"The prelim starts in two days. I think you should be here with him. I can take over—"

"I have never, not once, ever let anything personal get in the way of a case. I fell off my house's roof on a Friday once and was at a trial Monday morning. I don't lose, and I don't call it quits."

She nodded. "I understand. I'm just saying no one would blame you if you needed to take some time. I can handle it. And Jia and Will can handle it, too."

"They can't. Not this. Not against Russell Pritcher." I inhaled deeply and said, "Go home and get some sleep. No reason both of us should be here."

"I'm not leaving."

"Gates—"

"Forget it. I'm not leaving."

I squeezed her hand. "Thanks."

She leaned her head on my shoulder and we both stared off at nothing.

45

In the morning, my father was doing much better. Gates and I sat by his bed. He was out of it, but he was talking about some of the upcoming baseball games he was excited about.

"The Yankees," he said, his voice hoarse from the coughing. "That's the team. I saw them in 1966 at Yankee Stadium with my father and have never forgotten it. You weren't into sports and wouldn't have gone with me, but my father took me and I'll never forget it." He stopped for a while and stared off into space before saying, "I remember the smell of the popcorn and hot dogs. You don't get that smell anymore. Too many people there now, too much pollution in the air. But back then you could smell it. It would get on your clothes and hair, and you would smell it all day."

I sat and listened to him for a while, and when he stopped and closed his eyes to rest, I said to Gates, "You better get going. You've got an office to run."

"It's Saturday."

"We both know you don't take Saturdays off."

"How do you know that?"

"Because I don't, and you and I are the same."

She grinned, kissed me on the cheek, and left. I turned back to my father. He opened his eyes and said, "Wish I coulda taken you to Yankee Stadium," before his eyes closed and he was asleep again.

———

I was heading down to the cafeteria when I got a call from a number I didn't recognize.

"Hello?"

"Tatum, this is Russell. I got your number from your associate. Hope you don't mind."

"I do, but what's up?"

"My client has decided, against the advice of counsel, to meet with you."

"What're you talking about?"

"Anderson wants to meet with you and tell you his side of things."

I laughed. "You're kidding me?"

"I am not."

"Since when do you let your clients do anything against the advice of counsel, Russell? Gettin' a little soft in your old age, are ya?"

Silence on the other end.

"I can assure you, I vigorously emphasized this was a bad idea, but he insists."

"All right, I'll meet with him. Where and when?"

"It would have to be today. Preferably in the next couple of hours. I have an important appointment to attend to afterward."

"Yeah? You getting a massage or something?"

"Can you be down at the jail or not?"

I checked my watch. "Gimme half an hour and I'll meet you down there."

46

The jail wasn't far. Hell, nothing was far in this town. When I got there, I sat in the car a few minutes listening to Miles Davis. I wondered what my ex, Sarah Pascal, was doing back in Miami. Probably hauling in some drug dealer whose door she just kicked down.

Inside the jail, the guards were tackling somebody. The man, a tall skinhead with skull tattoos, was screaming at them to let him go. One guard lifted his legs out from underneath him, and the guy toppled forward and slammed his head into the wall. Another guard put his knee in his back and cuffed him.

"Never a dull moment, huh?" I said to the front-desk clerk.

"What can I help you with?" He looked up at me. "Oh, you're the new prosecutor. What can I do for you?"

Once he realized I was a prosecutor, his demeanor changed. It was something I'd grown accustomed to. When I was a defense attorney, they were the good guys and I was the scum of the earth for actually making sure the government had enough evidence before sticking someone in the electric chair. Now the shoe was on the other foot, and I had to admit, it felt damn nice.

"Thank you, yes, you can help me. I'm here to see Anderson Ficco."

He checked a list. "Of course. He's ready to go, but his attorney is running a bit late."

"Well, we have to wait for him. Why don't you just put us in the room and we'll stay quiet while we wait?"

He shrugged. "Sure thing."

A guard came out, huge guy with a barbed wire tattoo on his forearm, and led me back there. The room was all cement and green. A place interior decorators came to die. Across from me sat Anderson Ficco in an orange jumpsuit.

Like Steven, he appeared different than in photos and at the lineup. Sitting down, he looked practically crumpled over, skinnier. The droopiness of his eye was more pronounced, and I noticed now that his face was off kilter and that he had surgical scars underneath his chin. His eyes turned toward me, and he smiled and said, "Russell said you was really good lookin'. Bet bitches just line up at your house, huh?"

I sat down and glanced back at the door to make sure the guard was gone. "Sorry, I can't talk until your lawyer gets here."

He chuckled. "He said ya was slick, too. So ya from Miami, huh? Shit, only thing I ever seen from Miami is Cubans. No wonder ya moved back here. I been around them a shit-ton on my daddy's factory floor, and they thievin' as hell. Rob ya blind by the time ya turn around."

He blinked, and I noticed that his eyes didn't blink simultaneously. He grinned, and the chains around his wrists rattled as he brought his hands up on the table between us.

"I ain't killed her, ya know."

I didn't say anything. I knew the jail recorded these conversations, so I couldn't do anything that made it look like I was trying to speak with someone who was already represented, so all I did was raise my eyebrows a little bit.

"It weren't me. That shit-for-brains Stevie is who ya wanna talk to. He had a hard-on for Patty since they was kids. She was trashed, and he saw his chance, that's all."

The door opened and Pritcher walked in. He froze when he saw the two of us together. When the guard shut the door behind him, he sat down and said, "I don't even need to ask if you've been speaking to him without me present, do I?"

"Anderson, have I said anything to you?"

"No, sir, ya just been sittin' there while I talked some."

Pritcher opened a briefcase and put a digital recorder on the table. "The proper thing to do would've been to leave the room when you saw he was alone. I think this will be an issue we take up with the judge."

He hit record.

"I'm kinda in the middle of something," I said. "Can we get this over with?"

"Oh yes, your father. How is he doing? Heard he was hospitalized."

He caught me by surprise with that, and I didn't like being caught by surprise. "You heard that already, huh?"

The only people who knew were Gates and me and the hospital staff, which meant he had someone on the hospital staff feeding him information. Truth was, he likely had people everywhere in this town feeding him information. I knew this because, were I him, that's what I would do.

"I'd like it put on the record that my client is giving this interview against the strenuous advice of counsel."

"So noted. And I'd like it put on the record that your ponytail makes my skin crawl."

Anderson laughed. His chains rattled, and he smiled widely and said, "I ain't heard ya were funny. I like that. Wish I coulda hired ya, but my daddy payin' for it, and he says Russell here is the best. Don't seem like he done nothin' for me. I'm in here while he out there."

I took out my cell phone. I opened the recording app. "Tell me what you wanna tell me."

He glanced at his lawyer and his eyes blinked, one after the other. I looked down to his forearm and noticed the tattoo of the woman's naked body and the snake.

"We was at that bar in Vegas just drinkin' and havin' a good time. Me and Stevie. And Patty and Cecily get there like around midnight. Her daddy don't let her out much, so she sneaks out late at night. I hooked up with her a few times, so they came over—"

"Hooked up?" I asked. "What'dya mean *hooked up*? Sex?"

"Yessir."

"How many times?"

"Shoot, I dunno. Three times. It weren't nothing. But she ain't got no lovin' for Stevie, that's for damn sure."

I noticed his yellowed teeth. One of them had a chip, making it look jagged, like the outline of the mountains in the night sky on my drive to Vegas. For a rich kid, he certainly didn't take care of himself.

"I mean, he was always tryin' to hook up with her, and she don't care. Didn't pay him no attention. Until that night he killed her."

"Walk me through it."

He shrugged. "We was just havin' a good time is all. And when the girls came, Patty was all over me. I weren't in the mood, though, so I passed her on to Stevie. Thought it was 'bout time he hit that."

"So what happened?"

"We was there till one or two in the mornin'. Cecily left early, so we drove Patty home. Stevie dropped me off at home and then said he was gonna drop Patty off. And that's it."

"That's it?"

He nodded. "That's the Lord's honest truth."

I leaned forward a little. Normally, I could get inside the head of a little jerkoff like this and tear him apart, but not with Pritcher there. If I got too aggressive, he would shut it down and I'd miss my chance, so I had to word things as carefully as possible.

"I've seen pictures of Patty. She's beautiful. Some would say too beautiful for someone from this town."

He grinned. "She was hot. So?"

"So, sorry, Anderson, but you don't exactly strike me as a Casanova. No way she was hooking up with you all over the place."

I had to rattle him. See how he reacted.

Pritcher immediately jumped in. "Don't answer that, Anderson. There a question in there, Counselor?"

I leaned back in my seat. "You were accused of raping a woman when you were thirteen, weren't you, Anderson?"

Pritcher said, "Do not answer that. Tatum, I don't know what the hell you think you're doing, but that juvenile record is certainly not pertinent to this case."

"Who says anything about the case? I'm not looking to introduce it at trial. I'm just curious."

"Don't answer that, Anderson. This interview is over."

"Nah, I'll answer."

"You certainly will not."

Anderson looked at him, anger in his eyes. "Sit your ass down and shut up."

Pritcher, his face turning bright red, looked like he might strangle the kid. I waited for the fireworks, but none came. He sat down quietly instead.

"I didn't rape her."

"What happened?"

"She was a cleaning lady. I hit it, and she thought she could get some money outa my daddy. That's all. But then the sheriff went and charged me. He ain't sheriff no more, though," he said with his crooked smile. "And I ain't raped Patty. You wanna talk to Stevie."

"You were high that night, weren't you?"

He nodded. "Yeah, so?"

"So, high enough you wouldn't remember anything?"

"Hell no. I remember everything. Weren't that high. Just some mesc and pot. I can handle my own." He leaned forward. "And I'm tellin' you, I don't know nothin' 'bout what happened to Patty. Weren't me."

I folded my arms. "We found blood at the townhome you bought. If it's a DNA match to Patty, you are sunk."

"Blood? There ain't no blood there."

"Sorry, pal, bleach doesn't destroy blood. That's in the movies. My techs found it in a second."

He looked at his lawyer and then back to me. "There ain't no blood there. If there's blood, then Stevie put it there."

"Stevie put it there? Really? You're going for the conspiracy defense?"

He slammed his fist on the table. "That sumbitch. I'm gonna kill him."

"Why?"

"He put her blood there so you thought it was me if he got caught."

"See now, that's not what I heard. I talked to Cecily, who said you were acting out of your head that night."

"At first, yeah. But then Cecily left. She ain't seen me calm down with the pot. I just started playin' pool while Stevie and Patty made out. It weren't me that killed her. I ain't got no need to kill anybody."

"Why'd you confess?"

"Man, go back and look at that video. I ain't confessed to nothin'. Them cops put all sorts'a words in my mouth. I ain't said but twenty words to them, and none of 'em were that I did it."

I nodded and glanced at Pritcher, who shrugged. Truth was, Anderson was so skinny it was hard for me to imagine him bossing anybody around, least of all someone three times his size like Steven. The ex's story that Stevie was the violent one started making sense.

I couldn't risk taking Steven to trial and having him get up there and blame it all on Anderson while Anderson blamed it all on Steven. The jury would acquit one of them, or both of them. These were local boys with family connections all over the place. The jury's default position when the trial started—to draw blood—might reverse, and they might start looking for any reason to acquit. Normally a party situation for me, but from this side of the aisle, not so fun.

"Prelim starts soon," Pritcher said. "We should talk."

We rose and went out into the hall. I glanced back through the glass at Anderson, who spat a snot rocket onto the table.

"He's a charming little guy."

"Not the worst I've had."

"Gotta admit, I thought you'd pop him for talking to you like that, Russell. You don't seem the grin-and-bear-it type."

He nodded and glanced down at his feet. "We do what we have to do. Look, I believe him. Do you?"

"I don't believe anybody about anything. Makes life a lot easier that way." I looked back to Anderson. "But I spoke to his ex, and she's adamant that Steven killed Patty and that Anderson doesn't have it in him."

He folded his arms. "And when exactly were you going to send me this interview?"

"Relax, you'll get everything."

He shook his head. "I expect it all the second the prelim ends, and I'm going to be asking for a continuance for the trial date."

"We don't even have one yet, but okay. I'll stipulate. Whenever you want, as long as your boy is cooling his heels in here."

He exhaled through his nose and eyed Anderson. He pointed at me and said, "Investigate Steven. You've got the wrong man in there," and then turned and left.

I stood staring at Anderson, who looked over to me and grinned. He shouted, "Jay! I'm ready to go back to my cell."

47

Back at the office, I used Jia's computer to draft a power of attorney and a motion to declare incompetence for my father. I would have to have him evaluated by a psychologist that would write a report to the court, and so I listed the one I used for most of my cases. The one whose yacht I had paid for over the years with the amount of work I referred to him. Then I called him and he said he could be out in a few weeks.

"Tomorrow, Jerry. Preferably today."

"Well, if you insist, I'll make it work."

When I hung up, I went back to the hospital. Adam was awake and speaking with one of the nurses. I didn't interrupt and instead sat down in a chair against the wall. The nurse was laughing. At one point, Adam took her hand and gave it a gentle squeeze. She didn't resist but rather touched his shoulder and told him she would be back soon with his dinner.

"You can be quite the charmer when you want to be," I said after she'd left. "Too bad Mom and I never got some of that charm."

He turned to me, his expression going from happy to stern, and then he reached for the pudding on his side table. "Don't speak ill of your mother."

"I wasn't."

"I treated her like a queen. The best I knew how to treat a woman. They're not like men. They need certain things. Have certain sensitivities.

And if you point it out to them, they grow infuriated. You have to be careful around them, and sometimes you get it right and sometimes you get it wrong."

"Bullshit. I've defended enough abusers to know they always blame their victims because the alternative is for them to take responsibility for their own behavior."

"Yeah? What do you know about it? You never been married."

"I would hear you guys fighting sometimes."

He shrugged as he took a spoonful of pudding. "Everybody fights. So when am I getting out of here?"

No way in hell was I telling him I had just filed a motion to have him declared incompetent.

"A psychologist has to interview you first."

"Interview me for what?"

"Just to make sure you're making this decision with a clear head."

He stopped eating his pudding. "It's my damn body to do with as I please."

"No one's saying it's not your body. They're saying you might not be in the best position to evaluate your interests."

He tossed the pudding on the floor and started to get off the bed.

"You can't leave."

"The hell I can't."

"You still got IVs in you."

He ripped them out and started shuffling toward the door. I rose and stood in front of him. "You can't leave."

"Get out of my way. I'm only going to say it once."

"Adam, please, let me just talk to you."

"If you don't—"

"Just five minutes! Man, you'd think I'm talking to a four-year-old."

He folded his arms. "I'm listening."

"They need to make sure you understand what you're doing. Once the psychologist clears you, you can leave whenever you want. Just get the interview done and quit fighting me on it."

"Get out of my way."

I scoffed and stepped to the side. "Fine, you wanna go, go. But guess what? Without that interview and clearance from a psychologist, they're going to tackle you in the parking lot, drag you back in here, and tie you to that bed. So by all means, go."

He stood awhile, staring at me. Finally he shook his head and returned to the bed. I went looking for the friendly nurse to reattach his IVs.

48

The next day, a Sunday, nothing much would happen in River Falls but church. In fact, the entire town would empty and fill the pews at the local Mormon church. There was one Protestant church and one Catholic church in town, too, but only a sliver of the town went to those.

Gates called and asked if I wanted to go to church with her.

"I'll pass, but say hi to the big guy for me."

I essentially had the town to myself. My father never went to church. Only my mother had made me go.

I went to the hospital for a couple of hours. Adam and I sat in silence while he watched television, and then he told me he was tired, which was my cue to leave.

I got a text from Jia that Pritcher had filed three motions: a motion to suppress Anderson's confession, a motion to change venue to another city, and a motion to remove me as the attorney for conflict of interest. Just three. I was surprised: I could think of at least twenty motions I would file in this case.

Jia texted, **And don't worry about the responses to the motions, I'm drafting them now.**

Attached was one more request: to waive the preliminary hearing and hold a hearing on the motions instead. Jia called me after the text.

"Did you see?" she said.

"I did."

"Why's he waiving the prelim?"

"No idea."

The Art of Jury Trial as War, chapter 21: "Never, under any circumstance, waive a preliminary hearing." The defense didn't have to say a word, but the prosecution had to present sufficient evidence to convince the judge that they had enough to go forward to trial. Which meant it was like playing poker, where you could see the other player's hand but didn't have to show them yours.

"Something's not right. See if you can poke around and find out why he's waiving it."

"I'll see what I can do."

———

I'd been given a key to the office building but realized I didn't have the alarm codes. I was shocked to find there wasn't an alarm. Had I landed in *Leave It to Beaver*? People's entire criminal files were in this building. If they wanted to get rid of their cases, all they'd need to do was break in here and burn the place down, or at least steal their files.

When I opened the doors, I found heavy bars on the other side and on the windows. The same key opened the bars and I slid them open. Well, at least there was that.

The building was dark and smelled of dust and floor polish. I made my way down to the county attorney's offices. Here, it smelled like Gates's perfume. I checked her office to make sure she wasn't there, and the framed photos on her desk caught my eye. I sat in her chair. I had been curious to see more of what Gates's life had been like while I was gone.

The photos were of her parents, several friends, a couple of aunts and uncles . . . and one of two teenagers.

It was me and her at a water park in Salt Lake City that her father had driven us to. A photographer at the park was charging a buck to take photos, and we had one taken, my arm around her. We were fifteen. I thought we had tossed the photo that day because Gates said she didn't like how her hair looked. I'd thought it looked perfect and still did.

I went to the conference room, where a monitor and DVD player were set up, and took the Winchester file out of the drawer. I popped in the DVD of Anderson's confession.

"Look, we're just here to help you," Detective Howard's voice said. He sat across from Anderson in a small room, white walls with blue carpet. I'd already watched this video once and hadn't seen anything particularly unusual about it, but I turned it up and sat down anyway.

"We just want what's best for you, Anderson. I know your daddy, and I know how heartbroken he's gonna be with all this."

I watched Anderson. His eyes would close and shoot open in irregular rhythm: he was clearly high.

"I ain't done nothin'," he said.

"Don't stick to that, man. I'm telling you, don't stick to it, Anderson. This is going to go bad for you. And I really don't want it to. Now I know you went home with Patty, I know you had sex with her, but I don't know if you killed her. Tell us what happened after the sex."

"I ain't killed her."

"Did you have sex with her?"

"I don't think so."

The tape went on like this for half an hour: the detective suggesting things and Anderson seeming confused. When I'd first seen it, I hadn't thought it hurt us, but I hadn't seen it as particularly helpful either. Looking at it from the angle of Anderson being a drunken idiot and Steven actually abducting and killing Patty put it in a different light. I always watched these videos not with an eye toward the truth—the truth didn't matter—but for what a jury would see. That's the only thing that was of any importance. And what a jury would see was a high, confused kid being led along by an aggressive detective. Didn't matter, though, because the confession would never be allowed at trial.

"Haven't you watched this yet?"

I turned and saw Gates leaning against the door.

"Thought you were at church?"

"Ducked out early to see what you were up to. You weren't home or at the hospital, so I figured this is probably where you were."

"Russell filed a motion to suppress the confession and the video, so I wanted to take a look at it again."

"Is he going to win?"

"Oh, for sure. Look at this."

I fast-forwarded the video toward the end, to where Anderson said, "I wanna go home."

Detective Howard, bless him, said, "Not yet."

"It became a custodial interrogation right then, and he wasn't under arrest. They didn't Mirandize him, nothing. The confession will for sure be tossed."

"We got enough without it, don't we?"

"Well, Lyle's testimony puts Anderson there, we maybe got Patty's blood at his townhome, and if I cut a deal with Steven to testify against him . . . yeah, we could get a conviction."

"You don't sound convinced."

I clicked my tongue against my teeth. "I'm worried I might be prosecuting the wrong guy. Never had this problem as a defense attorney. My guys were always guilty."

She chuckled. "The ethics aren't quite as malleable over on this side, are they?"

I sighed. "No, they are not. The way I see it, I can cut a deal and get a conviction against Anderson, or I can try them both with what I have and rely on Lyle saying there were two of them the night he heard the screaming, even though he can't identify Steven as the other person there. It might be enough, but it might not. If I were Russell, I'd put Anderson up there to say it was all Steven. And then I'd put his ex on to say Steven's a creep-o and Anderson isn't capable of something like this. Then I'd hammer home that Patty was an escort at seventeen and who the hell really knows what scumbag killed her. Not a slam dunk for either one of us. So do I go for the single certain conviction, or do I try for both?"

She shrugged. "Your case. You decide."

"This affects you, too, you know."

"I know. But if I lose the election, I lose. Outa my hands."

I turned back to the video and watched Anderson. His eyes would roll back in his head and then he'd snap to attention for a few moments before nearly dozing off again.

"Can you get access to everywhere at the police station?"

49

We strolled into the station, chatting about Gates's time training the officers here when she first became county attorney. Only one cop seemed to be in the entire place. Gates began speaking to the officer on duty while I roamed around the offices. Howard's office interested me: it was nothing but posters of athletes and a girl in a bikini standing next to a Ferrari. The type of things a thirteen-year-old boy might have.

Gates came up behind me, put her hand on my shoulder, and said, "Back here."

We passed the janitor's closet and encountered a large room filled with boxes of files. It was gray and dark and smelled like mold. Stairs led down to another room filled with boxes and a hanging light bulb.

"Wow, Gates, could you *not* find a wet crypt to store all these in?"

"Hey, we don't have the budget of a South Beach PD. We do what we can. You wouldn't believe how hard it's been to even get the county to agree to scan all these and store them electronically in case there's a fire. It still won't happen for another year."

At the back of the room, she skimmed the boxes alphabetically before pulling out a large manila file. She opened it up, revealing Anderson Ficco's photo on the inside flap. He looked to be about thirteen or fourteen. His eyes were even.

"What happened to his eye?"

"Got injured playing football last year. Roscoe Mallory said he ran into a steel pipe that was lying around for construction near the field."

"Ran into a pipe?"

She shrugged. "Anderson said it was sticking out from the bleachers, and he slammed right into it. Almost blinded him. Here it is."

She handed me some papers. It was the police reports from Anderson's juvenile allegation that was dismissed.

Apparently, when he was thirteen, a live-in maid at their home had accused him of raping her. She stated she was asleep upstairs when she woke up to Anderson standing next to her, fondling her breasts. She slapped him away and told him to leave, but instead he climbed on top of her. She said it only lasted a minute or two before he quietly left the room. She reported it to his father, who said that it didn't happen, so she went to the police. When they interviewed Anderson, he said it never happened and that he was out back playing football with some neighbor kid. There was no interview with the neighbor. Miraculously, even without interviewing the sole alibi witness, the case was dismissed after it was filed.

I tried to find some follow-up interviews with the maid, Candace Blight, and couldn't see any. The detective on the case was a woman named Henrietta Trevor.

"Where's Detective Trevor now?"

"Retired. She lives in town still."

I flipped through the rest of the report. A SAFE kit had been done. No vaginal tearing—not unusual if the rape was committed by a skinny thirteen-year-old boy—no bruising, no semen . . .

"No semen?"

Gates glanced at the report. "Huh. Says the kit was done six hours after the rape. Not entirely impossible."

"No, not impossible for an adult that has some control over himself. But a thirteen-year-old kid? I don't think he'd have that kind of self-control. And no way he thought to wear a condom being that young." I closed the file. "Someone screwed that SAFE kit up on purpose. That's why there's no interview with this alleged boy Anderson was playing with at the time. Why bother if you know the case is going to be dismissed? We need to find out if Candace is still in town. How bugged do you think Howard would be if I called him on his day off?"

50

I met Detective Howard at Benson's and bought him a coffee and a
Danish to make up for calling him in on his day off. His bald head had
extra glisten today, and the sunlight seemed to shine off it like polished
steel. He wore a nice shirt and tie and carefully folded his suit coat and
set it down in the booth next to him. I knew it was his best suit then
and that he saved it only for church.

"You LDS?" I said.

He shook his head. "Catholic."

"Haven't met many of those in this town." I glanced at the burn
scars on his neck and he noticed.

"Iraq," he said. "IED went off on our Jeep. Piece of shrapnel cut
through my leg and I got this little present right here on my neck."

"Looks manly. I wouldn't sweat it."

He bit into his Danish. "Let's forget the chitchat for a minute and
just get to why you asked me here."

I took Anderson's juvenile file out of my bag and placed it in front
of him. He opened it and flipped through it.

"Guess I don't need to ask how you got an expunged file from our
archives without clearing it with the assigned detective," he said.

"No, you don't. And that's why I'm here. First, I need to talk to
the assigned detective. Gates said she lives in town, so that won't be
difficult for you. I need to know every detail that she left out of the

case notes. The most important is Anderson's alibi. Detective Trevor didn't interview the boy. Why? That's a massive, massive omission that only makes sense if you already know the case is going to be dismissed. Someone made it happen."

He nodded and flipped through the remaining pages of the file before closing it. "I can tell you why now if you like: because the maid probably had sex with the little twerp willingly, tried to get some money outa Anderson's daddy, and then stopped cooperating when he wouldn't pay up. Gold diggers come up with schemes like that all the time."

"Okay, well, how about we do our jobs and just make sure. Also, the alleged victim just disappeared after. I want to talk to her."

He slid the file over to me. "Great. Do it yourself."

I sighed. Did everything have to be hard?

"You don't like me, I get that, but this isn't about me. It's about that young girl rotting in a grave when she had her entire life ahead of her. Whatever people fixed this case for Anderson might be doing the same for Patty's case."

He leaned back in his seat. "Do you remember a cop on a case you had in Miami named Cynthia Phelps?"

I took a sip of coffee. "No. Why?"

"Well, she remembers you. You got her on the stand. It was her second year as a cop, pretty much a rook. You had her so shaken up she ran to the bathroom and puked and was cryin' for days after."

"I've made a lot of cops cry. Sorry, not ringing a bell."

"You found a conviction she had when she was sixteen, prostitution. See, she had an abusive boyfriend, drug addict that got her hooked on pain pills. He pimped her out one time when she was nearly unconscious, and when the cops arrested the john, they cited her. She'd run away from home, her parents weren't there, so she just pled to it. Didn't realize the cops had made a mistake in charging her."

"Mark, I'm not sure what you're getting at, but I want to talk about this case, not ancient history."

"Oh, you'll like this part. See, she cleaned up her life. Started going back to church, married a good man, had two kids, and joined the police force. But see when she joined, she thought juvenile convictions didn't count and didn't realize you still have to put them down on your application. So you found this conviction, somehow, and I can only guess that you bribed somebody, but you found it, and you brought it out in court. She got fired from the force, lost her pension, and couldn't find another job as a police officer. It broke her somethin' good."

"Look, if she was your friend, I'm sorry, but that's just the job. I did what I did to save my client. And don't lie on an application. What can I tell ya?"

"Well, she wasn't my friend." He leaned forward on his elbows. "Phelps was her married name. Her real name was Howard. Cynthia Melinda Howard."

I stayed quiet a second. "Sister?"

"Half sister. My family's from Tallahassee. Born and raised." He shook his head, staring down at the table. "She had a great career ahead of her. Our dad was a cop and our granddad was a cop. She had the brains for a good career. Much smarter than me." He took another bite of Danish and then pushed the plate away. "I liked Patty. I know her daddy, and I feel sorry as hell for what happened. But if my not helpin' hurts you even a little, you better believe I'm gonna do it." He tossed his napkin over his plate. "You can burn in hell for all I care, Counselor."

I watched him leave and stared down at Anderson's file. Well, I guess if you want something done right . . .

I called Will.

"Yo," he answered.

"I'm flying somebody out, like, today. On the next flight out from Miami I can find. I need you to book the flight and pick her up from the airport."

"Sweet. Girlfriend?"

"No, not exactly."

51

Nina Connor was the best investigator money could buy. A former FBI agent, and a freaking Israeli commando before that, she was tougher than any man I had ever met, and smart as all get-out. When I asked her why she never went into law, she said, "You don't get to punch anybody out as a lawyer."

"So what do you think?" I said to her over the phone after explaining everything.

"I'll be out as soon as I can."

I hung up and stared out the windows for a while before leaving the diner to check on Adam.

———

Adam was lying on his hospital bed staring out the window when I came in. Some food was on the side table. I put it on the tray and brought it nearer to him, and he said, "I'm not hungry," without looking at me.

"When'd you eat last?"

"I'm fine."

I noticed a bloody rag tucked between his leg and the sheets that he clearly was using to cough into. "The psychologist come yet?"

"He's coming this afternoon. I still think this is bullshit."

"Bullshit or no, you're not getting outa here without the evaluation, so you might as well do it happily."

He sighed. "I'm just tired, Tatum. Just tired. I want to go home."

"I know," I said softly.

The nurse came in just then and checked the IVs. "Hey," I said, "how about this, I'll go get us some burgers."

"I wouldn't recommend it," the nurse said. "He's got some nausea right now, and I don't think a greasy hamburger is gonna help none."

I nodded but said, "I'll be back soon."

Finding a burger place open on a Sunday in small-town Utah was like trying to find a Slurpee machine in the Sahara desert. I had to drive to Nevada to find a place that was open, and then I got two burgers with fries and headed back to the hospital. When I got there, Adam was already asleep, hair flopped down over his forehead. Softly, I brushed it away. It still amazed me how much he looked like me.

"Night, Pops," I said.

I slept uneasily and woke up at around eight in the morning. I checked my phone. There was a message from Will that he had tried to pick up Nina from the airport, but she had insisted on renting her own car.

I grabbed a round of coffees and took them into the office, having forgotten almost everyone here was Mormon and wouldn't drink it. I left them on the conference room table as I reviewed Pritcher's motions. The motion hearing was in an hour.

Jia was the first one in. She said, "Hey," and then went to work like a machine. Will came in a little later. He grinned and said, "I think I'm in love."

"Great," I said, not looking up from the files.

"It's Nina."

I looked up. "She'd eat you alive."

"I know. Isn't love grand?"

I closed the file and said, "I'll be in the courtroom."

———

Judge Allred's court hadn't changed. I'd come here sometimes as a kid and watch the proceedings. There wasn't exactly much to do in small towns, and watching someone you knew in handcuffs get lectured by a judge sufficed to pass the time.

The courtroom had several large windows, and the defense and prosecution tables looked almost new. I walked around and sat in one of the chairs of the jury box, which had wooden seats with blue cushions, seeing what the jury would see.

Pritcher came in a second later with his two associates. He grinned at me as he put his briefcase down on the defense table and said, "Gotta admit, the courtroom's nicer than I thought it would be."

"It's got its charms."

"Would you like to know my favorite courtroom? It was a small courtroom in Florence. I was defending a man accused of killing young women and posing their bodies in various ways. You don't even want to know the hassle of an American attorney getting special permission to try a case over there, but I did."

"Didn't know you spoke Italian."

"I speak six languages, actually. Haven't you done your homework on me? I'm disappointed, Tatum."

I rose and walked to the prosecution table as a bailiff came out of a door behind the judge's bench. "Sorry, Russell, you're just not that interesting."

Another bailiff came out a second later, pushing Anderson in front of him, and two bailiffs followed with Steven. The boys were seated at the defense table. The attorney representing Steven joined them and began whispering to him. Anderson and Pritcher didn't talk.

"All rise, Fifth District Court is now in session. The Honorable Beatrice Allred presiding."

Judge Allred came in and sat down and said, "Please be seated."

Though she had a computer, she still pulled out a couple of files, a notepad, and a pen before putting on her glasses and saying, "We're here for the preliminary hearings of *State versus Ficco* and *State versus Brown*, which I have signed an order striking and am setting this today for oral arguments on motions I received last week. I have received Mr. Ficco's motions to suppress and the State's responses, and I have received Mr. Brown's motions and the State's responses. After Mr. Ficco's motions today, we may address Mr. Brown's motions. Are we ready to proceed?"

Pritcher stepped around the defense table. "We are, Judge. Our motion on suppression of the admissions sets out the issues very clearly. The police, when they discovered the body of Patty Winchester, had no witnesses and no real evidence to indicate my client had anything to do with this crime. They had heard that he was seen with her at a bar in Las Vegas and that was it. Under *Thompson versus Keohane* and laid out plainly in our motion, the court must look at whether the interrogation was voluntary, where it took place, and the mental state of the suspect at the time of the interrogation. In this instance, as is shown on the video we submitted as evidence, the detective makes it clear that my client is not free to leave when he asks if he can go. The interrogation took place at a police station after my client was put in a police car and driven there. As I'm sure Your Honor saw on the video, my client was highly inebriated at the time of this interrogation, calling into question whether he had the wherewithal to even agree to a voluntary interview as the State is proposing."

I jumped in and said, "While I like fantasy as much as the next guy, Your Honor, in *Yarborough versus Alvarado*, the Court clearly states that the individual mental state, age, or personal attributes of the defendant are not factors for a trial court to consider in finding whether an interview was custodial. In fact, it lays out that the test is whether or not a reasonable person would feel free to leave. If you look at the video again, the defendant says he'd like to leave and the detective says, 'Not yet.' He doesn't say no, he doesn't physically restrain him, and at no point was the defendant told he was under arrest or had hand-cuffs placed on him. *Not yet* can be understood by its plain meaning in everyday language as an admission that he is free to leave but the detective would like him to stay longer to answer a few more questions voluntarily."

"That's an adorable interpretation of the facts, Your Honor, but *JDB versus North Carolina* again visited the issue and found that a child's age is a factor in determining custodial interrogation. Because the child is considered vulnerable to police persuasion. Here you have a similar circumstance in that my client was so inebriated he could barely keep his eyes open and you have a detective telling him he's not free to leave yet. I think the plain meaning of *not yet* is a de facto *no*. I don't think Miranda could've been more clearly violated had I tried to make a fic-tional scenario, and the fact that Mr. Graham is even arguing this shows how desperate the State is in twisting the facts to get an innocent—"

"Twisting the facts? I have said nothing that isn't true, and the detective in this case acted in accordance with—"

The judge held up her hand. "I've heard enough. Nice try, Mr. Graham, but it was a custodial interrogation the moment he told him he wasn't free to leave. The video and confession are out. As to the change of venue request, I am denying that, Mr. Pritcher."

"Your Honor, given my client's . . . *reputation* in the community, we feel it would be best were we to take this case to a more anonymous venue. I would ask the court to reconsider."

"So reconsidered and still denied. As far as removing Mr. Graham from the case, the only argument of the many you cited that I found somewhat persuasive is that Mr. Graham also has a certain reputation in the community, and garnering a conviction may seem more important than seeking justice." She looked at me. "Mr. Graham, a prosecutor is a minister of justice and should at all times keep justice in mind. If this case is somehow a publicity stunt for you to show the world, I don't know, that you can jump to the other side and still win, I promise, the sanctions I impose will not be pleasant. Having said that, if you want to leave this case, now is the time to tell me. No harm, no foul."

"No, Your Honor, I'm in all the way."

"Very well. Then I'm denying the motion to recuse Mr. Graham from the case." She looked to Steven's attorney. "Mrs. Boyce, I am granting the same orders for your motions. Though the detective in that instance did not state something as clearly as your client not being free to leave yet, the totality of the circumstances informed this court that a reasonable person in Mr. Brown's place would've felt they were in custody. Your motion for venue change and removal of Mr. Graham are also denied. Thank you, everyone, for your time."

I tapped the desk with my knuckles and turned to see Jia sitting behind me.

"You expected as much," she said.

"Yeah, but still sucks to lose at anything. Not exactly my thing, if you know what I mean."

She looked over as Pritcher whispered something to Anderson, and then he said, "Your Honor, one more thing, we would like my client to be arraigned today and to set the quickest jury trial date possible."

Steven's attorney stood up and said, "We would concur in that request, Your Honor."

After a preliminary hearing, or stipulation by the defense that they would waive it, the court had to give the client another arraignment, informing them of their rights and that the case was bound over now for trial. Usually the arraignment happened at a later date to allow the parties to exchange evidence and debate any motions that might be filed.

"Judge," I said, "while I appreciate Mr. Pritcher's zeal, the State is going to need time to prepare."

"Your Honor, this case has garnered national media attention. My client's reputation continues to deteriorate the longer the case goes on. Mr. Graham has had ample time to prepare this case. We waived our preliminary hearing and expect to have this case expedited. I have not addressed bail with this court in the hopes that we can have a quick trial date."

Judge Allred said, "Mr. Graham, you may be new to this case, but it has been lingering in my courtroom since before you. The defense is correct in that they have waived their preliminary hearing, and I see no reason you can't be prepared as quickly as they can, considering the State has actually had the evidence in this case quite a bit longer. Also, Mr. Graham, for future reference, I expect the prosecution on a case to be ready for trial the day they file charges. If you're not ready for trial, that means you're not ready to file charges against a citizen of this county." She took her glasses off. "I'm setting a jury date for three weeks from today. I assume all parties will be ready by then?"

Pritcher grinned. "Perfect, Your Honor."

Steven's attorney said, "That works."

"We'll make do," I said.

I watched as Anderson and Steven were taken back and Pritcher and the rest of the attorneys filed out of the courtroom. Jia had her arm up on the backrest in the audience pews, and when we were alone, she said, "He's got something."

"Damn right he does. Pretty good defense tactic is to drag a murder case out as long as you can and hope witnesses disappear or evidence gets lost. If he wants a trial fast, he has something that may not last very long that he needs to get on the record quickly. Our job, young lady, is to find out what it is."

52

For the next few days, I kept my head low. I wasn't in the office much. I found it distracting, and it didn't help my concentration to be in a conference room where I could hear the bureaucrats on the floor above me stomping around.

I sat in the corner at a coffee shop. It was small, with paintings for sale on the walls and only about ten things on the menu, but everyone here was young, and there was something about youthful energy that could pep up the middle-aged. Like a vampire sucking the blood of the young, I guess. Man, I was being morbid today.

I read through the Winchester file again and again. What the hell could Pritcher have that he would want to rush a trial? The guy had once dragged an assault case out six years with motion after motion, until the victim got so sick of testifying at various hearings, he forced the prosecution to drop the case entirely. If he wanted a quick trial, it meant he had something that was going to fry me.

A second later, a tall brunette in sweats walked in. She sat across from me and took a sip of my coffee.

"Sweats, Nina? The last time I saw you, you were in a Donna Karan nightgown."

"You've never seen me work. I don't wear anything that would make me stand out."

She took out a file from a gym bag and handed it to me.

I opened it up. "Summary?"

"Anderson's lying. I found his neighbors from 2013. One of them had a young daughter, but she was several years younger than him. No boys near him. The nearest boy his age was almost a quarter of a mile up the road."

"And the vic?"

"I believed her. I asked what she did during the rape, if she fought him. She began to cry and said she turned her head and stared at a spot on the wall until it was over. No emotion, didn't make a sound. That's a fairly typical response to shock and something that a lot of victims report. It's called disassociation. I can read people as well as you, and that woman was raped. The nurse that performed the SAFE kit passed away two years ago, so we won't know why semen wasn't found, unfortunately."

I flicked the file with my middle finger. "Clever bastard."

"What?"

"Anderson and Russell put on a show for me at the jail. Anderson was bossing around Russell, who pretended to be upset that his client was even talking to me. I knew he wouldn't take a client barking orders at him. He's too narcissistic for that. He once stabbed a client in the hand with a pen for getting too lippy."

"Really? How's that guy still practicing?"

"Connections and money go a long way. What about the detective that worked it, Henrietta Trevor?"

"Refused to speak to me about it. Unusual for a detective to not want to talk about an old case that got dismissed, isn't it? You'd figure they'd be bothered it was dismissed. Her eyes actually went wide and I saw her breathing speed up when I told her what I was at her house for. She's hiding something."

"Yeah, someone, I'm guessing Daddy Ficco, paid off the detective, the nurse, and probably the prosecutor, too, to make the case go away. I wouldn't want to talk about it either."

"Oh, I also got the expedited tire-track analysis you wanted. Tire tracks around the scene belong to a large truck of the same type Anderson Ficco owns. Can't confirm make or model."

"That'd be great, except that everybody and their mother in this town drives a large truck."

"It's something, at least."

I flipped through her reports while she took another sip of my coffee and leaned back in the seat. "I like this town. It's quaint."

"Try growing up here. That quaintness doesn't last long."

"I think you forget I grew up in Jerusalem. I would've loved a small town where nothing ever happens."

"Yeah, it had its charms, I guess."

"Why'd you leave? Typical story of a small-town genius who needs to experience everything?"

"I'm flattered you recognize I'm a genius, but no, I just felt suffocated. This town, any small town, I guess, can feel like a noose around your neck, and the older you get, the tighter that noose gets." I glanced over at the barista, who was humming along to a country song playing over the speakers. "I need one more thing. Russell's got something on this case. He asked for the quickest trial date possible and only filed three motions, even though I'm sure he could think up twenty more. I gotta find out what he has."

She shook her head. "Sorry, I can't. I have to be in Madrid."

"I'll pay double your fee."

"You know I don't work that way. A promise is a promise. I get a reputation for dropping clients and pretty soon I won't have clients."

She rose and kissed me on the cheek.

"What am I supposed to do without you?" I said.

She grinned and said, "You'll figure something out. You always do." As she was about to leave, she said, "Oh, and the eye injury, that's not from a pipe."

"What'dya mean?"

"I pulled the medical reports like you asked. Doctor said it was repeated blunt force trauma."

"Repeated? Like fists?"

"Yup. I think someone didn't like him very much."

53

It was afternoon when I got the call that they were discharging my father from the hospital. I rushed down there and found Dr. Langley in another patient's room.

"What the hell are you talking about?" I said.

"Mr. Graham, you can't be in here."

"The hell I can't. He's going to die without treatment."

The doctor told the patient he would be right back and said, "Outside, please."

We went out into the hallway, and I folded my arms as he took his glasses off and tucked them into the breast pocket of his white coat. "I'm sorry, Mr. Graham. I spoke to the psychologist, and he stated that your father is fully competent and in charge of his faculties. I have no choice but to follow the patient's wishes."

"I'll find another psychologist."

"If you wish, but I can't hold him here in the meantime. He wants to be released, and so we're required to release him. The nurse will have the discharge paperwork for you."

He went back into the other patient's room, leaving me in the hallway. I began to pace. How was I going to convince Adam to stay here?

When I went into his room, he was already dressed and sitting on the bed, a cap pulled down over his head.

"'Bout damn time. I thought I was going to have to walk home."

I stuck my hands in my pockets and said quietly, "You need to stay here."

"I really don't. That's the great thing about America, I can do what I want."

"Adam—"

"Don't Adam me. You don't get to tell me what to do. I'm your father. Now ya gonna drive me home or not?"

———

When I got to the office the next morning, Will and Jia were at a whiteboard brainstorming ideas about what Pritcher might have that made him want an expedited trial. Their list ran the gamut from surprise witness to dirt on the judge.

"I like the blackmail," I said, walking in, "but I've known Judge Allred since I was a kid, and she'd rather die than take a bribe, I think."

I took off my suit coat and leaned against Jia's desk as I stared at the board. Will said, "So the best one we have so far is that he's got, or knows how to get, some info on the potential jury. The jury gets called two weeks before a trial date in Allred's court."

I nodded. "And if he's got a clerk on the payroll willing to tell him who's in the pool, he can either research them or, more his style, outright bribe them. Okay, not bad. What else?"

Jia said, "Could be the escorting, but we don't think that's damaging enough to skip the prelim for. Plus, there's no need to rush with that. The only other plausible thing is that his investigators have found some piece of evidence we haven't."

"That reminds me, file a reverse discovery request. If he does have something like that, he'll be required to hand it over. I doubt it'll help since he's too smart for that. What he'll do is ask to have it introduced, and when I throw a tantrum, he'll say that he sent it the night before, which is when it mysteriously appeared on his desk from some anonymous source."

"Will that work?" Jia asked.

"Why not? It's worked for me several times." I scanned the board again and said, "Well, whatever it is, we've got to hope what we have is better: I'm cutting a deal with Steven."

"Seriously?" Will said.

"My investigator found out that Anderson was lying about the rape when he was a juvenile. He killed Patty, and he and Russell put on a little show for me to get me to buy his alibi at the jail. So he's probably the brains behind the outfit. Will, draft up an agreement for Steven. He's getting attempted homicide, one to fifteen, in exchange for his testimony at trial against Anderson. Then set an appointment and run down to the jail and have him and his attorney sign it. They have notaries at the jail."

"On it."

"Jia, we need to keep digging as much as we can and find out what Russell's going to spring on us. Talk to everyone, and I mean everyone, that's interacted with him since he got into town. Maybe they saw something or overheard something."

I scanned the board again and said, "I haven't gotten my ass kicked yet, and I do not want to start here of all places and against a weasel like Russell. Don't let me down, kids." I went to leave and Will said, "Where you going?"

"Just someone I need to see."

54

The cemetery was crowded with flowers. It was small and built on a hill overlooking River Falls. When I got out, I could see past the town to the red-rock mountains to the south and the Nevada border beyond that. I always forgot how small the town was until I looked at it from up high.

I climbed up farther on the hill and then stopped, unsure which way to go. I wandered around until I recognized a tree. A few paces behind that was the grave I was looking for.

The headstone said, "Marilyn Rose Graham. Beloved mother and wife."

I sat down in front of the headstone and picked some grass. I played with it, twirling it and feeling the texture. A breeze started blowing.

"You know what I remember most?" I said out loud. "You used to tell me I could always come to you. That mothers had special bonds to their sons and could always give them the best advice when they needed it." I tossed the grass on the ground. "I could sure use some of that advice right now, Mom. Because I feel like I'm lost at sea."

I inhaled deeply and rose, staring down at the grave a long time. I kissed my hand and then lightly touched the headstone before leaving.

———

When I drove to Adam's house, he was sitting on his porch. He was looking worse and worse. Pale with eyes rimmed red, his nose pink, burst capillaries from the intense coughing fits. More than that, he looked tired. A man who just wanted to lie down and not get back up.

I sat next to him and said, "I remember Mom out here mowing the lawn before it became my chore when I was ten or whatever. Never understood why you let her do it instead of doing it yourself."

"I tried, but your mother said I didn't do it right. That the lines on the lawn had to go up and down and be straight and that I went side to side too much. She had to have things a certain way. It would drive her nuts when they weren't that way. I tried to mow them straight for years, but it was never straight enough."

I looked to him. "She had OCD?"

"We didn't have words like that back then. People were just people. We all have our quirks. There's no reason to give it a name."

I looked over the grass. "Adam, you have to go back to the hospital. You're going to die."

He nodded slowly, not taking his eyes off the lawn, seeing some distant memory there. "I know."

"You know? What is that supposed to mean? You mean you're going to accept it and lie back and cough yourself to death?"

"Hey, I am sick of this holier-than-thou attitude from you. I'm an adult, and adults get to make their own decisions. I'm healthy and I'm goin' to stay healthy until it's time for me to go. And I ain't goin' on some hospital bed with a twenty-year-old doctor tellin' me how sorry he is for me. This is my home. This is the home I brought my wife to after our wedding and the home my father brought my mother to after their wedding. I ain't leavin' it."

I shook my head and rose. "Well, that's just great. But I'll tell you one thing, I'm not going to sit here and watch you slowly die. So you can count me out."

"Good. Go back to your fancy mansion and easy women, Tatum. You never really belonged in this town anyway."

"I got news for ya, Adam. Neither did you. Maybe if you had more balls, you would've done what I did and left instead of slowly dying here as a ranch hand."

His eyes widened and he turned away. I knew it was the sorest spot in his life, that spot that everyone feared and wouldn't look at too closely: the spot that revealed a life that had been wasted, and the realization that it was too late to do anything about it.

"Adam," I said, "I'm sorry. I didn't mean—"

"I'd like to be alone."

"Look, I get angry and I say—"

"I'd like to be alone, Tatum. Please."

I nodded. "Yeah."

55

The time before trial was a flurry of activity for me. Back in Miami, everyone knew to stay out of my way. When I got into the office in the mornings, there was a bagel and coffee sitting on my desk, and for lunch one of the staff would bring me a sandwich and soup, lay it on the desk without a word, and leave. Dinner was take-out Chinese and then some bourbon when the day was done at two or three in the morning while I sat in my office staring at the ocean. We had a mock courtroom, and the weeks before trial were spent there, running through arguments over and over until I knew every word I was going to say to that jury.

I didn't have any of that here. So I spent the days reviewing case notes, checking in with witnesses, practicing my arguments in front of a mirror, and helping Jia and Will realize that a trial was won or lost in preparation and how you framed the case to the jury in the opening arguments would determine which way the case would go when they read that verdict.

During the week before the trial, Gates and I went out a few times. Occasionally we had home-cooked meals at her house and a couple of times drove to Vegas for fancy sushi. My favorite thing was her laugh: I could always make her laugh, from the time we were kids. When I saw her at that restaurant, she stuck out like a diamond among coals. It wasn't just her physical beauty. Gates had whatever that beauty is on the inside that radiates out of some women. Men didn't have it. Whatever it was, I could sit in awe of it all day. Sometimes at night back in my condo, I wondered how the hell I had left her behind.

56

Something had been bothering me the past three weeks since my meeting with Nina, and I couldn't shake it: Anderson and Roscoe Mallory were lying about how Anderson's eye got hurt. The fact that the doctor told Nina that Anderson had likely taken a beating with fists, rather than running into a pipe, meant I was onto something, but I couldn't see what.

I parked at the high school and went in. Roscoe was out on the football field coaching about thirty young men. He had his arms folded and a clipboard hung from his fingers. One of the boys missed a pass, and Roscoe said, "Damn it, keep your eyes on the ball." He tossed the clipboard behind him near a gym bag and shook his head as he talked to one of the other coaches.

"Tatum," he said when he saw me. "What're you doing here?"

He held out his hand and we shook. "Oh, you know, nothing I like more than visiting the one place that holds my most painful childhood memories."

He chuckled. "You were picked on a bit, weren't you?"

"A bit? I showed up to freshman homecoming with a girl I found out only brought me there on a dare, and her boyfriend kicked my ass in the parking lot in front of the entire school. So yeah, there were some issues."

"Well, it's just jealousy. I was jealous as hell of your brains. I wasn't always nice to you, and I'm sorry about that."

"Water under the bridge, Roscoe." I looked out over the field. "Good team you got here."

"We got a shot at state. That boy there, Lopez, he's the best running back I've ever seen. He's got a sub-five forty dash."

"You're kidding."

He shook his head. "That kid's goin' pro." He looked at me. "What really brings you by?"

"Can we talk in private?"

"Sure thing."

He told the other coach to watch things, and we walked off the field and onto the bleachers. We sat at the fifty-yard line, and I looked out over the field. I'd never been to a single football game when I'd gone here, so this particular place held no memories for me.

"What kind of kid was Anderson when he went here?"

He looked out over the field. "Kind of a pain in the rear, to be honest. One of those kids you just want to get through the semester with and get him out of your class. Wasn't no better out here on the field. Always harassing the cheerleaders. Groping them and things. I had to bench him several times for pulling things like that."

"Any violence?"

"One time he got into a fight with one of our other players. Young black kid named David."

I nodded. "I can imagine why. Anything else?"

"No. He was a talker but didn't have too much bite. He weighed less than anyone on the team."

"What about you?"

"What about me?"

"You ever get into it with him?"

He chuckled. "Not to be vulgar, but if he walked between my legs people would think he was my penis."

I stared at him, and he grew embarrassed and looked away. "I just mean he's tiny. If I hit him, he would break."

"That isn't a no, Roscoe."

"No," he said sternly. "No, I never got into it with him."

"I read the statement you gave to the school about the injury. You said there was a pipe near the bleachers, and while he was doing laps, he slipped and hit the end of the pipe. But the doctor we spoke with suggested his eye injury was from repeated blunt force trauma. He thinks the most likely weapon was someone's fists. Now, normally I would just talk to other players on the team about what happened, but that's the funny thing: we did, and there weren't any other players around to witness what happened. Just you and him after school on the field."

He sighed. "Look, he groped one of the girls. I had him stay after and run laps as punishment."

"That's not in your statement."

He shook his head. "No, no, it wouldn't be. I . . . um . . . I didn't tell anyone."

"Why not?"

"He's a little punk, but he's the best kicker we've ever had, and we had a big game that Saturday. If I'd have gone to the principal with this, he would've been suspended. So I had him run laps."

"You let a sexual predator off the hook so you could win a game? Nice."

"Hey, football is all we got around here. It's important to this town, and sacrifices have to be made."

I rolled my eyes. "Yeah, it's right up there with world peace." I glanced at the field and saw the quarterback get sacked. "Who was the girl?"

"You wouldn't know her. She graduated last year and went to the University of Denver."

"I'd like her name."

"I'd rather not give it out. I promised her I wouldn't bring it up. She was really embarrassed."

I stood up and faced him, blocking his view of the field. "Listen to me: I have never, not once, lost a trial. And I'm not about to start now. And the way I win is that I know everything, and I mean everything, that is going to happen in that courtroom before I step inside. No surprises. If I walk in there and there's a surprise, you do not want to see what I'm going to do to you."

He shook his head. "No surprises. He groped her, I kept him after, and he slipped and hit a pipe. I don't know anything about medicine, but that doctor's wrong. I saw him hit the pipe, and I drove him to the ER."

I nodded. "I'll believe you, for now. But if you're lying to me, not going to state is going to be the least of your problems."

I walked off the field, took out my cell phone, and dialed Will.

"Hey, what's up?"

"Roscoe Mallory. He's lying about what happened to Anderson's eye, and I don't know why. I want everything you can find about him, and I mean everything. If he bought a porno mag at the grocery store, I want to know about it."

"I've known the coach since I was in high school. Everybody in town loves that guy. You really think he did something shady?"

"He just happens to mention to me right now that Anderson groped a girl but refused to give me her name. So either it never happened, or it's someone he doesn't want to tell me about."

"Someone like Patty."

"Right. Maybe Anderson groped Patty, then got a beating after, and Roscoe might be the one that administered that little can of whoop-ass. Beating a teenager up for groping a classmate—that's not a high school teacher reaction. That's the reaction of a lover. Which means—"

"Which means he might be on the list of Patty's clientele and maybe the obsessed one that was stalking her."

"Exactamundo, kiddo. So I need to know if he was seeing Patty and how often. And last I checked, high school teachers weren't millionaires, so let's dig into his finances and find out how he was swinging two grand for a date."

Will let out a long breath. "Man, Coach Mallory . . . that's crazy. You sure about this? I mean, you could be wrong."

"I don't know if I'm wrong or not, but it's too late to worry about that now. Let's find out what skeletons he's got lurking around."

"All right, I'll get on it. Oh, got the reports from the lab. No one ever found the hammer Anderson hit Patty with. The truck was cleaned with a blood cleaner. The forensics guys said it could have had blood, but the blood cleaner gets rid of all traces."

"Well, not the end of the world, but, man, Patty's blood on that hammer would've helped us."

He sighed again. "This is scary. Never been this invested in a case before."

I saw some young girls entering the high school, laughing and joking. Children. No older than Patty . . . or Bethany Bower. "Me neither."

57

That night I had dinner with Gates at her ranch. We ate hamburgers and watched a football game on television after. She sipped from her beer and set it down to check her phone.

"I stopped in to see your dad today," she said.

"Was he his usual pleasant self?"

"No. He couldn't talk. He'd lost his voice. I tried to get him to eat, but he just wanted his pills. Wouldn't eat anything."

I shook my head. "He's impossible to reason with."

"What're you going to do?"

I exhaled through my nose and stared blankly at the television. "Can we watch something else?"

She was quiet a second and said, "Tatum, what're you going to do?"

"I don't know, okay. I have no idea. I didn't sign up for this. I came out here to get away from my problems, not inherit everyone else's."

"Well, sorry we're such burdens, but he's your dad."

"That's not what I meant."

She rose and went into the kitchen and began washing plates off before putting them in the dishwasher. I rubbed my face and leaned my head against the couch cushions.

"How many hours a week you put into this ranch?" I said.

"About thirty."

"On top of everything with work?"

"Yeah."

"So what do you do for fun?"

She chuckled. "You'd think it was stupid."

"You know I wouldn't."

She stopped washing the dishes and dried her hands on a towel. "Come here."

I followed her outside and over to a barn. She slid open a massive door and inside was a truck and two cars. One of the cars, an old Nissan, was up on a mechanic's platform, and the engine was only halfway put together.

"You fix cars for fun?"

"Technically I build them. That's a Nissan body with a Mustang engine."

"You watch football and build cars, while taking care of a ranch. Why do I get the feeling I'm the girl in this relationship?"

"That's because you've bought into the lies about what a woman is. We're not trophies and we're not princesses."

"Hey, I ain't complaining. More power to you." I stepped closer and peered at the engine. "Where you even learn how to do this?"

"Self-taught. I think it'd ruin the fun to take a class." She adjusted something in the engine block and said, "I heard you visited Roscoe today."

"Yeah, and how'd you hear that already?"

"He called me."

"What'd he say?"

"He asked why you had come to see him."

"And what did you say?"

She pulled her hand out of the engine, and it was covered in grease. On a rack near the car was a bunch of towels, and she took one and tried to wipe the grease off. "I told him it was your case, and I was staying out of it. You know, he's a really loved figure in this town. One of the mayor's best friends."

"He's also lying to me."

"You sure about that?"

"I'm not sure of anything at this point, but yeah, I think he's not telling the full truth about Anderson. Something happened the day he was injured, and they're both lying about it, and I think it involved Patty."

She tossed the towel back over the rack. "Well, just be careful. If it gets out you're harassing him, whoever sits on that jury is not going to be happy with you."

58

That night, I couldn't sleep. One time I dozed off for a couple of hours and had a dream about Patty. She was lying in the ditch, but she was alive, trying to suck in breath through the dirt. A pool of mud was being created around her head from the blood pouring out of her. She stared at the moon as large clumps of soil were tossed on top of her.

I rose and went out for a walk. The night air felt like the heat from an oven: dry and searing. I went up to the gas station and grabbed a Diet Coke with ice. The attendant was asleep behind the counter, and I had to pretend to cough to get him to wake up.

"Sorry," he said, wiping the sleep out of his eyes.

"Late-night party?"

"Nah, just barely got this job. Ain't got used to workin' nights yet. Can't sleep durin' the damn day."

"You'll get used to it. You'd be amazed what you can get used to, believe me."

I left and wandered around the town. I came across a pasture that I remembered walking across to get to school with Gates. It had cows now and didn't back then. I watched the few by the fence until one of them came up to me and stuck her nose through the fence. I rubbed her ear until she turned away and went back to munching on grass.

———

I finally managed to get another hour or two of sleep, and when I woke I had dark circles under my eyes. I showered and changed into a black pinstripe suit with a red pocket square that I had bought in Las Vegas. When I looked at myself in the mirror, I saw the man who appeared in the newspapers, walking his client down a large hallway and out of a fancy courthouse, and I thought about something Gates had said when she saw me in one of the suits. She had lifted a hand and adjusted the lapel. "I think I liked you in cheap clothing."

"Why?"

"These suits . . . they're not really you. You're a country lawyer now, Tatum."

Going back into the bedroom, I tossed the suit onto the bed and changed into slacks and a blazer with a blue tie, and, sweet holy mother of crap, cowboy boots again.

The County Attorney's Office was empty when I got there. I sat in the conference room and began going through the file. Then I went out onto the cement steps of the building and read the file as the sun came up. I shut my eyes and rehearsed every word of my opening and closing in my head several times. I opened my eyes just as Pritcher and his crew were walking into the building. He told them to go ahead without him and stood in front of me.

"You sure you want to embarrass yourself like this?" he said when we were alone. "This will be all over the gossip sites and the *Miami Herald*."

"Helped in no small part by interviews with you about how I've lost my edge, no doubt."

"Oh, no doubt." He grinned. "That boy is going to walk."

I rose and folded my arms, staring into his pupils. "Show me."

59

Jia and Will were sitting behind me in the audience pews when the bailiffs brought out Anderson. Steven, who'd signed the plea deal earlier, would be brought in later to testify. Pritcher sat quietly at the defense table, unmoving. I didn't even see him blink.

"That was quite the show you put on at the jail a few weeks ago," I said, leaning over to him. "You had me sold."

"I have no idea what you're talking about," he said with a little grin.

"Even if it was a show, I would've expected you to crack his head open for talking to you like that."

He turned and faced forward again as the judge came out and the bailiff announced her.

Judge Allred took out her notepad and paper and a couple of pens and checked that they worked before she said, "Any pretrial motions to consider before we bring out the panel?"

"None from the State."

"None from the defense."

I glanced at Pritcher. *Really?* I would've had a laundry list of nitpicking evidentiary issues to bring up to the judge, hoping to get a few little things tossed at the last minute.

"Then let's bring out the panel."

All the attorneys stood. A group of forty people was brought in. I didn't recognize any of them, but a couple of them smiled at me out of courtesy. When they were seated, the judge said, "Ladies and gentle-men, we will now go through a process called *voir dire*. It is where we will be asking you questions about yourself in the hopes of making certain you can be impartial during this trial. I allow each attorney one hour to question you. Please be honest in your responses."

I got to go first. I'd read the questionnaires they were required to fill out beforehand, and they didn't have much useful information. Without my $600-an-hour jury consultants I had in Miami, jury selec-tion was limited in what I could get out of them.

I had no doubt Pritcher had flown out a jury consultant to poll the local population on the guilt or innocence of Anderson Ficco long ago and had come up with a list of traits people who thought he was innocent had.

I smiled at them and said, "Thank you so much for being here. I know a courtroom on a sunny day is not the ideal place to be, but, hey, at least we got warm water from a cooler over there for you."

Slight chuckle from the panel.

"This case involves details you're not going to want to hear. I've been an attorney now for almost two decades, and frankly, it was hard for me to learn about them. It involves someone in the community, this community . . . our community. But I have no doubt that you're going to be fair and impartial in this process, so I just have a few questions."

I asked if their parents were churchgoers, if they voted Republican or Democrat, if they'd ever been arrested, what their favorite shows and movies were, and what levels of income they had. I tried to picture where they had grown up and what the homes must've been like for them. Were they jaded by a rough upbringing? Or were they gener-ally optimistic about life and people? Did they value knowledge and academics, or did they view both with mistrust? I wanted to determine their personalities. To see who they would sympathize with more: a poor girl doing whatever she had to do to survive, or the son of a wealthy aristocrat who had everything handed to him.

When it was Pritcher's turn, he rose smoothly and gallantly strode to the jury like he was a knight here to slay the monstrous dragon. He stood in front of them and put his hands behind his back, a body posture indicating openness and honesty. His head tilted slightly to the right, as did most of the potential jurors', and he slouched just a little rather than puffing out his chest. It looked like he had worked extensively with body language experts, just like I had.

"I cannot thank you enough for being here today," he said. "There are parts of the world where men sit in an office and stamp files as guilty or not guilty, and that's as much of a trial that their citizens get. So all this," he said with a wave of his hand around the courtroom, "is a miracle. This entire system is set up to make sure innocent people, people like Anderson, are not sent to prison unjustly. So thank you for being part of that system with us today."

He then launched into his questions, which focused more on the types of books, movies, music, and art they enjoyed. He spent several minutes on where people liked to travel and their favorite cities in the world. Practically irrelevant, but it created a connection between him and the potential jurors. People loved talking about themselves, so Pritcher would stand in front of them, staring them in the eyes with full attention, and listen. Slowly, over the course of the hour, I could see that they began to trust him.

When he was done, we whittled the jury down to eight men and women and two alternates. Judge Allred said, "We will take a five-minute break to allow you to get a drink or use the facilities, and then we will begin with opening statements."

When the jury was led out, Pritcher turned to me and said, "Not too late. He'll take agg assault with probation."

"Probation for rape and murder? I'm not some newbie law school grad, Russell."

He shrugged. "Suit yourself. But when that jury says not guilty, remember I offered."

60

Jia, Will, and I convened in the hall. Gates had been in the courtroom and followed us out. She leaned against the wall with a grin on her face.

"What?"

"Nothing. It's just nice to see you in a courtroom again."

"Again?"

"I may have caught one of your trials on *Court TV.*" She checked her watch. "I have a meeting with the county council. I'll see you this afternoon. Day ends at one."

"What?"

"Judge Allred ends her days at one. I thought you knew."

"She finishes her trial days at one in the afternoon? This trial will take triple the time."

She shrugged. "It's how it works. Let me know if you need anything from me."

I watched her walk away, and Will said, "I think she likes you. She doesn't like very many people, you know."

"Appreciate the love advice, but let's stay focused on the game. Where the hell is Howard?"

"He should be here. There's a cafeteria on the top floor. The cops hang out there sometimes."

"Go get him. I want him sitting next to me before Russell finds him and starts messing with his head."

———

When Detective Howard joined me at the prosecution table, he was dressed in a shirt and tie and still had his badge clipped to his belt, but no gun.

"Where's your gun?"

"In the car. I don't bring it to court."

"Go get it and put the holster on the right side toward the jury."

"Why?"

"It gives you a sense of authority. Trust me on this."

He folded his arms. "Nah. I'm good."

I sighed and looked behind me. Hank Winchester sat in the back of the courtroom. He nodded once to me, and I nodded back. His face was empty of emotion, until he looked at Anderson. There was just a slight difference in his eyes and his brow furrowed.

On the prosecution table I had laid out several files and bags of evidence. Behind me, in the audience pews, sat Jia and Will.

One mistake prosecutors sometimes made was assigning too many prosecutors to a case, making the defense look like the underdog. O. J. Simpson had nine defense lawyers, an army. To get the jury on their side, the State should've had one prosecutor at their table, a newbie with no murder trials under his belt. *The Art of Jury Trial as War*, chapter 17: "Everyone thought the best attorneys were the old-timers with decades of experience, but the old-timers were weary, and juries could pick up on indifference." New, young lawyers, sweating and fumbling with papers because their hands were shaking, their voices cracking with anxiety, were the type of attorneys juries threw their arms around and protected. If LA County had put one of them on the case, OJ would've been enjoying his workouts in the yard at San Quentin.

The judge came in just then, and we rose and then sat. I watched the jury as they walked in: they tried not to look at either party. Pritcher seemed indifferent, staring off into space. His two associates sat quietly with their hands folded on the table. Anderson stared at the tabletop, tapping a pencil against his palm underneath it.

"We will now begin with opening statements. Mr. Graham."

"Thank you, Judge."

I rose and approached the jury. "The first time I went to the Supreme Court in Washington, DC, I stopped on the steps in front of the courthouse. It was about five in the morning, and I was the first one there. A cold mist hung over the city, and the moon was fading as the sun came up. As I stood there, I looked up, and at the front of the court, I saw the words *Equal Justice for All* carved into the stone. And I stood there in . . . awe. For most of human history, the law was just a way for the rich to systematically exploit the poor, but here, in the United States, that was turned on its head. Equal justice for all. I got chills staring at it.

"And I thought of it when I got this case, the case of a young girl, Patty Winchester, who died in the worst way a human being could die." I went to the table and pulled out a photo of Patty from the file, Hank's photo of Patty hugging him and her brother. "On May tenth of this year, this young girl, Patty Winchester, a high school senior at River Falls High, went to a bar in Las Vegas with her friend Cecily. She sneaked out and went with her friend, thinking they'd have some drinks at a bar that didn't check ID. And it's there that she met the man that would end her life." I pointed to Anderson. "Anderson Ficco."

I moved toward the jury and put the photo on the banister in front of them. "Patty knew Anderson and his friend Steven from school, and they started drinking together that night. Anderson also got high on mescaline and marijuana, as his friend Steven will tell you. He'll also tell you Anderson was out of his head. He was agitated and angry, harassing and groping the women in the bar. Cecily had a curfew and had to leave. Steven and Patty decided they were going to leave together, but Steven couldn't just abandon his buddy in that condition, so they took Anderson with them. And it was a mistake that would cost Patty her life.

"While driving, Anderson told Steven to pull over. Steven thought he might need to vomit or urinate, but instead Anderson pulled out a hammer from a toolbox in the back seat of the car." I hit my fist against my palm. "He smashed it into the back of Patty's head, fracturing her skull. Steven was in shock. He didn't know what to do other than take her to a hospital. But Anderson wasn't about to allow that. So he took out a gun, this gun," I said, as I went over to the table and held up the 9 millimeter in the evidence bag, "and stuck this gun into Steven's face and told him to drive. Steven, fearful that he might get killed, obeyed. Anderson led him to a townhome he secretly kept in Glassdale. He forced Steven to carry Patty's unconscious body into the townhome, and that's where her nightmare really began.

"For two days, in a psychotic drug binge, Anderson Ficco tortured Patty Winchester. He raped her. He cut her with a knife. He burned her with cigarettes. He knocked out teeth, and at some point, he began breaking bones. But that wasn't enough. He had to take her life, too."

Just then the door to the courtroom opened. I looked over and saw Hank Winchester leaving.

"After two days, when the drugs began to wear off, he panicked. He didn't know what to do, so he called his buddy Steven and told him that if he didn't come over and help him, Anderson would have to clean up loose ends. So again, Steven ran over because he was frightened Anderson would kill him. And what he saw almost made him vomit.

"The town house has a basement, and Anderson took Steven there. Patty was barely clinging to life. Blood was everywhere. Anderson forced Steven to help him take Patty up to the Hallows campgrounds. Patty was still alive when she was thrown into a ditch like refuse. It's at that point that Anderson killed her. But a gun and a knife would've been too quick. He wanted to enjoy it. So he crawled into the ditch and wrapped his hands around her throat. He crushed her windpipe as she screamed for help, and life left her body.

"One thing they didn't count on was anybody else being up there in the Hallows." I held up a finger. "But there was. A family, out camping. Their ten-year-old boy was looking for a toy he had lost when he heard screaming. He came closer to where the screaming was coming from and saw two men throwing dirt on a woman. And he saw one of the men, Anderson Ficco, climb into the ditch, and heard the screaming stop.

"The next morning, an elderly couple was out for a morning stroll when they noticed part of a leg sticking up out of the dirt. It was Patty's body." I pointed to Anderson. "Anderson Ficco tortured a young girl to death for fun. He didn't rob her, he didn't extort her family for money . . . he killed her because he thought it was fun."

I looked back toward the courtroom doors to see if Hank had come back, but he hadn't. I inhaled deeply and looked at the jurors.

"You're going to hear some other things in this trial that are going to be unpleasant. Patty was not perfect. She grew up poor and grew poorer as time went on. Her mother left her father with two young kids, and although Patty did her best to stay on the straight and narrow, there simply was not enough money to go around, and she couldn't sit there and watch her family lose their home or her father lose his mechanic shop. In an effort to help her single father, she sold the only thing she truly owned: her body. She worked as an escort. She sold herself for money to help her father and kid brother. But does that mean she's less deserving of justice than anyone else?

"Equal justice for all . . . Mr. Pritcher may tell you that those words apply only to defendants, but what about Patty? Does she get justice? Does anyone cry for her? Anderson Ficco, as you all know, comes from a wealthy family with a high-priced lawyer and a huge future ahead of him." I held the photo up higher to make sure all the jurors were looking at her. "Patty Winchester lived in a run-down mobile home. She was one of the voiceless in this country. She had no money, no power, no connections. Equal justice for all . . . does it apply to her? Does she get a voice?

"I think so," I said, putting the photo down and placing my hands on the banister. "I think you are her voice. No one else is going to speak for her. No one else gives a damn about her. But you can. You can do it by sending a message to people like Anderson Ficco that the powerless are not *things*. That having money and power does not mean you can use people and then discard them like trash when you're done with them. You can be that voice. You can send the message that people like Patty do matter." I looked each juror in the eyes. "Equal justice for all."

61

When I had sat back down, the judge said, "Mr. Pritcher."

Pritcher rose and buttoned the top button on his suit coat. He swaggered over to the jury and then folded his hands in front of his body, as though he were doing penance in front of them.

"When I was in law school, all I wanted to be was a prosecutor. My father was a lawyer, and he took me to court occasionally. One time, when I was eight years old, we were in the back of a courtroom not unlike this one, waiting for my father's case to be called. At the moment, a criminal case was being handled. The prosecutor rose and asked the judge that the defendant be taken into custody as he was a danger to the community. The defendant grabbed a pen off the defense table and lunged at the prosecutor.

"But the prosecutor didn't budge. He stared that man, a man easily twice his size, right in the face and didn't budge." Pritcher stopped and casually put his hands in his pockets. "Luckily the bailiffs tackled him before he could do any damage, but the impression on me had been made. I thought being a prosecutor would be the most noble profession I could dedicate my life to."

He took his hands out and began using them to help emphasize his words. I realized then that his body language control was better than mine. Being top dog sometimes meant you got sloppy because you weren't as hungry as those on the way up.

"After law school, I got a clerkship at that same prosecutor's office. And what I saw shocked me. Convictions were the law of the land. The bosses wanted as many as possible, because the positions were elected positions, and convictions looked good in the press. The incentives were pointing in the wrong direction, the direction of occasionally convicting innocent people for crimes they did not commit.

"I remember one woman very distinctly who we convicted of a shoplifting charge, and she was fired from her job and had to drop out of college because she couldn't afford it any longer. Several months later, we charged the manager of that store with fraud, because he had been stealing supplies. I asked him about the woman, and he admitted she hadn't stolen anything, that accusing her had been a way for him to deflect attention from himself.

"Three hundred and fifty-six people have been freed from death row in this country because of DNA evidence. Three hundred and fifty-six *innocent* people, like Anderson Ficco, whose lives were saved from a system that sees convictions as the ultimate goal. How many people have been executed or are spending life in prison who didn't have the benefit of DNA evidence?"

He went over and put his hands on Anderson's shoulders, showing the jury Anderson wasn't some monster but a human being.

"Anderson Ficco had nothing to do with Patty Winchester's death. Steven Brown has manipulated the prosecution into believing it was my client that committed these murders. You see, the prosecution has to choose a side. They know they can't get convictions in both Steven's and Anderson's cases, so they chose. Did they choose wrongly? They have no idea. They only know they need a conviction. This was the easiest path, the path of least resistance: believe the guy making up a phony story and use him to get a conviction on the boy that has no one to back up his story.

"We will present evidence to you today that Steven Brown is the man that murdered Patty Winchester. A young girl named Bebe Stewart will testify that Steven Brown was obsessed with Patty Winchester. So obsessed that Patty talked to the police about getting a stalking injunction against him."

What the hell?

I turned back and looked at Will and Jia. Will shook his head, his eyes wide with surprise.

Pritcher patted Anderson and moved back close to the jury. "She will testify that Anderson was always kind and respectful to Patty, and that on one occasion he even stuck up for her against Steven's advances." He held up a finger. "But it wasn't until that night, May fourteenth, that Anderson was simply not there to stop Steven.

"One thing the prosecution told you that is true is that my client suffers from addiction. He has since the time he was sixteen. If any of you have family members suffering from addiction, you've seen what it can do to the human mind and body. The night of Patty's abduction, Anderson was simply too out of it to fight for her, and Steven saw his chance.

"Steven Brown gave Anderson and Patty a ride back into town. He dropped Anderson off at home and then proceeded to take Patty, not to his apartment, but to the townhome that he knew Anderson owned. Anderson will testify that he had given a key to Steven, and that he didn't know when or how often Steven was there.

"When Steven arrived with Patty, she was highly intoxicated. He took her into the townhome, and for two days he stayed with her. For two days, he tortured that poor girl until she was close to death. Then he took her body with another unidentified person, whom Mr. Graham's detectives have been very conveniently unable to locate, if they've even tried, and dumped her in the Hallows. Anderson Ficco was nowhere near there. Anderson didn't know anything had happened to Patty until the police arrived at his door to arrest him. Anderson Ficco is innocent." He leaned on the banister in front of them.

"Anderson Ficco is *innocent*. Can you even imagine what it would be like to be convicted of a murder you didn't commit? To spend the rest of your life in a prison cell, knowing the man who actually committed the murder is free and roaming about, enjoying his life?

"There's a Bible passage in Genesis I'm quite fond of. Abraham is speaking with God, and God is about to destroy Sodom. It says, 'And Abraham drew near and said, Will you consume the righteous and the wicked? What if there are fifty righteous within the city? Will you consume and not spare the place for the fifty righteous who are in it? What if ten are found there?' And God answered Abraham and said, 'I will not destroy it for the sake of the ten.' That, ladies and gentlemen of the jury, is what the Bible teaches us. Better to let a city of the wicked live than to unjustly kill ten good men." He paused and looked at each of the jurors. "Better to let ten guilty men go free than to punish one innocent man. Anderson Ficco is that innocent man."

62

The judge called a ten-minute break. I took Jia, Will, and Howard out into the hall.

"What the hell was that?" I said to Howard, barely able to keep my voice down. "She tried to take a stalking injunction out against Steven?"

He shrugged. "I guess. I mean, I don't know."

"You didn't think to check whether one of our murder suspects had previously hurt the victim?"

"Hey, keep your voice down. It was a mistake."

I looked at Will and Jia. "And you guys didn't think to check?"

Jia shook her head. "I checked everything. If it was true, I would've found it in the system."

"Go back to the office right now and find out what the hell happened. Russell wouldn't just make that up." I turned to Howard. "And you, sit in the gallery seats with them. I don't want your taint on me when Russell destroys you on the stand."

He stepped close to me. "We got a problem, me and you?"

"A problem? Yeah, we got a problem. This asshole might walk because you were either too lazy or too stupid to do your job. Either way, you shouldn't be doing anything more than writing parking tickets."

He smirked. "You don't get it, do you? You're just a visitor here. No one gives a shit what you think."

He stormed off, leaving me fuming in the hallway.

———

When the jury was recalled and we were ready to go, I called Howard to the stand. He went up there without his gun and looked like a salesman at a jewelry store rather than a cop. Most cops I knew couldn't be paid to be without their guns, so he purposely didn't wear it because he knew it would bug me.

Howard was sworn in and sat down, pouring some water out of a plastic jug into a paper cup. He looked to Pritcher and then to me and winked. I couldn't imagine he would tank his testimony on purpose just to get back at me, but who the hell knew?

"Name, please, Detective."

"Mark Howard."

"And where do you work, Detective?"

The Art of Jury Trial as War, chapter 6: "Make sure, for every witness, that the jury sees them how you want them to, and the best way to do that is to label the witness and then use that label as many times as possible." To a defense attorney, the prosecution was always "the government," snitches were always "government informants," and detectives were "Mr. So and So." But the tables were turned now, and I had to make Howard seem respectable, so everything out of my mouth would be "Detective."

"I'm with the Ute County Sheriff's Office. I've been there for six years now. My current assignment is the investigation of felonies and violent misdemeanors."

"And do you recall the events we've been discussing that occurred on May tenth and fourteenth?"

"I do."

"Please tell us about them."

He cleared his throat and looked straight at the jury, as though he were talking to an old friend. Looked like the guy could be competent when he actually wanted to be.

"We got a call from a Kevin O'Brien. He and his wife were out walking their dogs up at the Hallows when they noticed something in the ground that looked like a human leg. He got a thick branch and moved around some of the dirt and discovered it was a body. They immediately called the police, and a uniform was sent out. I got the call about half an hour later that it was a suspected homicide."

"What happened then?"

"I went out to the scene and confirmed there was a body. I recognized her as Patty Winchester. I had known her father and had seen her on several occasions. I immediately called the station to get the forensic unit from the Washington County Sheriff's Office down there and then took Kevin and his wife's statements. While I waited for Forensics to arrive, I walked around the site to see if I could find anything relevant, and we found a small toy, a little monkey, that turned out to belong to Lyle Mallory, who'd lost it there. Nothing else was found that was relevant to this investigation."

"Describe the body for us."

He took a sip of his water. "The body wasn't decomposed very much."

"Objection," Pritcher said. "He's not a medical examiner, Your Honor."

"He's allowed to tell us what he saw, Judge."

"I'll allow it."

I looked back to Howard. "Go on."

"It was pretty bad. She had cuts all over her body, something a thin knife or maybe a piece of glass would do. And I noticed cigarette burns up and down her legs and torso. Her face and body were extremely bruised, indicating she'd taken quite a beating."

"Objection, again, Your Honor, Mr. Howard is not a qualified witness to speak to injuries."

"I'll lay some foundation, Your Honor."

"Go ahead."

"Detective, you've seen dead bodies before, correct? Both in your time as a police officer and as a soldier in Iraq?"

"Correct."

"You've seen victims of violent attacks?"

"Yes."

"How many?"

"In my whole career? I guess over fifty."

"You've seen bruising?"

"Yes."

"You've seen mutilations?"

"Yes."

"Was this body mutilated?"

"Beaten and mutilated, yes, quite severely." He looked to the jury. "Honestly it's the worst I've seen."

I questioned him for over an hour about speaking with Patty's father, which led them to Cecily, who led them to Anderson and Steven. Of course, I couldn't talk about the boys' confessions, which were nothing more than Howard aggressively getting them to say what he wanted anyway, so we glossed over that part, and then I said, "Thank you, Detective."

Pritcher stood up silently and approached the detective. He didn't stand at the lectern, but instead put his hands behind his back and stood a few feet from Howard.

"I have a copy of your police report, Mr. Howard. Would you mind telling me where in there it states she had cigarette burns over her body?"

"It should be in the attached supplemental."

"The supplemental report you filed a few weeks ago?"

"Yes."

"Did Mr. Graham ask you to file that?"

He hesitated. "Yes."

"But you didn't file it on your own before then?"

"No."

"And it wasn't in your initial reports?"

"No."

"It's clearly relevant to the case that the victim had cigarette burns all over her body, wouldn't you say?"

"Yeah."

"But you didn't include it?"

He shook his head. "I did not. But it's because—"

"You also didn't include the part about the dozens of lacerations, did you?"

"No."

"Again, a relevant fact that anybody looking at this case would need to know, correct?"

"Correct."

"And you hid it from your reports?"

"I wouldn't say I hid it, but I didn't put it in there. Can I explain why?"

Pritcher took a step closer. "You knew the victim?"

"I did."

"You felt bad when you saw her?"

"Yeah, of course."

"Emotion can cloud judgment, can't it, Mr. Howard?"

He nodded. "Yeah, it can. But I was thinking clearly here."

"Thinking clearly without putting in that she was covered in cigarette burns and had cuts over every inch of her body? I would hate to see what your investigations are like when you're not thinking clearly."

"Your Honor—" I said.

"Mr. Howard," Pritcher quickly added, "you found my client, Anderson Ficco, within six hours of finding the body, is that right?"

"Yes."

"And you arrested him a couple of hours later after interrogating him?"

"Yes."

"So eight hours. Within eight hours you had an arrest on this case?"

"Yes."

"And you were emotional."

"I didn't say that."

"So your testimony to this jury is that you saw a mutilated corpse of a girl you knew, and you were calm, cool, and collected?"

"Yes."

"Really?" Pritcher went to his associate, Tomomi, and got a large color photograph from her. He showed it to me, and it was of Patty standing in front of her school with another girl her age.

"You recognize this photo, Mr. Howard?"

"Yes."

"Who took it?"

Howard bit his lower lip and glanced at me. "I did."

Son of a bitch. Did everyone know what the hell was going on here but me?

"Why did you take it?"

"It was . . . I have a niece, and Patty and her were friends. That's my niece in the photo."

"More than friends, weren't they? You stated to a uniformed officer on the scene that they knew each other since third grade, correct?"

"How did you . . . yes."

"And I'm guessing Patty was over at your niece's house occasionally?"

"Yes."

"And she was over at your niece's house sometimes when you were there?"

"Yes."

"So you knew Patty since the third grade as well, correct?"

He hesitated. "Yes. I guess."

"You knew her well?"

"Yes."

"You cared about her, Mr. Howard?"

"Of course."

"And yet you saw her mutilated body and you were cool as a cucumber, right?"

Howard didn't respond.

"There were tire tracks around the body, weren't there?"

"Yes."

"Did you have an expert identify the tracks around the time of the murder?"

"Yes, we discovered that—"

"Uh-uh, Mr. Howard, I didn't ask if you looked at the tracks under orders from Mr. Graham several months after the homicide. I asked if at the time or around the time of the homicide you had these tracks analyzed."

He hesitated. "No."

"Seems important, doesn't it?"

"It is, yes."

"But you and the forensic unit didn't do it."

"No, we did not."

"You should've done it."

"Yes, we should've."

"Just another mistake for the pile, right?"

He didn't respond.

"Did you look around for signs of any witnesses?"

"Yes, we didn't find any."

"But there was one, correct? Lyle Mallory."

"Yes, that's correct."

"Another mistake, right?"

"I suppose so."

"Before arresting my client, did you talk to people near him about Patty's and his relationship?"

"No."

"You didn't talk to a Ms. Bebe Stewart?"

"No."

"Ms. Stewart informed Mr. Graham that Anderson was not the killer, and it was in fact Mr. Brown, didn't she?"

"Objection, Your Honor, hearsay," I said.

"Sustained."

"Mr. Howard, do you have any disciplinary proceedings against you?"

"No."

"Ever had any?"

He glanced at me. I had looked up his records from the Utah POST Academy, and they were clear.

"No."

Pritcher went back to his table and brought out another photo. I hadn't seen this one before. A blonde woman standing with Howard outside a baseball stadium.

I stood up and said, "Your Honor, the State would object to the use of this photograph. I haven't seen it before, and a reverse discovery motion was filed."

"For impeachment, Your Honor, no notice required."

"I'll allow it if it pertains directly to impeachment."

Pritcher approached Howard. When Howard saw the photo his eyes went wide. This wasn't good.

"Who is she, Mr. Howard?"

"She's . . . um . . . April Mannis."

"A former lover, correct?"

"Yes."

"A former lover who accused you of rape, correct?"

"Objection, sidebar!"

"Approach."

I stormed over to the bench. "Judge, if true, Mr. Pritcher had an ethical obligation to disclose that information to me."

"Impeachment, again, Your Honor. I don't have to disclose anything to the State if their own witness is up there lying, and I catch them in the lie."

"The lie itself isn't what I have a problem with. Mr. Pritcher knew about this alleged incident, didn't inform us, and gathered the photograph without handing it over. Rule seven is clear that all material evidence must be handed over by the defense to the State when the defense intends to use that evidence in trial if a reverse discovery motion has been filed."

"I didn't intend to use it. If he had been honest, I would've just moved on."

"You're so full of shit, Russell."

"Up yours."

"Boys, calm down. Mr. Pritcher, you had an obligation to turn this over. I'm striking all of the testimony from the record and excluding the photograph."

"Thank you, Judge," I said.

I went back to the prosecution table while the judge informed the jury to disregard everything they'd just heard. We had about as much chance of them forgetting everything as Santa Claus landing on the roof and giving us all presents, but at least they wouldn't hear more about Howard's ex.

Pritcher continued pounding on Howard. After forty-five minutes, Howard was red faced and sweating. Pritcher brought up things I'm sure Howard had no idea people could find out about. Like a shoplifting charge he'd had at age eleven and the fact that his father, drunk, had once put him in the hospital with fractured ribs and a busted nose. Information I would've gotten if I'd been given my normal six months to a year to prepare a case, along with my team of investigators.

When Pritcher was done, the judge looked to me. I debated getting Howard off the stand, but I could tell the picture of his ex had lingered:

Howard looked like a rapist up there, so I had to afford him the chance to explain. I rose and said, "Tell us about the rape allegation."

"It's untrue. Completely false. April and I only dated for like a month, and I called it off with her because she kept getting arrested. She had a severe alcohol and drug problem. I have personally arrested her over a dozen times, and she filed the report against me after the last arrest. Internal Affairs already looked into it and decided it was bogus. I wasn't even in the city at the time she's claiming it happened." He looked at the jurors. "As a police officer, we get a lot of complaints filed against us by people that feel the system has treated them poorly. We're the face of the system to them, so it's always us that gets it. Almost all of the accusations end up being proven false by witnesses. It's just part of having the job."

"Thank you, Detective."

The judge said, "Mr. Pritcher?"

"Nothing, Your Honor."

Thank crap.

"You're free to leave, Detective."

He stood and then hurriedly got his jacket and exited. I didn't notice any of the confident swagger he normally had. He didn't even look back at us.

"Next witness, Mr. Graham."

63

The next witnesses were the O'Briens. I had them up to describe the condition of the body and how exactly they found it. Nothing earth shattering. I finished up with each of them in about fifteen minutes and moved on.

The ME from the state crime lab was next, but by the time we took a break, got him sworn in, and had gone through his qualifications, it was almost one. The judge called it a day fifteen minutes early and released the jury, telling them not to discuss the case with anyone else. I asked to have the jury sequestered, and Judge Allred laughed.

As everyone filed out of the courtroom, Jia came up to me and said, "That made Howard look like an idiot, but Russell didn't contradict anything Howard had said."

"It's just the first little gash. He's going to attack and attack until the gash becomes a gaping hole in our case, and the jury starts thinking they can't trust us. What do you got on the stalking injunction?"

"It's legit. It didn't come up on a regular search, though, so I searched by initials. According to the system, a 'PW' tried to take out a stalking injunction against 'SB' four months ago. I thought it's gotta be them. I doubled-checked the birthdays, and it's Patty and Steven Brown. I don't know why someone entered it with just the initials since no one searches that way. Probably a new clerk at the court or something."

"Do you have a copy of the injunction?"

"No. Nothing was there. I've never seen that before."

"It means the report was taken, but no injunction was ever filed."

"Who would do that? I mean, I can see Nathan Ficco having the ability to get it dropped, but Steven doesn't have any money or connections besides Anderson."

"No idea who, but job number one for you is to dig deep and find out who took that report when Patty came in."

"So can we not use Steven now?"

"We don't have a choice, he's our star witness. And there's no actual injunction, just a report, so it's not official. We go with the game plan we got for now."

We walked out of the courtroom, and I turned my cell back on. I saw I had a missed call and a voice mail.

"Lunch?" Will said.

"I'll catch up. You guys go ahead."

I checked the voice mail in the hallway: it was from a Dr. Thomas. The doctor that had treated Anderson's eye injury.

I returned the call. "Doc, hey, this is Tatum Graham with the County Attorney's Office. Just returning your call to my call."

"Yes, what can I do for you? You said it was urgent."

So far, Will hadn't dug up any evidence that Roscoe was involved with Patty as more than a teacher, and he also hadn't been able to confirm that the girl Anderson supposedly groped was Patty. If I were able to prove that Anderson had gotten in trouble for groping her, it would help me counter the stalking allegation against Steven.

"So, Doc, I'm in a bit of a bind and need some clarification. I know my investigator and associate already spoke with you, but I was wondering if there's anything else you can tell me about Anderson Ficco's eye injury that could help me. Did they find the pipe, or did his father speak with Coach Mallory or—"

"Speak with him?"

"Yeah. Do you know if his father spoke with Coach Mallory about the injury? I know you don't live in River Falls, but Coach Mallory is pretty recognizable."

"I know who he is. He was here with him."

I could take a lap around this place. "You're sure?"

"Yes, I've been to several of the football games."

"Did he say anything to you?"

"Say? No. We just discussed Anderson's history and the injury itself. When we were finished, they thanked me and left. Oh, I did ask if Coach Mallory was injured because of the blood. There was blood all over his clothing, which I assumed was from Mr. Ficco."

An electric shock went through my guts. "Doctor, did Coach Mallory have any hand injuries or was he wearing gloves when he came to the hospital?"

"You know . . . I don't completely recall. This was a long time ago, Mr. Graham."

"Well, thanks anyway. You've been a big help."

I hung up and checked my watch before deciding to drive over to the high school.

64

I got to the high school around two in the afternoon, and it looked like school was getting ready to get out. As I was walking up, a bell rang and kids started filing out of the place.

The front office told me Roscoe was finishing up teaching social studies upstairs, so I went to his classroom. He was speaking with a student who had stayed after class, and I waited until they were done and the student had left.

"Tatum, back again? You must not be as traumatized by this place as you let on."

"Varies day by day." I glanced around the classroom. On the back wall was a time line of various events throughout history, starting with the founding of America.

Roscoe began collecting his papers. "So what did you need?"

I folded my arms and approached him but didn't get too close. "I had an interesting talk with a doctor today. Dr. Thomas. You remember him?"

"Can't say I do."

"He was the doctor that treated Anderson's eye injury last year when you took him in."

He put his papers in his bag and then looked at me. "I don't know what you're talking about."

"That hospital has video," I lied. "When I get that video and watch it, what's it going to show me, Roscoe? I'm getting it this afternoon, so it's best we not lie to each other right now."

He sighed and sat down in his seat, rubbing his head. "I was just trying to protect him."

"Tell me what you know, and maybe we can help each other."

"This can't leave the room."

"We'll see. What happened?"

"It's Anderson's father."

"What about him?"

"There was no pipe. I swore to Anderson that we would make something up and stick to the story." He exhaled and looked down to his desk. "His father was upset over something Anderson had done. It didn't even seem like a big deal to me, an arrest for DUI. I mean, it is a big deal and it isn't. Kids do stupid things. So when practice was finishing up, I was speaking to Anderson about how to go about fixing it when his father showed up."

"And?"

"And he was furious. I'd never seen him like that. I tried to calm him down so the three of us could talk, but there was no talking. He grabbed Anderson and pinned him against the wall with one hand and pounded him with the other. I mean, just pounded the poor kid. I managed to finally pull him off, and when I did, I noticed the brass knuckles."

"What?"

"He was wearing brass knuckles to beat his own son. What kind of man does that, Tatum? Beats his own kid to the point he deforms him?"

I was silent a second. "Assuming I believe you, why didn't you call the cops?"

"You don't know how much influence the Ficcos have. I mean, I guess you probably do, but it's gotten even worse since you left. I mean, Nathan owns like half the land around this town. Whoever he wants elected to office is who's going to get elected to office. The sheriff was elected almost exclusively by money the guy donated to him."

Huh. Guess that would explain how Pritcher is getting such good intel. He wasn't bribing anyone. He didn't have to: the sheriff's office was probably handing him the information on a silver platter.

Roscoe rose and picked up his bag, slinging the strap around his shoulder. "I'm sorry I wasn't honest with you before, but I want to keep my job. I have a child to support. If Nathan Ficco wanted to, he could have my job with a snap of his fingers. And Anderson made me promise not to tell anybody. He said it would be worse if his father got in trouble, so I respected his wishes."

I nodded as Roscoe walked out of the room. His story struck me as plausible. And I preferred thinking Roscoe hadn't been involved with Patty.

I took out my phone and texted Will to meet me at Nathan Ficco's house.

———

Will was there before I was. I parked next to him in the horseshoe drive-way and got out. We walked up to the door and he said, "What's up?"

"You're just here as a witness. Don't say anything, and whatever you do, don't upset him. We need him talking."

A housekeeper answered and I asked for Nathan. Without a word, she left to get him. Nathan wore a full business suit, though he was retired and it was the middle of the day.

"I'll refer you to speak to my attorney, gentlemen."

"Mr. Pritcher is technically Anderson's attorney, Mr. Ficco. And we just want five minutes of your time. No more."

"I will not help in this witch hunt to condemn my son."

"I'm not asking you to. I want to ask about something else that may be related. Five minutes, and then you'll never see me darken your doorstep again."

He shifted his gaze from one of us to the other and said, "Fine. Five minutes."

We entered the home and followed him to his study. He sat down in a chair. There was a glass of whiskey next to him, and he took a sip and said, "Do you want a drink?"

"I'm fine, thanks. And the pope here doesn't drink." I folded my arms. "Where's Mrs. Ficco, by the way?"

"Out. Now what is this about?"

"She's been out every time we've been here."

"Yes, women can actually leave the house, Mr. Graham. Miracle of miracles. Now what do you want?"

"I want to talk about Anderson's eye injury."

"Why?"

"Call it curiosity."

He took another sip. "The damn fool never was very coordinated. When he was six I tried to teach him how to ride a bike, and he broke his leg falling off. He's fragile." He raised his glass to take a sip. "Might as well have had a girl."

"Well, regardless, what do you know about what happened?"

He shrugged. "Just what he told me. He tripped on the field and hit the jagged edge of some pipe."

I nodded and glanced around the study. "You got any brass knuckles around, Mr. Ficco?"

"Any what?"

"Brass knuckles. You know, metal, several holes for your fingers to fit through?"

He chuckled. "You think I injured Anderson's eye? Trust me, Mr. Graham, if I wanted to hurt him I wouldn't need brass knuckles to do it."

"See, 'cause I heard you showed up to the football field and did a little number on your son."

"That's preposterous. Who told you that? Roscoe Mallory?"

"Does it matter?"

He stared at us a moment. "I wasn't going to help you anyway, Mr. Graham, but perhaps you need to look a little more closely at dear Coach Mallory."

"For what?"

"For the fact that he was sleeping with Patty Winchester."

Will and I glanced at each other. "Bullshit. You would've said something to help your son from the beginning."

"Mr. Pritcher recommended not saying anything and instead surprising you in court with it when he called Roscoe to the stand. But seems appropriate now. He became obsessed with her. Patty once confided in Anderson that she was frightened of him." He finished his whiskey. "Drop the charges against my son and go get the real killer. That's what the taxpayers are paying you for. Now get the hell out of my house."

Once outside, we stopped on the porch and I looked back at the Ficcos' home. Near the roof was a wasp's nest tucked under the gutter.

"Looks like you were right," Will said.

"We need confirmation. You didn't find anything?"

"Not much. Got Roscoe's bank accounts, and there weren't any large transfers in or out in the past year. But there were three charges to the State Street Motel downtown. The times were all in the afternoon."

"Go talk to Cecily. If anyone might know if Patty was sleeping with him, it's her. Then head down to that motel and show Roscoe's and Patty's pictures to everyone that works there and see if they ever showed up together."

"What about the eye injury? You still think Anderson's dad hurt him?"

"Roscoe said he beat him with brass knuckles over a DUI arrest."

"DUI? I don't remember that coming through the office."

"Which means either Roscoe is lying or Daddy used his influence to get rid of it. I need you or Jia down at the station digging through the files. And then pull Nathan Ficco's criminal history. I specifically want any times where the Department of Child Services was called out to investigate reports of child abuse."

"Got it. Out of curiosity, though, why are we so interested in his eye injury? I mean, however it happened doesn't change the fact that Anderson murdered Patty."

"It's an unknown, and I don't like unknowns. They have a nasty little habit of coming back and biting you in the ass."

65

That night I headed over to my father's house. He was in the kitchen frying potatoes and eggs. Will had called me and said that Cecily was up in Zion National Park and she would be back tomorrow. I'd told him to hit up every one of Patty's friends with Jia and find out if anyone knew anything about her sleeping with Roscoe.

"Don't people knock anymore," Adam said, "or is that not the custom in Hollywood?"

"I didn't live in Hollywood." I stood in the doorway of the kitchen and watched him. A rag with blood on it was lying on the counter, a beer next to it. "Adam, you can't drink with your pain meds."

He waved me off. "In my day we drank with everything, and we weren't keeling over dying every five minutes. Now they're warning us against this and that, and people are dying younger and younger. Gotta be tough and take some pain. Take small pain now and you can handle big pain later when it comes." He coughed into his rag a few times and said, "And the son of a bitch always comes."

He scooped the eggs and potatoes onto two plates. He said, "Come eat. You're all skin and bones."

"Not really hungry right now."

"You will be later. Just sit down."

I sat down across from him, and he dug in. I took a couple of bites but couldn't eat. He noticed and said, "Stress is a helluva thing. Eats you in your sleep."

"Who says I'm stressed?"

"Since you were a kid you've had a tell. You raise your right eyelid when you're stressed, like you're trying to stretch it or something. It's a tic. Your mother thought maybe we should take you to a shrink, and I told her that was ridiculous."

Man, he was right. I didn't even remember because it had become so natural I didn't notice it anymore.

"So this starting over fresh, it working out for ya?" he said.

I shrugged and took another small bite of eggs. "Does it for anyone?"

"I don't know. I've never done it. I was born in this town and I'll die in this town."

"You regret that?"

He was silent a second. "Sure, who wouldn't? But I have a feeling that you only want what you don't have, and once you trade for it, you realize it's worse than what you got now." He took a sip of beer. "Or maybe change is always best. What the hell do I know? I'm just an old fool dying by himself."

I stared at him a second. "You're not by yourself, Adam."

My phone vibrated. It was a text from Gates asking if I wanted to have dinner tonight. I responded that I did, and Adam said, "She really likes you, ya know."

"Who?"

"Please. Who else would be texting you? She was broken when you left. Her dad told me she cried for days. Wouldn't come out of her room. You could've at least said goodbye to her. I know it shook you to see her in the hospital all broken up like that, but you could've said goodbye."

"Well, hindsight's twenty-twenty, isn't it?"

"Yeah," he said quietly. "Unfortunately."

66

After dinner, Gates and I walked around her property. We stopped at a fence overlooking a small valley, and I could see several cows huddled around a calf. The evening sun was dimming, and it gave everything a soft orange glow. Clumps of dandelions swayed with a light breeze. It was quiet. The type of quiet you can never get in a city.

"I forget how loud it is in cities until I'm out of them," I said. "I'm not sure we were meant to live in proximity like that. There's some argument that we're actually not the dominant species on the planet. Wheat is. That wheat forced us to abandon our hunter-gatherer lifestyle and to cultivate it in huge quantities over most of the earth and to make sure it's the main part of our diet so we'll always have it around. And the worst part is it's forced us to live in close proximity so we'll be better at cultivating it."

She chuckled. "You're so morose. I love it. It's like being around a depressed teenager all the time."

"I'm not morose. I'm a realist. There's a big difference."

She leaned on the fence and stared at the cows. "You know what convinced me to stay here? That one right there. I call her Dallas. She was a calf when I was preparing this place for sale. I was out here one night making a repair to the fence, and she came up to me. She put her nose through the fence and wouldn't leave until I rubbed it. We sat there like that for a long time. Just . . . connecting. I texted the buyer right then and told him I wouldn't be selling."

"That's what changed the trajectory of your life? A cow?"

"Never know how angels show up in your life to lead you down the right path, do you?"

I scoffed and leaned on the fence with my forearms. "Well, tell whoever my angel is to show up and give me a hand with this case."

"I reviewed it this morning. Things seem to be going fine. You've got Steven after the medical examiner and Cecily Gilbert after Lyle. Seems like a good case to me."

"Something's not sitting right with Anderson's eye injury. He didn't just fall on a pipe. Something happened. And either Roscoe is lying about it or Nathan Ficco is. One of them doesn't want me to know the truth, and it's connected to Patty."

"Nathan will say and do anything to help his son. I wouldn't believe a word he says, particularly over Roscoe. But . . ."

"But what?"

"But then again, you never really know what people are capable of when nobody's watching."

67

The next day in court, Jia and Will sat behind me, and I didn't have Howard sit next to me. It was just me, Pritcher, and Anderson at the tables.

"Mr. Graham," Judge Allred said, "I believe the floor is yours."

"Thank you, Judge. The State calls Steven Brown to the stand."

The bailiff went to the back and brought out Steven. He wore a suit and wasn't cuffed. He was so large he took up almost the entire witness booth.

I rose and stood in front of the lectern. "Name, please."

"Steven Brown."

"You live here in River Falls, Steven?"

"Yessir, born and raised."

"You know why we're here?"

He glanced at Anderson, who was staring right at him with a smirk on his face. "Yessir."

"Please tell us."

"It's about the killin'a Patty Winchester."

"Tell us what you remember about that night."

"Well, we was going down to Skid Row. It's a bar in Las Vegas. We go there sometimes 'cause they don't have great bars over here in Utah. They don't really check for ID neither, so it works out. So me and Anderson go over there, and we meet up with Patty and her friend

Cecily. We knew 'em from school. And Patty was really drunk. Like really drunk. Hittin' on all the guys in the bar. Rough guys, like bikers and such. And so Anderson and I was worried about her. Like them guys was takin' a likin' to her, and they didn't look like they would take no for an answer."

I got a chill as I stared at him. Something in his voice was off. I stepped around the lectern and went up close to him, my arms folded as I stared into his pupils. I was close enough I could smell him, and I saw his pulse pound in his throat and the sweat glisten on his forehead. "What happened next?"

"Cecily had to leave. She said she had to work in the mornin'. So me and Anderson was left with Patty."

"Describe what state Anderson was in mentally."

"Mentally? I don't know. He was fine. Bit too drunk, but that was a frequent occurrence."

"Any drugs?"

"I suppose. Yeah, he was probably high, too. He likes mescaline."

"So Anderson is drunk and high, and you guys are left with Patty. What happens then?"

"We drank a little, played some pool, and then I decided to drive 'em home. Patty and Anderson were both too drunk to drive." He swallowed and looked at Anderson and then looked away. "Then I dropped him off at his house and her at her house and that was it."

My stomach felt like it dropped into my feet. "What did you say?"

"I said I dropped them off at their houses and then went home. Next day Anderson called me and asked if I'd heard from Patty. He wanted to call her and apologize for actin' like an ass last night. I told him I dropped her off and ain't heard from her."

I stepped closer to him. "Do you remember speaking with me a couple weeks ago at the jail, Mr. Brown?"

"Yessir."

"Do you remember telling me that Anderson was high on mescaline, and that while you were driving home, he hit Patty over the head with a hammer?"

He hesitated. "I do. I was lyin'."

"You were lying?"

"Yessir. I was in trouble and thought if I blamed Anderson, I could get out of it. But my conscience got to me, so I'm tellin' the truth now." He looked to the jury. "Anderson ain't had nothin' to do with Patty dyin'."

"Conscience?" I said, almost laughing. "Your conscience got to you? That's just fantastic. So you lied to an officer of this court, correct?"

"Yessir."

"But you're telling the truth now?"

"Yes."

"Your Honor, permission to treat the witness as hostile?"

"Granted."

"Mr. Brown, Anderson kept a townhome separate from his home, as Detective Howard testified to, correct?"

"He did."

"And a lot of blood was found in that townhome?"

"Yeah, I guess it was."

"Patty went missing after that night you two were with her?"

"Guess so."

"And a lot of blood was found in the townhome?"

"Yes."

"Tire tracks belonging to a vehicle similar to Anderson's truck were found in the Hallows where Patty's body was found, correct?"

"Yes."

"Cecily said in her statement that Anderson was so drunk he was harassing every woman in the bar. You aware of that?"

"I'd heard she said somethin' like that."

"Patty was extraordinarily beautiful, wasn't she?"

"Yeah, she was."

"No offense to you, but far more beautiful a girl than you or Anderson were used to spending time with. Outa your league, wouldn't you say?"

"I don't know. I guess. Hell, everyone had a crush on her. That ain't nothin'."

"You just said you drove them, right?"

"Yes."

"So you were sober?"

"Yeah, I just had one beer."

"And you, perfectly sober, saw how out of control Anderson was, correct?"

"I don't remember if he was. Sorry." He looked to the jury. "I'm sorry I lied. I'm just scared. I ain't never been in trouble before. But Anderson ain't have nothin' to do with Patty. I don't know how blood got in his townhome or if it's even Patty's, but I for sure dropped him off at his house and then dropped her off at her house. That's the Lord's honest truth. I don't know what else to tell ya."

I glanced back at Pritcher, who smirked.

"No further questions for now," I said.

68

I asked for a recess after Steven's testimony. I turned to Howard, who was sitting behind me. He blew a kiss at me, the pleasure at my humiliation exuding from his face like a warm glow, and left. Jia and Will sat there dumbfounded. I joined them in the gallery.

"You don't seem that shaken up," Jia said.

"Oh, don't let my calm veneer fool you, I'm about to bust up this courtroom. The Jolly Green Giant sandbagged us. Pritcher probably coached him before I was even on the case. I'm guessing he was promised they could both get away with it if they stuck together."

"That's a felony for an attorney to advise someone to perjure themselves."

"Welcome to the practice of law. What's legal and illegal doesn't matter. It's what you can show a jury. And we don't have squat to show anymore."

Pritcher gathered his things and came over. He patted my shoulder and said, "Better luck on the next case."

When he and his associates had left, I rose and walked over to the jury box. I put my hands on the banister and stared at the empty seats.

"So what now?" Will said.

"Now, we go with what we got. Lots of blood was found in Anderson's townhome, tire tracks belonging to a truck like his were at the scene, Lyle is going to testify that he saw Anderson dump the body, and I'll get Steven back up there and tear him apart. We don't need much else. We just gotta hit hard in closing that Steven is lying now to protect himself and his buddy, and that he was telling the truth when he told me Anderson killed her. And when this is over, we're asking Judge Allred to revoke our plea arrangement since Steven lied and putting him on trial for the homicide, too."

Will was staring at his phone. "Um . . . boss?"

"Unless that's a text from Anderson saying he's ready to give a full confession and get me some cowboy boots that don't make my toes feel like they're in a vise, I don't want to hear it."

"You're going to want to. It's a text from a patrol officer at the sheriff's office. Lyle's mom called them and said Lyle never made it to school this morning."

"What?"

"She says she saw him off, but then the school phoned to ask why he was absent."

"Go tell the judge I need to call it a day. Jia, you're with me."

We rushed down to Nikyee's house. She answered the door in a panic, her hands trembling, her eyes red and wet with tears.

"He never got to school," she said, her voice quivering. "He never got there. It's never happened before."

"It's okay. We're going to find him. Now, could he have gone to a friend's house?"

"He only ever goes to two friends' houses. I called their mothers. They haven't seen him. Their kids are both at school."

"Who else walks the same route as him?"

"Our neighbor . . . our neighbor does. Her name's Jill."

"Which neighbor?"

"Right over there."

I hurried to the house next door and knocked. After a few seconds, a woman with frizzy blonde hair answered.

"Hi, Tatum Graham. I'm with the County Attorney's Office. We're trying to find Lyle next door. He never got to school. I was hoping you could let me talk to Jill?"

"Oh my gosh, yeah, of course. She's at school, though."

"Mind giving the school a call and getting her on the phone?"

Jill was pulled out of class, and a few minutes later I was able to speak to her.

"Jill, hi, I'm a friend of Lyle's, your next-door neighbor. He never came to school today, and I was wondering if you've seen him."

"Yeah. He gave me some gummy bears today. I asked if I could have some and he said yes."

"That's nice of him. Where did you see him last?"

"Near Nimbley Park."

I looked to her mom and said, "Nimbley Park?"

"It's about halfway between the school and here."

"What did you see at Nimbley Park, sweetheart? Did Lyle leave the park and head home?"

"No, he got into the car."

"What car?"

"I dunno."

"What color was the car?"

"Blue."

"Was it a big car or a small car?"

"Small."

"Do you remember anything else about the car?"

"Umm . . . it had a bull on the back."

"A bull? What kind of bull?"

"A red bull on the window."

"A red bull. Okay, and did you see who was in the car?"

"No."

"Was there more than one person?"

"I dunno. I just said bye and went to school."

"Okay, thanks for talking with me, sweetie."

Nikyee was standing a little behind me on the lawn. I turned to her and said, "Blue car with a bull on the rear window. Ring a bell?"

"Oh no. That stupid bastard."

"Who?"

"Roscoe. He's got a blue Nissan with a Chicago Bulls sticker on the back."

"Has he ever picked up Lyle like this before?"

She shook her head. "No, we have strict visitation rules. He took him outa state once without telling me, so we got an order from the judge that he can't see him without my permission." She took out her phone. "I'll call him." It rang a few times. "Voice mail. I'm gonna head over there and get him. Thank you for your help."

I stood on the lawn and watched her walk away. Jia said, "Well, that was a lucky break."

"Luck, my ass. He's running."

"Coach Mallory?"

I nodded. "He blamed everything on Nathan to get me outa there. Must've slept on it and decided it was best to hit the road. Call Howard, get out a BOLO call on his car, and call his credit card companies and get an alert whenever he tries to use one. We need to catch him before he leaves the state, or we're not seeing him or Lyle again."

69

Court was called off for the rest of the day, and the jurors were released to go home. Pritcher didn't object. I could just picture the little ferret laughing it up tonight over drinks about how he'd run circles around me.

I sat in the conference room and tossed a tennis ball against the wall, catching it with one hand on the bounce. The BOLO—be on the lookout—call had gone out for Roscoe and his car, and an AMBER Alert had been issued for Lyle. A police unit was sitting outside the high school and another one outside Roscoe's house. But I didn't think we'd see him anywhere near there.

Jia and Will came in. Will said, "Okay, last time anyone saw him, he was leaving the high school. Vice principal said the coach came in this morning to tell him he had to cancel his classes for today because of a family emergency, and he wasn't sure if he'd be in the rest of the week."

Jia said, "Got a list of his known relatives. Sister in Arizona about three hundred miles away and an uncle in California."

"Call the police departments in whatever towns the sister and uncle live in and ask if they'll put a unit outside the homes. Tell them it's for a child abduction case. If they're resistant to help and don't seem too inquisitive, tell them you're FBI."

"Local cops hate the feds," Will said.

"That's a myth they portray on crime shows. Every cop wants to join the FBI, so they're willing to go out of their way to help them and get brownie points."

"On it."

As Jia and Will left, I yelled, "And make sure to get them a photo of Roscoe and Lyle."

When I was alone again, I began bouncing the ball. I received a text from Gates.

No??? was all it said.

Yes

That lying scumbag. I'll string him up myself

What's the point? Let's just find the kid

I'm sorry I told you he could be trusted

Don't worry about it. You didn't know

I rose and tucked the phone into my pocket. All I could do now was wait for the cops to do their jobs and snag him somewhere along the way to his sister's or uncle's place and for Will to get a warrant to search his home.

I decided I couldn't just wait in the office for the police to call me, so I went to Adam's house.

I knocked and opened the door. No one inside. I went up to the bedroom, and Adam was fast asleep. No pills or booze around, so hopefully it was just a nap and he wasn't blacked out.

As I went down the stairs, I stretched my neck from side to side. Tension had built itself up in me and came out of my head in intense, throbbing headaches. No migraines yet, but I was sure they weren't far away.

I searched the medicine cabinets in the bathroom and didn't see any ibuprofen. I went into my dad's office and glanced around. I remembered he used to keep medicine he used only for himself in his desk.

One of the lower drawers was locked—Adam never locked anything. I looked around the room for keys. Back upstairs, I wriggled his keys out of the pocket of his pants, which were lying on the back of a chair, and went downstairs.

I tried each key in the lock. The sixth or seventh one finally worked, and the drawer popped open.

Inside were letters and a couple of medals from his days in the army. A bottle of ibuprofen was tucked in the back. I grabbed it and was about to close the drawer when the name on one of the letters caught my eye. It was addressed to my father in my mother's handwriting.

I flipped through the letters. At least five of them were from my mother, though the return address wasn't anywhere I recognized. I took out my phone and googled the address. It was the state hospital in Saint George.

I read a couple of them. They were mostly my mother telling my father about her day, though I couldn't remember a time when my mother had been away long enough to write him. I looked at the dates . . . I would've been nine, a year before she died in the car accident.

The third letter made my heart stop. It read:

> *People here are treating me well. They look at me different. I guess being in a place like this people just think you're crazy, but they're kind. I met another woman in here who tried to take her own life, too. We've been talking a lot about it, and it helps. I'm hoping I will be out of here soon. Please, please, please don't tell Tatum about*

any of this. You know how he worries about me. Just tell
him I'm visiting my mother and will be home soon. And
hug him and tell him his mother loves him very much.

I skimmed through the remaining letters from my mother, my heartbeat starting to thump in my ears. More descriptions about her days and how the people in the hospital were treating her. Then I turned to the letters at the bottom of the stack.

Three letters, all from women, all written to my father. Several of them mentioned weekends together and how they felt about him. One thanked him for the trip to Mexico and hoped she would get to see him again soon.

I took out the drawer and dumped the contents onto the floor. Tons of papers, bills, receipts. One particular envelope looked old and worn. I picked it up. All it said on the front was "To Adam."

Inside was a single sheet of paper containing my mother's handwriting:

Dear Adam,

I'm so sorry. I don't know what to say. I know there're no
words that will comfort you. The pain you will feel can't
be fixed. I don't know what else to do. I feel like I'm on
an airplane that's crashing, and I can either jump out
or crash with it, but the ending will be the same. You're
going to blame yourself because of the other women, and
I blamed you for a long time, too. But in the end I don't
think that was it. I think this is how it was always sup-
posed to end.

I don't know what you should tell Tatum. He's my
heart. I wish I could get him to understand that he was
the only reason I stayed as long as I did. Don't tell him
about this. Tell him something else. I don't know what.

But I don't want him to feel this. To think his mom didn't love him enough to stay. He won't understand it now. Maybe when he's older, you can tell him the truth.

I'm not going to do it in the house, I don't want you to have that memory there. I'll call the ambulance first and tell them where I'm going to be so you can have a funeral, if it helps. If it doesn't, please just save the money and have me cremated.

Goodbye, Adam. I hope you find whatever it is you're looking for.

Marilyn Rose

I threw the letters as hard as I could at Adam's face. He groaned and rolled over and looked at me, his eyes bloodshot.

"What the hell do you want?" he said, still groggy.

"You disgusting bastard."

"What?"

"I read these damn letters, Adam. How many were there? Huh? I counted three women here, but there's no way that was it. Those are just the ones that wrote you."

"What the hell are you doin' goin' through my private things!"

"She . . ." My voice choked and I couldn't get the words out. I had to swallow and stared at him as his eyes lowered to the floor. He sat up in bed. "She killed herself, didn't she?"

He nodded slowly but wouldn't look at me.

"And you never told me?"

"What good would that have done?"

"What good? *What good?* You don't think I had the right to know my mother killed herself? You had me think it was a car accident!"

"What's the difference? Other than it causing you pain you didn't need. I was protecting you. She was protecting you."

"She killed herself because she loved you and was loyal and you were out nailing anything that moved."

"Hey, watch your mouth."

"I mean, Mexico? You took one of your women to Mexico? For my entire childhood I don't remember you taking Mom and me out to dinner, and you took someone to Mexico?" I got close to him. "How many, Adam? How many women?"

"That's none of your business. I was a vibrant, healthy man. I had needs."

"Needs? What about her needs? What about the needs of the woman that cooked for you, and cleaned for you, and took care of you when you were sick, or when you'd get home so drunk you could barely stand? What about her needs?"

"You don't know what it's like to be married to a woman like her. She was depressed all the time. Cryin' all the time. Most days she couldn't get outa bed except to see you to school. She was living for you, not for me. You didn't see that side of her, she hid that from you."

"She wasn't supposed to be living for either of us. She should've had her own life."

"She didn't want anything. All she wanted was to take her medications and lie in bed and die. That's what it was like being married to her. You wanna get real? Your mother and I didn't have sex for eight years. Eight years! Can you go eight years without sex, Tatum?"

"Who gives a shit about sex! She was the love of your life."

He chuckled. "Boy, you really do live in a fantasy land, don't you? No one has a love of their life. That's why people are miserable. They think they're gonna find their soul mate, and they toss whatever good they do have waiting for one, and when one doesn't come, it leaves 'em empty."

"Thanks for your pontificating, Socrates. Now how about we discuss how you killed my mother."

He climbed out of bed, rage in his eyes. "I," he said slowly, "did everything I could for that woman. I worked my fingers to the bone to make sure she never had to work, I gave up trips and cars and everything I ever wanted to make sure we had enough money for her medications. For years I went without affection or intimacy because I wanted to stay loyal to her. But there's only so much a man can take. I was lonely."

"Everyone's lonely, Adam." I folded my arms. "Did you go after her? Did you even try to stop her?"

"Stop her? What the hell you talkin' about? I didn't even know until I got a call at work that they'd found her body."

"How . . ." The words choked me, and I had to stay silent a second before I could speak. "How did she do it?"

Adam rubbed his chin and looked down to the floor. "She, um . . . she went up to the Hallows with some pills. When they got there, she'd been dead awhile. There was nothing they could do."

My eyes grew wet, and it felt like my throat was closing up. I had to swallow to make sure I still could. "She . . . killed herself at the Hallows?" I said quietly.

He nodded and looked at me. "Yeah."

In a flash, the pain, as it sometimes did, turned to anger. And all that anger was directed at the man standing in front of me. The man whom I blamed, whether fairly or unfairly, for the death of my mother.

"How many women?"

"What does it matter?"

"How many? How many did she know about?"

"None of your damn business."

"How many?"

He tried to push past me, but I wouldn't let him. "How many did she know about?"

"Get outa my way."

"No! How many?"

"Get outa my way. I'm not going to ask again."

"No. How many!"

He reached back and slapped me across the face.

The room turned silent, even the sound of our breathing muted. We stared at each other, and I saw the rage in his eyes start to dissipate. I took a step back and then left the house.

70

I drove to a small park in the middle of town. I used to come here as a kid. My mom would bring me when Adam was at work. A golf course was nearby, and sometimes I'd gather a few golf balls and try to sell them back to the golfers. She'd let me take the money I'd earned and buy candy at the gas station.

I got a text from Will. All it said was Better get down to Roscoe's house.

I sighed and stared awhile longer at the ducks drifting lazily in the pond. What a life they had. Eating, sleeping, and lying around in the sun.

Give me ten minutes, I texted back.

———

When I arrived at Roscoe's house, two units from the sheriff's office were already there. Will was speaking to them outside. When he saw me, he came over.

"Talked to a neighbor that says he left in a real hurry and had his car packed to the brim." He looked up at the house. "Guess we know who the man was with Anderson that night. It explains why Lyle didn't identify Steven at the lineup. Poor kid was protecting his dad. Can't imagine that was easy for him to lie to everybody."

We walked inside the home. A one-story rambler. The furniture seemed untouched, but some of the cupboards in the kitchen were open along with a few drawers. It looked like someone had been searching for something. In the bedroom, clothes were everywhere. On the nightstand was a photo of Roscoe and Lyle holding the head of a buck that had been killed.

"There's something else," Will said. "There's a gun safe in the hall closet. It's empty."

"Great, the psycho's armed, too. Can anything else go wrong with this case? Would you like to arrest me as well and just put me out of my misery?"

"Hey, I'm just telling you what I found, boss. Take it easy."

I exhaled and sat down on the bed. "I know. It's not your fault. Look, there's nothing we can do here. Just keep one unit stationed outside in case he shows up."

"Should I modify the BOLO to armed and very dangerous?"

"Cops have itchy trigger fingers as it is. You do that, and Lyle might get caught in the cross fire. We need to get Roscoe when he's not paying attention." I rose and paced around the bedroom, kicking aside some clothes on the floor. "So if I was a murdering psychopath, where would I go and hide with my son?"

Will glanced into the closet. "Relatives are the best bet. Still checking out that sister and uncle."

"I agree, but it's also the most obvious bet. He might realize that and go somewhere less obvious."

"Mexico?"

"Maybe. Let border security know and send them down a photo. And shoot one up to the Canadian border, too, just in case."

"Cool. Anything else?"

"Yeah, I'll be at the bar if you need me."

———

I sat at a bar near Benson's and sipped a beer. Despite the early hour, there were a few people there, older men with dark circles under their eyes. One woman sat in a corner and drank by herself, absently staring out the window. The entire place reeked of mold and rot that wafted up from underneath the floorboards.

Adam would come here almost every night after work while I was growing up, and I couldn't imagine why.

Gates walked in and sat down at the bar next to me.

She looked at the bartender. "Diet Coke, please." She waited until she got her drink before turning to me and saying, "It's not your fault. We'll find him."

I shook my head, staring down at the white froth at the bottom of my glass. "That's not what I'm thinking about."

"What then?"

I inhaled deeply and looked at her. "My mother didn't die in a car accident."

She glanced away and couldn't look at me.

"Holy shit, you knew."

"Tatum—"

"You knew, didn't you?"

She kept staring down at the bar top. "I heard my father talking with Adam after it happened. Adam said he wasn't going to tell you, and my father said that was a bad idea. That you might hear it from someone at school if it got out, and then you wouldn't trust him again."

"Why didn't you tell me?"

"I didn't want it . . . I don't know. No one else was going to tell you, so I figured I shouldn't. It wasn't my place."

"Yeah, okay, when I'm nine, maybe. How about when I was seventeen? You didn't think that might be something I'd want to know?"

"I don't . . . no. No, I didn't think that'd be something you'd want to know. Why would you? What good would it have possibly done for you?"

"It was the truth."

She scoffed. "Look who's lecturing about the truth. And by the way, maybe I would've eventually told you if you hadn't run away while I was in a hospital bed, unsure if I was going to wake up again each time I fell asleep."

I stared at her a second and then threw a fifty on the bar.

"Tatum—"

"No, don't."

I left the bar and didn't look back.

71

I stopped at a pharmacy and picked up some antacids. I popped two of them and drank them down with a Sprite in my car. The parking lot was empty, and I sat and listened to an eighties station for a while. My Tesla needed a charge, and the nearest station was over thirty miles away, so I grabbed an energy drink and guzzled half before driving out there.

The station was at a Starbucks in a little town called Hurricane. I waited inside at one of the tables. My head was pounding again, and I stretched my neck from side to side. I wondered what Sarah was doing right now in South Beach. I wouldn't say I missed her—missed wasn't the right word—but there was some emotion that I couldn't quite explain.

I picked up the phone and dialed the first few numbers and then stopped and put the phone down. That wasn't my world anymore. Neither was this. I felt like I was drifting above the ground with nowhere to settle.

Once the car was charged, I headed back to River Falls. The trial was continued until the day after tomorrow, so I had about a day and a half to figure out how to best destroy Steven's testimony. We still had the ME, a blood expert, a forensic tech, Cecily, and another officer to go before we rested. And I'd be recalling Steven to dismantle what he'd caught me off guard with. There was still a chance. Assuming of course we could find Lyle. Without the kid, I didn't think we had enough to convict Anderson of anything.

Back at the office, I sat in the conference room. The office of the previous prosecutor had been cleared out, but it didn't have any windows and only two bright lights that looked like they belonged in a supermarket. I grabbed the tennis ball I had left on the table and bounced it against the wall.

Jia came in a while later and folded her arms but didn't say anything.

"More bad news? Did the ME disappear, too?"

"I . . . um . . . wanted to talk to you about something. I know it's not the right time, but I need to do it now." She sat down. "Something kinda fell in my lap."

"Don't say it."

"My friend referred me to a firm, and I did an interview a couple days ago. It's a big firm in Salt Lake. It's double the salary, and I'd be learning civil litigation as well as some criminal, which they said I could head up since they don't have anybody there specializing in it. It's a good opportunity."

"Civil litigation is two people yelling at each other about money for years until one of them caves or a jury decides who's a little more right than the other guy. Does that sound interesting to you? And we're in the middle of a freaking murder trial. I need you."

She nodded. "I know. But . . . they want me to start on Monday. Hit the ground running and all that. I'm sorry. I let Gates know, and I thought I should tell you in person." She rose. "I really enjoyed working with you. I hope you win this case. I really do."

I thought about trying to convince her, about berating her and saying she was abandoning Patty, that she was betraying her duty . . . whatever. But I didn't. Truth was, I was the one who probably put it into her head that she should be in a big city.

Just like that, she walked out, and I sat there with the ball in my hand. I tossed it hard against the wall, and it bounced back and hit me in the chest.

———

It wasn't long before I couldn't handle being in the office anymore. Everything seemed to be unraveling. I decided the best course of action would be to rent a dune buggy, go out into the desert like I used to do when I was sixteen, and ride in the sands until the world's problems melted away.

The ATV rental place wasn't far from the City and County Building, so I walked over. On the way there, I saw Pritcher standing outside Benson's with his two associates. He was wearing a tracksuit and sneakers.

"You raid *The Sopranos'* wardrobe, Russell?"

He chuckled, and his two associates said something about seeing him tonight and left.

"Quite the bombshell for your star witness to change his testimony last minute like that." He grinned. "I must admit your face was just priceless. I wish I could've taken a photo. It'd be nice to have that on the cover of the *Miami Herald.*"

"It ain't over till it's over."

He shrugged. "What's this I hear about your number two witness absconding? Do all of your players run off before the game even begins?"

I stepped close to him. "If I find out you had anything to do with that boy disappearing—"

"Please. This case should never have gotten this far. Don't blame me because your reach exceeded your grasp. Face it, Tatum, prosecution just isn't your thing. Leave it to the bureaucrats who don't care if they get a conviction or not. Losing all the time will eat at you until there's nothing left. Just a bit of friendly advice."

"Here's a bit of advice for you: if I find out you had anything, and I mean anything, to do with that kid taking off, I will personally make sure they take your bar license, and I'll prosecute you myself."

He smirked and tapped my shoulder. "You're just adorable when you're angry. Take care of yourself. We wouldn't want you having a heart attack before the verdict comes back, now would we?"

He started to walk away and then said, "Ever wonder what dogs taste like? Like spicy beef."

"What?"

"I heard you love dogs. I've eaten dog before. Got to butcher it myself before the meal. They taste like spicy beef. I'll have to take you to this little restaurant in Saigon so you can try some."

I watched him walk away and knew I was too angry to be rolling around in a dune buggy. I got a call from Will just then and I said, "Give me something."

"Officer up near Fremonton saw a blue sedan with a Chicago Bulls sticker on the back pulled over on the side of the highway. He's there now. I was going to head up and check it out before I called you."

"Will, I could kiss you. I'm heading up to Fremonton. Keep me updated."

"Hey, did you hear about Jia?"

"One emergency at a time. Meet me up there."

"You got it."

72

Fremonton was about twenty miles out of town. On the way up, I saw two Utah Highway Patrol cruisers pulled over on the side of the road with a blue sedan in front of them. The sedan was packed so tightly with clothes and knickknacks the back window was completely blocked out. Will was with the troopers.

"Found the car abandoned on the side of the road," one of them said. "Looks like they took off on foot."

I eyed the desert around us. Sand dunes for as far as I could see. "With a ten-year-old kid? Seems like that'd be a last resort."

Will was looking into the windows of the car. He opened the door and searched inside for a second. "No keys."

"Which means he probably planned on coming back. Someone might've picked them up here." I stared out in each direction and saw a dirt path leading up over a hill. "Where's that go?"

"Nowhere," the trooper said. "Nothing really out here. Some abandoned shacks against them mountains, I guess."

I looked to the car and walked over. Clothes, food, a computer and television, and several framed photos. Things someone would grab if they didn't plan on coming back.

"He left everything," I said.

"Maybe he saw one of the troopers?" Will said.

I thought a moment, then popped the hood of the car and went over to the engine. I took out the oil dipstick, undid the gas cap, and dipped it into the fuel tank. Only the very tip was wet.

"He ran outa gas." The only conceivable path that he could've taken was the dirt trail. "Hope you can hike in your loafers."

———

The troopers called for backup and one of them, a Trooper Smith, came with us, and we headed up the trail. Once we got over the hill, the sound of traffic faded, and there was nothing but a breeze blowing over loose sand.

An old farmhouse with a worn-out fence was up ahead about a quarter mile. It had an empty horse pen and a garage that looked like it was about to fall over.

"Why would he run up here?" Will asked. "He had to have known we'd search the place with his car right there."

"He probably planned on stashing Lyle up here since he'd know the BOLO call would be for a man and a kid. Then he'd hitchhike or walk for gas somewhere."

We stopped a couple hundred feet from the house. The windows were broken out, and the white paint had faded and chipped until there was almost none left. A welcome mat was visible in front of the door, covered in dirt and sand, the letters fading.

Trooper Smith said, "We should wait."

I glanced back at him. "We should. But I have no idea what he's going to do with that kid."

"I can't let you go in there. Sorry."

I nodded, watching the house. It looked like a strong gust of wind could blow it over. "Let's at least get a little closer while we wait."

We walked toward the house a bit more before we heard something inside. The door opened and Roscoe stood there, a Glock in his hand.

The trooper drew his sidearm, and I stepped in front of him, my arms out to show Roscoe I wasn't armed.

"Roscoe, everyone needs to relax. We are not here to hurt you."

"I didn't want this."

"I'm sure you didn't. No one does." I hesitated and bit my lip. "Where's Lyle, Roscoe? Is he all right?"

"Of course he is."

"Good. Why don't you send him out here with us so he doesn't get hurt? Then you and I can talk."

He mumbled something, the gun still pointed at the ground. If he raised it even a little, the trooper would likely push me out of the way and fire.

"I'm scared, Tatum."

"I know you are, pal. Listen, I'm not going to let anyone hurt you or Lyle." I turned to the trooper. "Put your sidearm away."

"Can't do that."

"Put your damn gun away, Trooper. Now!"

He eyed me and then lowered it but didn't put it back in the holster. I turned to Roscoe and said, "Can I come in?"

Will was about to say something, and I held up my hand for him to be quiet.

"Just you."

"Okay. I'm walking toward the house now. I'm unarmed, Roscoe."

I approached, my heart like a drum in my ears. I undid my jacket and took it off, dropping it on the ground to make sure he could see I wasn't armed. I kept my hands high as I approached. When I got to the door, he stepped to the side and let me in. He shut the door behind me. Some old furniture was inside, covered in dust and cobwebs.

"Where's Lyle?"

"He's safe. I would never hurt him. Hell, Tatum, what kind of person do you think I am?"

"The kind that kills young girls, apparently."

"Is that what you think? That ain't me. I would never hurt Patty."
He swallowed. "I loved her."

"You loved her?"

He nodded. "We'd been together a long time. I would see her
whenever I could. She said she loved me, too. That we would get married when she turned eighteen next year and run away together. She'd
been saving money for it, too. I was broken when she died. Couldn't
work, couldn't eat or sleep. You know how long it took me to be able
to get outa bed again?"

"Then why'd you run?"

"When you came to the school, I knew you'd find out, and I would
lose everything. I mean, forget prison, I'd be on the sex offender registry. I could never work as a teacher again, could never see Lyle again.
I'd have to live with them scumbags in the trailer parks outside'a town
'cause that's the only place there ain't no kids . . . I don't want that,
Tatum. I'd rather die right here."

"Easy, pal. No one's dying today." I took a deep breath and looked
around the house. Rusted nails thrust out from the floorboards, and
broken glass lay in front of all the windows. "Picked a helluva place for
Custer's Last Stand, didn't ya?"

He sat down in an old chair, staring at the floor. The gun hung
limply from his hand. "I ran outa gas. You believe that? You see in them
movies people on the run, and they never stop to get gas. Little things
are what always hurt ya in the end, ain't they?"

I nodded. "They sure are." I glanced at some stairs leading up. "Is
Lyle upstairs?"

He nodded.

"Anderson's eye, was that really his father?"

"I didn't lie about that. Nathan Ficco is a sick son of a bitch. I tried
to help Anderson out. If I hadn't . . . I don't know. Maybe what happened to Patty wouldn't have happened."

I stepped close to him. "Roscoe, give me the gun. The cops are on their way, and they're going to be looking to shoot. Don't die here. We can cut a deal. Maybe even keep you off the sex offender registry or do a reduced sentence or something. There's no need for you to die. Especially since you'd be leaving that kid upstairs without a father."

He nodded and laid the gun on the table next to him, his eyes wet with tears. I slowly made my way to the table and then picked up the gun. I let out a long breath and felt relief wash over me, my muscles like jelly.

"She didn't love you, Roscoe. She was just trying to provide for her family. I'm sorry, but that's what it was. You ruined your life for nothing." I glanced up the stairs. "Roscoe, moment of truth, was it you with Anderson up at the Hallows burying her body?"

He looked up at me and was about to speak when something flew through the open space where a window had been. It sizzled and smoked. A flash grenade.

"Get down!"

The grenade popped and filled the room with acrid smoke. The door burst open. Several officers in full SWAT gear surged in. They tackled Roscoe and flung me to the ground.

73

A SWAT van, several UHP cruisers, and two units from the sheriff's office waited below. They had cordoned off one lane of the highway, and I sat on the hood of a cruiser until I saw Lyle being led down. I hopped off the hood and went up to him.

"You okay, son?"

He nodded.

"We're gonna get you back to your mom, okay?" I looked to the officer and nodded. Behind him I saw Gates speaking with a news crew from the local station. She saw me, said a few more words, and then came over.

"You okay?"

"Sure. Nothin' like a giant's knee in your spine to perk you up in the afternoon. Better than coffee."

She grinned and wiped a bit of dirt from my face. "What the hell were you thinking going in there? You're not a cop."

"I wasn't thinking."

She sighed and looked around. "What a mess. All because one man couldn't keep it in his pants."

"Hey, the Trojan War was started because one man couldn't keep it in his pants." I looked over to the SWAT van where they were loading Roscoe.

"What now?" I said.

"Now I'm going to offer a deal to him, Anderson, and Steven, and whichever cracks first and tells me what happened doesn't get the death penalty. I'm sick of playing around. And we need to interview Lyle and see if he was covering for his dad being there the night of the murder. I have a feeling all three were involved in this."

"I'm not sure Roscoe was. I got the feeling he actually thought he was in love."

Will ran over. "Talked to Anderson's ex again like you asked."

"And?"

"He had motive," Will said. "When I asked Bebe about Coach Mallory, she admitted Anderson knew he and Patty were sleeping together, and that Patty wanted to stop. The coach flipped out, and Patty threatened to report him for statutory rape if he didn't leave her alone. Bebe said Coach Mallory started showing up everywhere, trying to hold Patty after class, catching her at the gym, standing outside her house in the middle of the night, stuff like that. Bebe said she didn't tell us or the cops because the coach is a nice guy, whatever that means, and she didn't want him to get into any trouble."

"So the mayor showed up in Vegas and made a scene at the bar, but Roscoe was probably the stalker Diana told us Patty was scared of."

"Jilted lover takes revenge," Gates said.

"You could be right," I said, "but I don't see him torturing and killing her. For starters, there's the blood in Anderson's basement. Roscoe couldn't have tortured someone in his own place without the neighbors hearing."

"Anderson and Roscoe are the best bets, with Steven covering for them. Steven played football for four years under Roscoe, and so did Anderson. All his players would do anything for him," Gates said. "He killed Patty and got Anderson to help, and they got Steven to cover for them."

"Maybe. We'll know soon enough. Will, get Roscoe down to the station. I'll meet you there. Make sure Howard doesn't get anywhere near him and screw this up. I want first crack at him. And tell Nikyee I'm coming by tonight to talk to Lyle again."

Gates waited until Will had left before she said, "People aren't going to be happy that we're amending our case and going after the local football coach taking the team to the state championships."

"I'll talk to the press once we know for sure who did what. I'll take the hits, not you. It'll be fine."

She nodded and glanced over at Lyle as his mother pulled up and he ran to her. "About your mom," Gates said, "I shouldn't have—"

My phone rang. It was Pritcher. "Hold that thought." I answered and said, "Yeah, Russell, what is it?"

"Congrats on your bust."

I looked over to a few of the troopers gathered around the SWAT van. We hadn't been here more than two hours, and Pritcher had already gotten word.

"Yeah, I'm sure you're thrilled."

"I assume the charges against my client will be dropped."

"Gotta hammer out a few things first."

"Good. Oh, I should tell you, a friend of mine from New York will be defending Mr. Mallory. He's on his way to the airport right now and asked that I inform you. He of course sent an email to your office and the sheriff's department informing them that Mr. Mallory is represented, and I'm recording this conversation."

"What? Why would you get him a lawyer?"

"Who says I did? Take care, Tatum. And if charges aren't dropped against Anderson by tonight, I will be filing a motion to dismiss the case in the morning."

I hung up. There went the only shot I had at getting a confession from Roscoe.

So far it seemed like prosecution was little more than eating crap every day.

I got a call just then from a number I didn't recognize.

"Hello."

"Mr. Graham?"

"Yes."

"This is Kate Bailey, I'm a nurse over here at Saint Mark's."

My heart dropped. "Yes?"

"You should probably get down here, sir. Your father was just brought over in an ambulance."

74

I rushed down to the hospital. My father was in the intensive care unit. I headed up there, and they let me into his room. It stopped me cold.

His face was white as a sheet of paper. His hands lay limply by his side and some blood had crusted on his lips. He was unconscious, and they had already dressed him in a hospital gown. Dr. Langley came into the room and stood with me a second before he said, "He collapsed walking to his car. Luckily one of his neighbors saw and called 911. I don't know what would've happened if he hadn't come in when he did." He paused. "Mr. Graham, his lungs are filled with fluid and blood. The cancerous tissue is simply going to grow until he suffocates to death. We have to operate to save his life, so while he's unconscious and can't give consent—you're the next of kin."

"Do what you gotta do."

He nodded. "I'll have someone come in with some paperwork for you to sign."

I approached the bed. I couldn't take my eyes off my father. I pulled up a nearby chair and sat down. Once, my father had reminded me of a lion. Strong and healthy and aggressive. He looked like a withered leaf now, as though he could fall apart right there in the bed and a breeze would blow away the pieces. It hit me then that he was going to die, and I wondered why it had taken so long for it to dawn on me that this was real. Maybe I couldn't face death until it was right there in the room with me.

It made me think of my life. What would be left when my father was gone? I had no other family. In truth, despite everything, it was just me and him in the world. And I'd screwed it up, too, along with everything else. What the hell was I really even doing here? I had no place as a prosecutor. I had no place in River Falls. It had been a subconscious impulse to come back here, just because I didn't know anywhere else.

I slumped over and put my hand to my head. The headache was back, and I rubbed my temples. I looked at my father's pale face.

He had his watch on still, and I took it off his wrist and held it in my hand. My mother had bought him this watch and had me give it to him as a Father's Day gift. I played with it in my hands for a bit and then couldn't control myself anymore. I wanted to collapse into darkness and not crawl out again. To get away from everything and everyone and disappear.

I put my head on my father's chest, wrapped my arms around his body, and I wept.

75

I woke up in the chair across from my father. The soft hum of his monitor filled the room, followed by an occasional beep. He was awake now and staring at the ceiling, his eyes bloodshot, his lips cracking from how dry they were. I poured some water from the sink into a plastic cup and brought it over to him. He took a few sips, and I put it on the side table and pulled up the chair again.

"Dad?"

He looked to me, his eyes red and wet.

"They, um, they're going to need to get you into surgery as soon as possible. They need to drain your lungs and cut out as much of the cancerous tissue as they can. I've already signed the paperwork since you were unconscious. It's a done deal, so I don't want to hear anything about . . ."

His eyes closed again.

"Sorry. I, um, I'm going to be right here when you wake up."

His eyes opened again, slowly, and drifted over to me. "What about your case?" he said, his voice hoarse and slow.

"It's a mess. Someone else looks guilty now, and whether they did it or not, whether they colluded or not, I'll probably have to drop the charges against the kid I thought it was. I'm going to hand it to Gates and quit." I looked out the window and could see the sun speckling the bark of a tree through the leaves. "I shouldn't have come back here.

I don't know what I was thinking. I'm going back to Miami. It's where I belong."

He swallowed. "Do you know the myth of Sisyphus?"

"What?"

"Sisyphus. The Greek tragedy."

"I've heard it, once or twice."

He swallowed and had to take a breath. "My father told it to me once. He said Sisyphus died but came back to earth for revenge. He was supposed to return to hell but realized, only after he was already dead, how beautiful the trees were, or wading into a cool stream, or the birds and the sunlight on his face. So he refused to return, and the gods punished him. For eternity, he would have to push a rock up a hill, and it would keep tumblin' back down. He would never be able to get to his goal."

He had to swallow again, and I got some more water for him. He took a few sips.

"I thought Sisyphus must be miserable, but my father said no, he was happy because he decided to be. He decided that the one thing the gods couldn't take from him was his choice to be happy. It's like that for us. We try to find happiness out there, and we just end up suffering for it." He took my hand. His skin was clammy and his fingers trembled. "You have to choose your own happiness, Tatum. I had the chance with your mother, but I went outside our marriage and looked for happiness there, and you know what I found? Nothing. Nothing is ever as good as you think it's gonna be, and nothing is ever as bad as you think it's gonna be. Don't make the mistake I made."

"Excuse me," the doctor said from the doorway. "We're ready."

I nodded and stood up. I bent down and kissed Adam's forehead. He squeezed my hand the best he could, and I left while they prepped him for surgery.

76

I was in the waiting room sipping a Diet Coke and popping ibuprofen when Gates came in. She was in sweats and sat down next to me. She took my soda and pulled a long drink before giving it back.

"Don't you have some voter thing?" I said.

"Town hall. I cancelled it."

"You can't do that. The election's next month."

"Elections aren't everything."

"Gates, go to the town hall."

"You sure like to tell other people what to do, don't you?"

"It's a gift."

She leaned her head on my shoulder. "I haven't eaten all day. You wanna grab something while we wait?"

———

We sat in a booth at the hospital cafeteria, and I stared out over the road as cars drove by. Gates ordered for us. My cell phone was off, so I put it on the table. She turned it on and flipped through it, taking a picture of herself and making it the screen saver before handing it back to me.

"Really?" I said.

"You're too arrogant to ask."

I grinned. "I am." I turned the phone over in my hands. "You know I almost came back that first week I was in Miami."

"Really? Cold feet?"

I shook my head. "No. I loved it. The sunshine and orange trees, the beach, the restaurants, the art museums, all of it." I hesitated. "I wanted to come back because there was someone here that I felt I shouldn't have left behind. Someone that I saw hurt, and it cut me so deeply I didn't know what else to do but run."

She lowered her eyes to the table. "That person probably would've liked to have been invited."

"Would that person have come with me?"

She shrugged. "Who knows? She was young and adventurous then. Anything's possible to the young."

I exhaled loudly and leaned back in the seat. "Life's a helluva trip, ain't it? It takes years to look back and realize you should've gone left when you went right."

"Maybe. Or maybe there's only one road, and it takes you where it takes you."

"Funny you say that. You know what my dad told me just now? That we make our own happiness in life." I grinned. "He said his father told him the myth of Sisyphus. Don't know where the hell my grandpa would've learned that because the only thing I remember about him is that he preferred horses to cars and dropped out of school in the third grade."

"Don't knock cowboy wisdom. Those guys worked from sunup to sundown, hard lives, and you learn a lot about yourself when you have to do that."

I hesitated. "I think I might be done, Gates. With the case and with the job. I never should've taken it, and I'm sorry."

Gates took a swallow of juice before putting the glass down and staring into it. "You know why I hired you? I didn't have to, you know.

I've dealt with a few murders myself and could've handled this, no problem."

"Why?"

"For you."

"What'dya mean, for me?"

"You needed this. I felt like you had a hole inside you when I saw you that first time. You looked like a lost little boy." She grinned. "It was the same look you used to have when we were kids and you'd get us lost in the forest but pretend to know where you were going because you thought I would get scared." She reached out and lightly touched my hand. "You need this. For whatever reason. And I'm not saying it's trivial; it's just your personal reason that no one else will understand. But you need to finish this. If you don't, I think you will regret it the rest of your life."

77

It was the next morning before Dr. Langley came out and sat down with us. He exhaled and said, "The surgery went well. He had several tumors the size of dimes in his right lung, and we excised all of them. After we drained his lungs, he was able to breathe on his own quickly. He's very strong. He's resting in post-op right now, but you should be able to see him, probably, later today."

I nodded. "Thanks, Doctor."

He rose and said, "He told me to tell you something before he went under, in case he didn't make it. He said to tell you he's glad you came back."

I finally forced Gates to leave and do what she had to do. I didn't want her sitting idly by with me all day.

Evening came quickly, and I didn't even remember the day passing. I sat in the hospital waiting room, staring at the lighting in the parking lot from a window in front of me. A nurse came out and told me my dad was still sleeping after the surgery and that it might be best to come back in the morning.

I left the hospital and wasn't sure where to go. I sat in my car awhile with the windows rolled down and thought about what Gates had said. I exhaled, started the car, and headed to the police station.

It was quiet when I got there. The female officer at the front nodded to me and said, "How are you, Mr. Graham?"

"Hangin' in there. Hey, need to review a file from last year for a case. Would that be possible?"

"For a deputy county attorney? Of course."

She led me to the basement, where Gates and I had been before. Except now I wasn't looking for a juvenile case for Anderson; now I was looking for the DUI that had disappeared into a black hole.

"Happy hunting," she said as she headed back up the stairs. "Lemme know if you need to check out anything."

"Thanks."

I scanned the files, slowly running my fingers over the names as I made my way down. Nothing about a DUI received by Anderson was here; I knew Jia would have found it if it were.

If an officer wanted a case to disappear, it wasn't hard. But the one thing an officer couldn't get rid of as easily was evidence that the traffic stop had occurred. They had to call in to dispatch that they were pulling someone over. There might not be a police report, a booking sheet, or an inventory of the car, but there had to be a dispatch log letting the station know the officer had pulled someone over and why.

If Roscoe were telling the truth about Nathan Ficco injuring Anderson's eye, and I did find a DUI stop that was never filed, then that meant whoever had pulled him over had buried the file. And whoever that was probably also had buried the stalking injunction that Patty tried to take out against Steven, and who knows what else, to protect Anderson Ficco. Someone may very well have been sabotaging this case from the beginning.

Toward the end of the row were the miscellaneous files. If an officer pulled someone over, there'd be a recording and then a transcript made and filed by the dispatcher. If an officer wanted a case to go away without it leading back to them, the officer would just not send it in to the prosecutor's office and instead would funnel it here to be destroyed. And they couldn't take the file themselves, because when the staff went through the files to destroy them and it wasn't there, it would raise too many questions. Better to leave it here and wait until the end of the year when most departments cleaned out their archives.

I caught a lucky break since they were filed alphabetically; otherwise I'd be here all night.

I found a file with the name ANDERSON B. FICCO. It was dated ten months ago. I pulled it out, and it consisted of nothing but a dispatch log stating the officer had pulled Anderson over and then concluded there wasn't enough evidence of driving under the influence and let him go. My eyes scanned up at the top of the sheet for the officer's name . . . DETECTIVE MARK HOWARD.

It wasn't entirely unusual for a detective to pull DUI duty in a small town like this with few police officers, but that this particular detective happened to pull over the son of the richest guy in town, who was now being charged with murder, set off alarm bells.

I took the file and hurried back upstairs. There was one more file I needed to see.

———

Jia opened the door after a couple of knocks. She was in workout clothes, and I could hear music.

"Tatum? What are you doing here?"

I lifted the file. "Take a look at this."

She opened it as I stepped inside. Her house was large, far larger than a single adult needed, and barely decorated. The TV and the couch were really the only luxuries.

"Howard?"

"He's our puzzle piece," I said. "Howard busted Anderson for a DUI and buried the case. Which means Roscoe was telling the truth, and it wasn't him but Nathan Ficco that jacked up Anderson after he found out about the DUI. And I think the botched murder investigation was purposeful. I went back to Howard's personnel files: he was with Atlanta PD for seven years before moving out to Utah, Robbery-Homicide for two of those years. No way a detective with his experience would bungle a homicide this bad, and it had nothing to do with him trying to be sensitive to Hank or his niece knowing Patty. Howard sold himself out to Nathan Ficco on the DUI, and I bet he did it again on the murder. Nathan Ficco cleaned up after his son just like he did for his rape case when he was a teenager. But I need something before I can prove any of that: I need to show Howard got some sort of compensation for this."

She closed the file. "You want his bank records."

"Yes. And I happen to know a young woman who can get me things faster than anyone I've ever had work for me."

"Tatum—"

"Hear me out: You can work for a big firm anytime. Anytime. With your brains and your experience here, if that's what you really want, you can do it whenever. But someone told me today that I needed this case, and that if I abandoned it, I'd regret it the rest of my life. I have a feeling you need it, too. That you're going to be sitting in a crappy little office going over your one thousandth lease termination and wondering what would have happened if you'd stuck it out and seen this case through. Don't live with regrets." I folded my arms. "Trust me, I know."

She sighed and said, "How long do I have?"

"I already got Judge Allred to give us one more day before resuming the trial."

"All right. Give me until noon tomorrow, and I'll find something."

78

That night I slept at the hospital. The chairs were uncomfortable, and I woke up at least three times with kinks in my back. The chairs had armrests, so I couldn't lie across them. Eventually I just lay down on the floor and tried to get a couple of hours' sleep.

In the morning, I asked the nurse if I could see Adam, and she said I could. I went up to his room, and another nurse was there, checking incisions and IVs. He lay with his head propped up and his eyes closed. He looked even paler than before, his lips blue, the veins in his face protruding. A thin sheen of sweat covered his skin. I sat down next to him and rubbed my lip with the back of my index finger.

"He sedated?" I said.

"Just a little nap. Should be about time to wake up, though."

I leaned forward and said, "Dad? Can you hear me?"

Nothing. I was about to go sit in the recliner in the corner when his hand opened. I took it, and we sat quietly for a few minutes while the nurse finished checking everything and then told me she'd be back in a little while.

I held his hand until his eyes opened. He took me in a moment, and then they shut again and he tried to speak, but no words came. I didn't know if he could have water, so I just waited until he said, "Am I dead?"

"Don't think so."

A small grin came to his lips. "Get me a drink, will ya?"

"I'll ask."

"Whiskey on the rocks."

"It'll probably be ice chips, but let me see."

I went out and checked with the nurse. She said he could have fluids and that they would bring something by. As I was heading back, Jia called me.

"Yeah."

"Down here at First Ute Bank. Guess what I got?"

"Those nasty lollipops that are always three months too old?"

"Better. Detective Howard's bank statements."

"I'm not even going to ask how you got a judge to sign off on a warrant for a decorated detective before ten in the morning."

"What can I say? Allred loves me. She made me some coffee in her chambers while she signed it for me."

"I'm sending her a fruit basket when this is over. So what do you got?"

"I'm taking photos and sending them to you now."

I waited a few minutes in the hall. The nurse came to my father's room with a tray that held ice, water, and juice. She set it on the nightstand. My phone buzzed and I opened the text messages.

Jia had sent me Howard's statements from last year up until now. I flipped to September, ten months ago. Normal transactions at first, and then toward the bottom, a deposit in cash of $5,000.

I skimmed the rest. Jia had circled a payment of $30,000 in cash deposited into the account three months ago, around the time of Patty's murder.

I called her.

"Either he won a lottery or there're payments from Anderson's father in here."

"Gotta be. I know how much he makes, and those two big deposits are like more than half a year's salary for him. And there's another cash deposit every month for a thousand. Never more than that, always a thousand."

"It's a retainer fee for his unique services."

"Ugh. And to think I thought he was cute."

"Corrupt cops can be cute, too."

"So what now?"

"Now I'm going to go have a little talk with the fine detective."

"I'm coming with."

I glanced at my father, who still had his eyes closed. "No. I need you to tear this guy's life apart. I want to know everything about him starting from the time he was born."

"Will can do all that. I'd rather be there when you confront Howard."

"I know, and you'll get your shot at him, but for now I need you guys to dig up anything else you can. And maybe put in a heads-up to the police department over in Hurricane that we may need a couple of their guys down here to make an arrest soon because of a conflict of interest. I'm not sure who we can trust out here to slap cuffs on one of their own."

"All right, I'll see you at the office, then." She hesitated. "Be careful."

"Hey, careful's my middle name."

———

Vail told me that Howard's shift didn't start until noon, so I managed to get his home address under the guise of needing to talk to him because he wasn't answering his phone.

Detective Howard lived in a large house surrounded by several acres of property. I had to drive up a dirt road to get there, and there were no other homes nearby. It was on the outskirts of town, in the space between River Falls and Glassdale, away from everything. He had a barn near the main house and a garage with several cars, including a Corvette and an expensive Dodge truck.

I took my phone out of my pocket and turned on the audio recording app, then slipped the phone into the breast pocket of my shirt. As I got out of the car, Will pulled up in his truck.

"Heard you could use a hand," he said, stepping out.

"I told Jia—"

"I know, but you gotta be nuts if you think we would've let you walk in there and confront Howard by yourself. He hates your guts. You need someone there to calm things down if they escalate."

Didn't sound like there was going to be much debate, so I said, "Just don't say anything. I need him to make admissions, and the slightest hint that we're looking into him could cause him to lawyer up."

"Lips shut, I think I can manage that."

We went to the front door and knocked. No one answered. We rang the doorbell. I tried the door, but it was locked. There was a window near the porch, and I looked around before taking off my jacket and wrapping it around my fist.

"What're you doing?" Will said.

"Baking a cake. What's it look like?"

"We don't have a warrant. We can't go in there."

"Will," I said, pointing to the door, "this guy helped Patty's killers. Sabotaged the investigation from the beginning. Lied to us constantly. And we're the only ones that know it and the only ones that would want to see him prosecuted. This is a huge embarrassment to the mayor and the sheriff. They're going to do everything they can to raise doubt that he had anything to do with it. If we don't stop him, he's going to get away with it, and do it again. We can't let him have a badge anymore."

He sighed and put his hands on his hips. "Fine, but you gotta wrap it tighter than that or you're gonna get cut."

I grinned as I wrapped it tighter and then approached the window. I cocked my fist and shattered the glass. Moving aside some of the broken pieces with my jacket, I unlatched the window and lifted it, making sure to check that there wasn't a sensor indicating an alarm.

Inside was warm and had a stale, rotting stench. Like no one had opened any windows for years. I went to unlock the front door and thought it might be best not to get Will involved in this, so I left it locked.

"Hey, Will, wait out there for me. If I'm not out in ten minutes, call it in. Do not come in here yourself."

"Aw, man, I don't need protecting."

"Yes you do. I don't care if I get disbarred, but I do care if you do. Ten minutes."

"Fine. Ten minutes."

The house was cluttered and messy. In the corner were stacks of boxes filled with everything from bills and papers to clothes and dishes. Howard was a hoarder. The kitchen wasn't much different, with overflowing boxes stacked against the wall. The sink was full of dirty dishes and the kitchen smelled like rotting food. On the table was a half-finished breakfast.

I wandered around the living room and entered the bedroom. The bedroom was where it all was. Anything that had ever happened to anyone, good or bad, came out in the actions in here.

I checked the dresser drawers and didn't find anything and then tried the closet. It was a mess, with shoes piled on top of old dirty clothes, piled on top of blankets and pillows, but I saw nothing out of the ordinary.

The bed was large. I got down and checked underneath it. There was a box about the size of a suitcase. I pulled it out. The box looked like it had been homemade from some pinewood. It had a little lock on it. I took it out into the kitchen and put it on the table. Then I searched the rest of the house for tools. In the garage, which was attached to the kitchen, I found a toolbox. I got a thick screwdriver and a hammer, then slipped the screwdriver behind the lock and hammered the top with one careful shot after another. Eventually, the lock snapped and I opened the box.

79

Inside the box, the first thing I noticed were the porno mags. At least ten of them. And not *Playboy* or *Penthouse*. Things like *Torture Chamber* and *Taboo XXX*. Some of the most violent BDSM I'd seen. A few of them looked foreign, and the women in them didn't appear to be faking the pain.

I took the magazines out and searched the rest of the box.

There was a handgun with the serial number filed off. I carefully took it out and placed it on the table. Some medals from the military were in a glass casing, as was an award for valor. A couple of recognitions from the sheriff's office and an old worn photo of a mother with a small boy. Howard. The mother looked straight ahead, no expression on her face, her hands carefully placed on the small boy's shoulders. Howard had a steely expression on his face, no smile, and I could see the burn scars on his arms and neck, the ones he had told me he had gotten in Iraq, and I knew, somehow, that it had been his mother who had given them to him.

At the bottom of the box was a large manila envelope. I took it out and unclasped it. Inside were printed photos of a woman on glossy photographic paper, the woman bound and bloody. But not like in the pornography. These photos were gritty and had bad lighting: taken personally by an amateur.

When it hit me who the woman was, it felt like I'd been punched in the chest. I couldn't breathe. I threw the envelope down and rushed out of the house.

80

I pushed open the door and Will stood there.

"It's Howard," I said. "He has photos of Patty in there being tortured."

"You're kidding."

I shook my head and glanced around the property. "We need to find him."

"You think he killed Patty?"

"I'd bet my life on it. You should see what else I found in his house." I paused. "If Lyle saw two men there, the other man was Howard. I wouldn't be surprised if Howard invented a car theft so he had an excuse not to be at the lineup."

"So that would mean Lyle's the only person that could identify him, right? I mean, he's known about Lyle for a while, but what if Howard thinks we're getting close?"

"Then Lyle would have to go." I put on my sunglasses. "I'm going to head down there and check up on them. Get a unit there just in case, would ya?"

"Sure thing."

I drove down to Nikyee's home.

I knocked and no one answered. Looking inside the windows, I didn't see movement, and when I called Nikyee's cell, no one picked up.

"Come on, answer. Answer answer answer answer."

I went around back to see if there was another way in. A back window, which connected to a bedroom, was unlocked. I pulled off the fly screen and crawled inside.

The house was quiet. I went into the living room and shouted, "Nikyee, are you here? Lyle?"

I waited a few seconds but didn't hear anything. I went into the kitchen. Didn't look like anyone was home. I would have to wait here until they came back so I could get them somewhere safe. I glanced at the dining table and saw some food, two plates of spaghetti. One of the forks had fallen on the floor and sauce had spattered over the wall.

I felt something just then—a small prickling on my neck—and knew I wasn't alone.

I turned. "Where are they, Mark?"

He didn't have shoes on, only socks. He held a black .45 and had a grin on his face as he leaned against the kitchen counter and stared at me.

"Are they dead already?" I said.

He tilted his head to the side, mocking me.

"Talk to me. I'm here. Where are they? I can help you get outa this."

"Yeah? You can help me, huh? How are you gonna help me? You gonna give me life in prison instead of the needle? Doesn't seem like much help."

I swallowed and glanced at the door behind him, wondering if I could make it out of there before he got any rounds off. "How much did he pay you to do it? How much did Nathan pay you to kill an innocent girl?"

"*Pfff*, there wasn't anything innocent about her. We ain't worse the wear with her gone, you ask me."

"Was it just the thirty thousand? That's all you got for killing someone?"

He shrugged. "Ficco promised me another thirty after his son was acquitted." He made a clicking noise against his teeth with his tongue. "See, then it looked like I wouldn't get my money. Deal was Anderson wasn't going to get anywhere near convicted, but damn if I never saw that little boy out in the woods that day. You got me with that, Counselor. You really did. I just about shit my pants when I found out someone saw us up there." He chuckled. "Man, that lawyer pulled a number, though, didn't he? Convincing Steven to get up there and lie. That dipshit didn't have anything to do with this. I was just gonna make sure he got convicted for it."

I nodded. "I figured it was just you and Anderson. I'm guessing Anderson didn't have it in him to kill her."

He shook his head. "Nah, his dad's right about him. No balls."

"And, um, wild guess, you didn't grow up in Florida and don't have a sister I screwed over."

He chuckled. "No, man. But you had to think I had a reason to not help you. Worked nicely, yeah? Only problem was the photo Pritcher showed the jury of my niece. It was just some picture I found in Patty's room when I went there pretending to look into the case." He chuckled. "I was scared it could've been the daughter of someone on the jury. That would've put an end to our case real quick, wouldn't it? But I tell you what," he said, laughing, "I sent that lawyer every dirty thing about me, and then when I lied about it up there and he caught me, your face, aw, man, your face . . . I just about made my tongue bleed biting it so I wouldn't burst out laughing."

I tried to take a step closer to him, and he lifted the gun and said, "Only if you want a hole in your head."

I held up my hands. "Easy. We can still work this out."

"Bit too late for that." He sighed and rubbed the side of his head with the gun. "Don't know what to do with you, though. There're gonna be a lot of questions, ain't there? Don't suppose you haven't told anyone yet about our little secret?"

I didn't say anything.

"Thought so."

"I've known a lot of men like you. You're gonna kill me no matter what I do, so we might as well get it over with."

"Men like me?"

"I found your toy box with Patty's pictures."

He was silent. "You were in my house?" he said calmly.

"Bet you just couldn't believe your luck, huh? Here you are masturbating your whole life to this stuff, and this opportunity just falls right into your lap. And, man, I bet Nathan was crazy pissed, wasn't he? He pays you to take care of her quickly and quietly and instead you keep her for two days and mess everything up for him. And on top of that, like a genius, you took photos and kept them at your house. Skipped the lecture at the academy on what constitutes damning evidence, did we, Detective?" I had to delay until the cops got here, without pushing him so far that he decided to pull that trigger. "It was your mom, wasn't it? Those scars you told me were from Iraq."

I saw the muscles in his jaw flex from biting down.

He ran his tongue over his lip. "You know, I was just going to pop you, but now that you've been in my house and violated me sideways, I think I'm going to take my time."

"Fine, but I have to know: why did Nathan want her dead?"

"Why do you think?"

"I'm guessing he was cleaning up another of Anderson's messes."

"You are sharp, Counselor. I'll give you that." He looked down to the gun. "Can you imagine having a son like that? Dumber than a box of hair. Anderson had a thing for Patty, but she didn't give him the time of day. Wasn't interested in him at all. So they're driving home from Skid Row and fighting about it, Anderson high as shit and pissed because she's been paying attention to Steven, and during the fight she tells him she slept with his daddy." He chuckled. "Imagine what that felt like for him? Can't hook up with the girl of his dreams, but his fifty-nine-year-old daddy did. So the dumb shit grabbed a hammer and hit her with it. Cracked her good, too."

"And then they drove to the townhome, where, I'm guessing, he called Daddy, and Daddy called you."

He nodded. "Called Nathan crying like a little girl, saying he was going to prison. So I go down, and she's still alive. Can't even kill someone right."

I shook my head. "And you saw your chance for some fun and told him to take off and you'd take care of it."

"Always fantasized about something like that. Having another person as just . . . your toy. And then when I was done, I called Anderson to get his skinny ass over and help me, and we took her up to the Hallows. But too many people saw them together that night he hit her, so we couldn't just hope no one would go looking for her. We had to have an arrest and an acquittal. Double jeopardy so they couldn't get arrested for it again if someone found something or one of the dumb shits told somebody about it." He was lost in thought a moment. "I killed before, but never like that. Never up close where you could see their face. I can see how certain people would find that addicting."

"She was just a kid, Mark."

"A kid don't whore themselves."

"She thought she was helping her family, and she might've pulled herself out of that life if you hadn't killed her."

He shrugged. "It wasn't my call, honestly. I went over there to bury a body, but when I saw she was alive I called Nathan, and you know what he said? He said, 'Just kill the bitch and I'll pay you more.'" He chuckled. "He is one coldhearted bastard."

I had to keep him talking as long as I could. "It's the wealth."

"How you figure?"

"There was a man in ancient Rome—a rich man, friend of the emperor—named Pollio. A slave dropped a glass container at a party once, and Pollio threw him into a pool filled with eels that ate him alive. Pollio was a man who lived in a world where he didn't expect glass to break. That's what causes uncontrollable anger: unreasonable expectation. And no one has more expectations about how the world works than the rich, and when it doesn't work that way, they lose it." I hesitated, comprehending just then that I had never applied that to myself. "Trust me, I've seen both sides."

He stared at me a moment. "Yeah? How much money you got anyway?"

"A lot," I said, trying to keep my voice calm as I realized how I was going to get out of this. "Enough so you'd never have to work again in your life. So I'll tell you what: my life in exchange for my money. All of it. You can have it. I don't care."

"Yeah, I take your money, and you put out an international warrant for me. Money ain't no good if I gotta hide in barns and holes in the ground to stay outa the pen."

"Gentlemen's agreement, then. I'll give you, say, a million dollars, and we'll keep that part between us. In exchange," I said, chuckling nervously, "you don't kill me, of course, and you agree to testify against Nathan. I'll give you full immunity."

"There's no way Gates is gonna let you give me immunity."

"She trusts me on this." I lowered my hands. "So what's it gonna be? Immunity and a million bucks in exchange for my life and testifying against Nathan, or killing me and living life on the run?"

He tapped the gun against his leg. "I want the money now. Right now. And I want an immunity agreement drafted and signed by you and Gates before I do anything."

"No problem. I'm going to reach into my pocket and take out my phone, okay?"

"For what?"

"I need to transfer the money to a local bank. I'll get a money order made out to you. And by the way, this time, don't use your own bank when you go deposit it, huh?"

He nodded and lifted his weapon. "Do it."

I quickly googled the number to my bank in Miami. I showed him the phone so he saw the number, and I put it on speakerphone.

"Miami First National, this is Karen speaking. How may I help you?"

"Hi, Karen, I need to make a transfer out of state, please."

Howard lowered the gun. The second he did, I dropped the phone and grabbed the chair from the dining room table. I swung it as hard as I could into his head. The chair shattered against him, raining splinters over me. Howard flew off his feet and hit the counter. I sprinted for the door.

I was outside when the first shot went off. I ran around the house. There wasn't time to get to my car, so I dashed for the barn and went through the open doors as a round went into the wall of the barn.

The barn was two stories, filled with tools and hay. A ladder went up to the second floor, and I quickly climbed up as I heard his feet on gravel behind me. I looked around the second floor for any weapons, and the only thing I saw was a pitchfork. I grabbed it and ducked behind a bale of hay near the ladder.

"Counselor," he said. "Get your ass down here and I'll make it quick."

I lifted my head a little over the hay and saw him looking to the ladder on the other side of the barn, blood running down onto his neck from the large gash on the side of his head. He went over to the ladder and looked up at the second floor, then lifted his weapon and started to fire randomly through the wood.

"Counselor, I got all day, ya know. And I got plenty'a clips. I'ma hit you eventually. Just come down now and save us a day, would ya?"

Carefully, he began climbing the ladder. It was only a matter of time before he made his way over here, and I certainly was not bringing a pitchfork to a gunfight. I slowly put it down and started to crawl toward the ladder.

"You know what? I don't feel like chasin' you around. I think I'm going to Gates's house."

I froze.

"I've seen the way she looks at you. And I bet you're just stupid enough to actually care for a bitch, ain't ya? How 'bout I go over there and cut her tits off? What do you think, Counselor? You think she'd like that?"

He looked around and then headed back to the ladder to climb down.

"Wait." I rose, my hands in the air. "Wait, I'm coming down."

If I had to die, I had to die, but that was the one person in the world I wasn't going to let die with me. I climbed down the ladder as he did the same. He came up close and pressed the muzzle of the gun against my head. I closed my eyes and held my breath.

"Here's the deal. I want that million bucks."

I opened my eyes. "No way you let me live."

"No, no way. But . . . I give you my word I leave Gates alone after I get that money."

"No offense, but your word ain't exactly the most reliable."

"Yeah, but what choice you got?"

I swallowed. "Good point."

He reached with his free hand for his cuffs, and that's when I slapped the .45 away. I tackled him as it went off, the crackle of the gun deafening me. We hit the ground, and he elbowed me in the face, cracking my nose. I lifted myself off him and swung down with blow after blow, but it didn't seem to hurt him. I cracked him in the teeth, knocking one loose. Blood oozed from his mouth, and he laughed.

He flung me off him like a doll and rose to his feet. I lay out of breath, my knuckles bleeding, on the dirt floor.

"Forget this bullshit," he said. "You're too much trouble."

He lifted the gun.

81

I looked into that gun and thought of Gates. Of the life I should've had. Most of my life had been spent acting like someone else. They say that depression is your mask, telling you that you're tired of the role you've been putting on for everyone else. My mask had had enough and was just tired. I closed my eyes and pictured Gates the night we rode under the moonlight on her ranch, the smell of grass in my nostrils.

"Mark!"

I opened my eyes and saw Will enter the barn with two officers. The cops had their guns drawn. One officer stepped forward and said, "Mark, put your weapon down."

Howard grimaced. "Shit, Jim, this here's the killer. This son of a bitch killed Patty Winchester. When I found out, he came after me, man."

"If that's true, we'll work it out. But for now I need you to put your weapon down."

"It's *him*, Jimmy. He's right here, and you're gonna let him go?"

"Mark," he said, coming within a few feet of Howard, "please put the weapon down. I don't want to fire, but I will if you don't give me a choice."

Howard chuckled and lowered the weapon to his side. He looked at me and said, "What'd I tell ya, Counselor? You can't rely on nobody."

He lifted the gun to his head, the muzzle pressed against his temple. I jumped up. "No!"

Howard pulled the trigger. Warm blood hit my face as his body tumbled over. The officer he'd called Jim stood in shock for a few moments before he put his gun away and checked Howard's pulse. There was no need. A hole the size of a tennis ball had blossomed on the right side of his skull. His dark black blood was mixing with the dirt and making a thick mud.

Will ran up to me. "You okay?"

"We need to find Lyle," I said, brushing past him to get out.

"Hey, wait a second. Tatum, stop. Tatum!"

I turned around.

"We found them. They were in the basement. They're both okay. You saved them, man. You came in right before Howard did anything. They're okay."

I nodded. Will put his hand on my shoulder and said, "Let's sit down."

"Better idea, let's lie down." I got down to the ground, my heart a second away from bursting out of my chest, my stomach a pit of acid about to burn through the skin. I lay back on the dirt and stared at the light coming through the cracks in the roof of the barn, then turned on my side and vomited.

———

When the ambulance arrived, Lyle and Nikyee were checked by a paramedic. I went over to her.

"If you hadn't come in—" she said.

"Hey, no use playing that game. We're all still here."

"Tatum!"

Gates ran up and threw her arms around me. "That was the stupidest damn thing I ever—"

"Can you do me a solid and save the yelling for later tonight? I think I'm about to pass out."

She stared at me, anger and worry in her eyes, and then said, "I think I have to fire you. You're too reckless."

"Hey, won the trial in a weird sort of way, right? That's all that matters."

"Is it?"

I grinned. "No, it's not."

82

I was there when Nathan Ficco was arrested a week later. The audio recording I had of Howard spilling his guts, and the transfers Jia had established from an offshore account owned by Nathan Ficco's construction company into Howard's account, were more than enough for a conviction. He tried to hire Pritcher, but Pritcher said, rightly, that because he had defended Anderson, it would be a conflict for him to represent Nathan as well. He couldn't care less about conflicts, I'm sure, but Judge Allred would've thrown a fit, and I had a feeling he'd had enough of River Falls.

Pritcher stood with me outside Nathan's house as a deputy with the sheriff's office helped Nathan out. Nathan's hands were cuffed behind his back and a news van was there, the cameraman slowly striding along with him until he was put in a police cruiser.

Thanks to Jia's brilliant digging around in everyone's bank accounts, we'd also been able to connect withdrawals of $2,000 in cash from half a dozen men in town that lined up with deposits of $1,000 in Patty's account the next day. I guessed that the other $1,000 went straight into Farah's pocket.

Horace Webb, Gates's opponent for county attorney, and good friend of both the mayor and Nathan Ficco, had actually been stupid enough to write Patty a check and put "services rendered" in the "memo" line. The story was statewide and had even gotten some national press on the cable news networks. That kind of publicity would be enough to win the election for Gates.

I'd also made a call to the Attorney General's Office about a little bar in Las Vegas that was engaging in the trafficking of underage girls. Too bad. Despite the horror of what she was doing, I'd liked Farah.

I had Steven Brown charged with perjury but would be cutting a deal for probation with him. Turned out the stalking injunction Patty had supposedly filed against him had been faked by Howard.

"You do know," Pritcher said, "that Anderson was an unwilling accomplice in all this. His father and Howard were the ones that pressured him to, allegedly, help in the killing and burial of Patty. And he certainly, again assuming he was actually there, did not kill her himself."

"He almost killed her by hitting her with a hammer, Russell. And then he covered up her death afterward." I thought a moment. "But he certainly wasn't the brains of the outfit. Considering his age, I'll cut him a little slack. Aggravated kidnapping and attempted murder, five to life, but I'll stipulate to fifteen years and write a letter to the parole board. The offer's good for today. Otherwise I keep the homicide charges and go forward on conspiracy to commit homicide and accessory after the fact. Might even hand it over to the feds and let them seek the death penalty."

He nodded. "No need, he'll take it." He motioned toward Nathan with his head. "What about him?"

"Him, I'm going to put in prison for the rest of his life. And I'm going to charge every man that took advantage of that girl with statutory rape. Including the mayor." I grinned. "He's giving a press conference this afternoon, and he's getting a little surprise visit from the boys in blue when he comes off that podium."

I gazed at Nathan Ficco in the back of a police cruiser. Venom was shooting out of his eyes at me, and I winked at him. I turned away and folded my arms, staring at Pritcher.

"I'm just willing to bet I'm not going to find any evidence about how you convinced Steven to lie on the stand, but if I do, Russell, I'm coming after you, too."

He chuckled, his eyes never wavering from mine. "Well, I would say it was a pleasure, but it certainly wasn't. I still think you're a traitor to your profession, but you seemed to do well in this one instance." He brushed something off my suit. "Take care of yourself, Tatum."

I watched him leave, and then I turned to Nathan's house. Anderson and his family would have to find a life without Nathan, but from what I'd seen, Nathan was a tyrant anyway. They would be better off.

Will came out of the house and over to me and said, "Arrest warrant was executed properly. I think we should start holding some seminars on the Fourth, Fifth, and Sixth Amendments for the city and county cops. They need to learn what they're doing."

"Cool. I think I know the perfect prosecutor to head that up, too."

"Me? I don't know. I'm not very good at public speaking."

"You'll do great. Besides, you gotta have the backing of the cops if you're gonna be mayor one day."

"Mayor?"

"Call me psychic, but I see politics in your future. And I think this town could use someone like you."

I turned to get into my car and Will said, "Tatum? Thanks, man. For . . . I don't know. Just being here, I guess."

"You can buy me a beer tonight when we go out to celebrate."

83

It was in the afternoon that day when I sat on Gates's porch and looked out over the meadow behind her house. Some cows were roaming around, and I could see her horses in the pen by the fence. Dandelions dotted the landscape, and farther out were trees and then a valley. She came and sat down in the rocking chair next to me.

"You know the local paper has been bugging me about getting them an interview with you."

I waved my hand. "Hate that stuff. Always have. Besides, you're a much prettier face for the media."

"It wouldn't hurt to get your name out there. I mean . . . if you're planning to stay."

I inhaled deeply and looked out over the grass. "I think I'll be around for a while. My dad gets out of the hospital today and I want to be there. I don't know him, and he sure as hell doesn't know me. I thought maybe we could change that."

She watched me a second and said, "I think he would like that." She sipped water out of a bottle she was holding. "Guess who else will be staying?"

"Jia. I know."

"How do you know?"

"She texted me and said she turned the job down. It's a good move for her. I don't think she'll stay here, but she needs to cook a little bit in the fire of the courtroom before she heads out to bigger and better things."

"Better?"

I grinned. "Well, at least bigger."

She reached for my hand. I took hers, and we sat quietly a minute and watched the grass and the cows before I said, "I have a surprise for you."

"What?"

"I'll show you."

———

We pulled up to the City and County Building.

"What is it?" Gates said.

"Wouldn't be a surprise if I told you."

Once inside, she was going to head downstairs, and I said, "No, up here."

Gates and I took the stairs to the third floor. The floor was massive and people were boxing things up. Some movers were there as well, and Gates glanced around and said, "What's going on?"

"The city manager's office is moving downstairs. And guess who'll be moving up here to the nice offices?"

"Are you kidding me? How'd you manage that?"

"Easy. I bought the building."

She chuckled. "What?"

"I bought the building. What? It's a good investment. I looked at the demographics, and the town is slowly—albeit very, very slowly—growing. One day I can leave this building to my kids."

"Kids? Who are you and what have you done with Tatum?"

I approached her and took her hands in mine. "I don't . . . I screwed it up once. You don't get many second chances. I'm not going to screw it up this time."

I kissed her, and as I did, one of the guys from the city manager's office walked by and said, "Get a hotel. And don't think I'll forget you're moving us into the basement. Better make sure your lawns are up to code, 'cause I'll be watching."

"Hey, don't make me move you guys into the bathrooms."

He scoffed and mumbled to himself as he went down the stairs. Gates grinned at me. "You make friends wherever you go, don't you?"

"It's a gift."

She wrapped her arms around my neck, and we stared into each other's eyes.

"What do you think about dogs?" I said.

"What?"

"Dogs. I was thinking it's time I got one."

"Well, Adam mentioned something about wanting grandkids actually."

"Let's just start with a dog and see how he does, shall we?"

She grinned and kissed me, and it seemed like she was the only person in my world. And I knew I could be perfectly happy with that.

ACKNOWLEDGMENTS

I'd like to give a special thank-you to my awesome team at Thomas & Mercer and Amazon Publishing. You guys rock.

ABOUT THE AUTHOR

 Victor Methos knew he would be a lawyer at the age of thirteen, when his best friend was interrogated by the police for over eight hours and confessed to a crime he didn't commit.

After graduating from the University of Utah S. J. Quinney College of Law, Methos worked for a special kind of lawyer—the kind who put up neon signs and would do anything and everything to win. Afterward, he sharpened his teeth as a prosecutor for Salt Lake City before founding what would become the most successful criminal defense firm in Utah.

In ten years, Methos conducted more than one hundred trials. One particular case stuck with him, and it became the basis for his first major bestseller, *The Neon Lawyer*. Since that book's publication, Methos has focused his work on legal thrillers and mysteries. He currently splits his time between Salt Lake City and Las Vegas and continues to defend the poor and the weak against the strong and the powerful.